Counting on a Cowboy

Counting on a Cowboy

A Four of Hearts Ranch Romance

Debra Clopton

THOMAS NELSON
Since 1798

Published in Nashville, Tennessee, by Thomas Nelson. Thomas Nelson is a
registered trademark of HarperCollins Christian Publishing, Inc.

Thomas Nelson titles may be purchased in bulk for educational, business,
fund-raising, or sales promotional use. For information, please e-mail
SpecialMarkets@ThomasNelson.com.

Scripture quotations marked NIV are taken from the Holy Bible, New
International Version`, NIV`. Copyright © 1973, 1978, 1984, 2011 by Biblica,
Inc." Used by permission of Zondervan. All rights reserved worldwide.
www.zondervan.com. The "NIV"and "New International Version" are
trademarks registered in the United States Patent and Trademark Office by
Biblica, Inc."

Publisher's Note: This novel is a work of fiction. Names, characters, places,
and incidents are either products of the author's imagination or used
fictitiously. All characters are fictional, and any similarity to people living
or dead is purely coincidental.

ISBN: 978-0-7180-7782-2 (mmpb)

Library of Congress Cataloging-in-Publication Data

Clopton, Debra.
  Counting on a cowboy / Debra Clopton.
    pages ; cm. -- (A four of hearts ranch romance ; 2)
  ISBN 978-1-4016-9051-9 (softcover)
  I. Title.
  PS3603.L67C67 2015
  813'.6--dc23
            2015006796

Printed in the United States of America

15 16 17 18 19 20 OPM 6 5 4 3 2 1

Always to my family—those with me now
and those who've gone before me . . . but
are forever and always in my heart.

CHAPTER 1

"Wake up, Abby," Abby Knightley demanded of herself through a huge yawn. Sitting straighter, she gripped the steering wheel of her car as if her life depended on it—and it did.

Abby's stomach knotted at the thought . . . her first-hand knowledge of just how truly life could change in the blink of an eye. She knew getting behind the wheel was always life or death. She'd suffered great loss—she pushed the memories away, unable and unwilling to go there. She blinked back the sting of tears and berated herself for driving while tired. For putting herself in this situation.

She almost pulled over to the side of the deserted road to sleep. But thankfully her GPS reported that her destination, the small Texas town of Wishing Springs, was only about five miles ahead. She could make that . . . just a little farther. And that was the only reason she was still driving . . .

Her eyes blurred and she eased her foot off the gas pedal as the worry gripped her further. She should have stayed in Houston after being delayed so late. But she hadn't wanted to. She'd feared that if she didn't leave right then, there might have been another delay tomorrow. And then another one. With so many friends and family trying to talk her out of moving—like today, Abby might not have ever summoned up the determination to leave again if she hadn't finally gotten in her car and driven off.

Of course the fact that she'd sold her home and had a moving company haul her belongings off to storage was a pretty good sign she was going somewhere. But *Wishing Springs, Texas?*

"That *hole* in the wall," her friends called it in horror.

Abby cringed thinking about their response to her decision to make a new life for herself.

Her head bobbed and she yanked it up, realizing her eyes had closed. She shot them open, shook herself, and—too late—saw the hulking, *huge*, black cow—or was it a buffalo in the middle of the road?

"Holy Toledo!" Abby shrieked, yanking the wheel with all her strength, only to realize she was now heading straight toward a *cowboy* standing in her high beams.

Time slowed as she hit the brakes. He stood like a Western movie legend come to life. His brows dipped, his jaw tensed, his eyes connected with hers through the windshield as time stopped in that split second it took her to register the danger.

She cranked down hard on the wheel as flashbacks of another wreck crashed over her.

She managed to swerve, sending her car careening into the ditch, across the rough ground, then through the barbed wire fence.

On impact with the fence post, the car's air bags exploded—smacking Abby like a hard right hook to the face.

Stars filled the sudden, brief blackness.

Face throbbing, Abby fought off passing out—*had she missed him?*

Had she run him down? Dazed, with icy fingers of fear clutching her heart, Abby struggled with her seatbelt and almost had it off when her door flew open.

"Are you okay?" the very much alive cowboy asked, his voice gruff.

"*Yes.* Are you? Did I hit you?" Relief surged through her so strong she barely felt the pain of her face from the impact of the air bag. No sooner had the relief hit her, then anger, then the familiar panic sent her clawing to get out of this car.

"What were you thinking?" she demanded, pushing him back so she could escape the confines of the car. Surprise froze his expression as he backed up. She glared at him. "I could have *killed* you! Just what were you doing standing in the dark out here in the middle of nowhere? Have you gone crazy?"

He blinked in obvious surprise at her attitude, then a slow grin built until it caused a deep dimple to appear beside lips that suddenly had her gaze glued.

"Now calm down," he said in an easy drawl that caused her pulse to skitter unexpectedly. "I'm okay and you're okay, so no need to be upset. I was trying to herd that escaped steer off the road before someone came along and had an accident. I'm sure sorry I didn't get him in before you got here."

"It's dark. I didn't see you. I could have hit you." Her stomach lurched at the close call and her hands shook as she grasped her hips.

Concern etched his features. "But you didn't. Come on now, breathe before you go and give yourself a stroke or something. My truck's down there." He pointed into the distance.

Abby spotted headlights pointing out into the pasture. "Way down there," she accused. "I can barely see them."

"Look, the steer started out down there, and then bolted. I ran after him on foot—big mistake. I'm just glad you didn't get hurt because of it."

"Well, I could have been," she retorted, not able to let being upset go as easily as he seemed to think she should. She knew, understood, what could have happened all too clearly. Her mind filled with the sound of screeching tires, she closed her eyes and fought the memory off. Heard the screams—her screams—

"Hey," he said kindly, his hand, gentle and warm, wrapped around her arm, causing her to jump. "We're all okay. That's all that matters."

She met his eyes and blinked, remembering where she was. "I, I just wasn't expecting something like this."

"You're whiter than a sheet. You may need to sit down. You have a few cuts on your face still bleeding a little bit. I'm sure it all hurts pretty good too."

Blood? Abby yelped. Her heart dropped to her knees and she swayed. She might have fallen if his strong hands hadn't closed more securely around her arms, holding her up.

"Hang on, breathe," he said, easing her back into the car's seat. He wasted no time pushing her head forward between her knees. "Come on now, this will pass. How are you doing down there?"

She sucked in a couple of shallow breaths. "I'm f-i-i-i-ne," she said, drawing the word out, trying to sit up, but he resisted, holding her firmly. "Really, I am. As long as I don't see it," she called, trying to sit up again. This time he let her. She carefully made sure to keep her eyes off the mirrors. "Is it bad? Is it going to drip? I can't see it drip." Flashbacks surged and she focused on him as he crouched in front of her. She hated the panic she could hear in her voice and the panic of threatening memories clashing inside of her. Memory of her loss . . . of Landon.

Unable to go there, she focused hard on the cowboy's blue eyes sparkling in the light of the interior car lights. Familiar eyes, she suddenly realized. "It's not bad. Not much more than a scratch, but let's get rid of it before it—" He halted as a drop of blood landed on his wrist and in the glow from the inside car light she saw the dark red stain spread out on his tanned skin.

She gasped. "Not good—"

Then everything went black.

. . .

Bo Monahan caught the woman as she went limp. "Whoa," he said—as if that would stop her from falling out in a dead faint. It was just a small amount of blood from a cut at the corner of her full bottom lip. Just a drop on his wrist. He got a little queasy around a lot of blood, but this wasn't as big as a dime.

She'd slumped forward into his arms—he'd automatically swung her up and now held her. Her feet dangled over one arm and her head lolled against his chest. Her dark hair tickled his jaw. Suddenly at a loss, relief surged through him when he saw lights coming down the lane leading up to the ranch.

Jarrod was on the way.

Bo had just found the escaped steer about five minutes before and called his brother for backup while he ran in pursuit. This poor gal had just happened to come around the corner a few moments too soon. The ornery bovine had bolted right in front of her car and all Bo could do was watch.

"Wake up, pretty lady," he urged. A slight September breeze was blowing, but despite it not yet being cold in Texas this time of year, her cheek had an icy chill—her face pale in the bit of light reaching them from inside the car. She had a Sarah Evans face—one of those faces that was beautiful, but give her a baseball cap and she became the girl-next-door type. He couldn't seem to take his eyes off of her. Though he sure wished she'd open her eyes and let him know she was okay.

Seconds later Jarrod's headlights flooded over them, blinding him as hers had done. Jarrod, his older brother, stormed out of the truck, stalking through the glaring beams.

"You didn't say anything about an accident. Have you called 911?" He stared at the woman in Bo's arms.

"No time. It just happened. That blame steer was in

the road and this lady had to swerve to miss it. She was shaky, but fine after the accident. This isn't from the wreck. She saw a drop of blood from that small cut on her face and she fainted."

"You sure that's all that's wrong?" Jarrod pulled out his cell phone. "I better call 911. Have them send out an ambulance just in case."

"She didn't hit anything other than those two fence posts. The air bag deployed and probably busted her lip. But call anyway."

"No," she groaned, and moved in his arms. Her lashes fluttered, and then Bo found himself looking into soft blue eyes.

"Well, hello again," he said. "Glad you're coming back to us." He smiled to reassure her, though he was far from happy that one of their steers had caused this. She could have been hurt bad if she'd hit the nearly two-thousand-pound animal at the speed she was traveling.

"I'm fine," she said, her eyes starting to focus. She studied him. "You're Bo Monahan."

He'd never had a problem with ladies knowing who he was—until after his new sister-in-law had put Wishing Springs on the map. Maggie was an advice columnist in the Houston area and there had been a TV special done on her and his brother Tru. If that wasn't bad enough, she'd written a crazy article on single men in his small town and since then, women had been showing up in Wishing Springs in packs.

Like day trips to see the "cowboys." Made him feel like the newest animal in the zoo.

And he wasn't especially fond of feeling like he was on display.

Until that had all started, Bo had enjoyed it when a woman approached him and already knew his name. These days not so much.

Jarrod hiked an eyebrow at him, telegraphing their shared reaction. The only difference was Jarrod ran the ranch cattle operation and upkeep while Bo ran the ranch's custom-made stirrup business. Because the stirrups could benefit from the publicity, Bo had been idiot enough to agree to be interviewed on the show.

So now he was recognized and looked for by all the day-trippers here and sometimes when he went out of town for any reason. He was a little touchy on the subject these days.

Jarrod, on the other hand, had flat out refused to be on camera—the cattle business got plenty of publicity without showing him. The stirrup business needed all the free publicity it could get and so there you go—Bo had been on the program.

"Yes, ma'am," he answered though his thoughts rambled. "That's me. How are you feeling?"

"Fine," she said, disgust in her voice. "I passed out, didn't I? I hate when I do that."

"I can sure see where it would get to be bothersome."

"Real bothersome." Her fingers began drumming against his chest as she seemed to think hard about something. He realized he wasn't finding the feel of her in his arms bothersome at all. Matter of fact, he didn't mind that she knew who he was.

"It just takes a drop. Do you know how hard it is

to avoid seeing a drop of blood? It's tough." Her brows suddenly dipped and her gaze dropped to his chest and her hand lifted. She gasped. "You're holding me."

Taken off guard by her only just realizing that, he laughed and so did Jarrod. A complete look of horror flared red across her face.

"Well, you don't have to look so horrified. I'm not as bad as all that."

"That depends on who you ask," Jarrod drawled. "How about we take you to the ranch, ma'am, and get you something to drink while you get your wits about you."

"No. No, I couldn't. I have a room in town at the Sweet Dreams Motel."

She wiggled in his arms and he knew he should put her down but found the thought unappealing so instead he said, "And it will be there after you've had some sweet tea and are steady on your feet." Bo wondered if her eyes were as soft a blue as they looked in the dim light.

"But—"

"No buts, ma'am," Jarrod said. "Bo."

"Might as well not argue with my big brother. He's pretty used to getting his way when he spells it out. And I happen to agree with him. I'll take you up to the house and let you get steady while I get that blood off your face. Unless you want us to take you to the hospital."

"No, really, I'm fine. It was just the blood. My face isn't throbbing any longer either. You can put me down now."

Jarrod moved to the front of her car and voiced what Bo had also figured. "I don't think your car is drivable."

With Bo close beside her, she moved to stand beside Jarrod. "Oh my word," she gasped. "My car."

"Looks like this is going to need hauling in, all right." Bo bent to look at the metal fence stake sticking out of the radiator.

"Yeah, I'd agree. I'll go round up the steer before it causes any more trouble. You've got this, don't you, Bo?"

Bo didn't miss the mild humor in his brother's question. Jarrod could read him like headlines on a newspaper and had already picked up on his interest and curiosity toward Abby. "Yeah, got it."

"I'll see you later, ma'am. If you need anything let us know. And don't worry about any of this—we'll take care of all of it."

"Thank you, and please call me Abby."

He tipped his hat. "Abby, you take care."

Looking less pale, she watched Jarrod walk to his truck and take out a rope then head into the shadows for the steer.

"Will he get the cow by himself? Do you need to help him?"

"Nah, Jarrod's a pro. He'll have that troublemaker caught in a flick of his wrist. Let's get you to the house and that lip of yours doctored. Might need an ice pack for your face too."

"Thanks. That might actually feel good."

"Hang here for a minute while I jog down there and get my truck."

"Sure," she said, staring into the distance where his truck sat. "I'll be here. No hurry."

Attraction needled him as he jogged away. She was pretty. But he'd sworn off dating right now. That his last relationship had ended badly still had him hesitant about dating right now, so he was taking a break. Plus, his plate was too full with work and Pops. Not to mention the irritating matter of the man-watchers all around. The big question: Was she one of them?

By the time he got back to her, she had her purse over her shoulder and her trunk open. He grabbed her two suitcases and set them in the back of his truck.

She paused before getting into the cab as he held the door open. "Really, you can just take me to the motel in town, if you don't mind."

"I'd feel better if we knew you were completely steady before I take you to the Sweet Dreams and drop you off." He held her elbow and assisted her as she got into his truck.

He felt responsible for her safety now. Besides, what if she did accidentally glimpse herself in the mirror before she cleaned her face? She could faint and hit her head on something. She could end up in the hospital or worse. He couldn't be responsible for that.

After he started up the drive, he asked, "Have you always fainted so easily at the sight of—well, you know? It's just plain dangerous."

Her expression shadowed and she looked away from him out the dark window. Even in the dim lights of the dashboard, he hadn't missed the look of sadness that had deadened her eyes.

"No. I . . . I had an accident and it's been like this ever since. My doctor says it will get better one day. Time will help."

She didn't sound all that sure about it. Bo wondered all the way to the ranch what kind of accident might cause someone to start fainting at the sight of blood. He didn't ask, though. His gut was telling him it was a deep subject and one she probably didn't share with strangers.

But he sure was curious.

CHAPTER 2

Okay, here you go. Sit right there and I'll get you a warm wet cloth and you can clean that bit of dried . . . off your face—or better yet I'll do it for you."

"Um, no. I should be able to do it, but I might need you to direct me." Abby gave a wavery laugh as she sat down at the kitchen table feeling out of place. If she hadn't been so sleepy, she would have seen the cow in the middle of the road before it was too late.

She stared around the kitchen of what Bo had said was his grandfather's home. She knew from the interview she'd watched on TV that Pops was the Monahan brothers' beloved grandfather and that he had been a very respected champion in the cutting horse industry, as well as one of the best trainers in his day. His grandson Tru had followed in his steps. Bo seemed to own and operate a custom stirrup business, according to the show. They'd mostly interviewed him for his thoughts on the bet that his brother and Maggie Hope were involved in.

It felt a little odd having just met the man and yet already knowing a fairly good bit about him. She'd been so dazed and upset over the wreck that it had taken her a moment to realize who he was.

She wondered what people would think when they learned that she'd come to town because of Maggie Hope's column. Her therapist had gotten her started reading the column, trying to help her see positive ways to deal with trouble. Maggie had a way of giving hope in her column. Abby had needed that—still needed it. She was hoping to meet Maggie. To thank her for inspiring her in her darkest moments . . . Still, what would people think? That she was weird?

As weird as her friends back in Houston had seemed to think?

At the memory of her friends' disapproval, Abby bit her lip. She tried to give them grace and know that they thought they were wanting the best for her. After all, she'd practically locked them out of her life, she'd been so withdrawn. Her moving away was hard on them.

"Ow," she groaned, only then realizing she'd clamped hard on the split at the corner of her mouth. She was glad she didn't taste fresh blood.

She watched Bo turn on the faucet then rummage around in a drawer. He pulled out a cloth and ran it under the water.

"Pops is asleep or I'd introduce you. He enjoys meeting new people, but at about nine p.m. he starts yawning these days." He pulled the rag from the water and squeezed it. "Okay, a nice warm rag to get rid of that blood."

He must have decided that the actual word wasn't going to have her falling out on the kitchen floor, Abby thought, almost laughing it was so . . . cute. That thought had her glancing at the wall clock. "It's almost eleven-thirty—I hope the motel is okay with me arriving so late at night. I got delayed leaving Houston." She tried to focus on what she was saying rather than her handsome rescuer, but that was impossible.

He pulled a chair near and sat down across from her. Their knees were nearly touching. He held the damp rag in his hand, poised to get the blood, startling her that he was so willing to help.

"May I?" He gave a cocky smile that shocked her to her toes. "Wouldn't want you to have to do this in the mirror and pass out on me again."

She nodded and sat very still as he went to lay the cloth against her skin, but when his warm fingers gently cupped her jaw, she jumped and her pulse bucked.

"Sorry, I didn't mean to make you jump." He apologized and laid the cloth against her lower lip.

Despite the soothing warmth, Abby tensed and couldn't breathe under his gaze as she felt his gentleness.

He lifted the cloth, staring at her as if searching for a sign that he might be hurting her, then, as if satisfied that he wasn't, he carefully placed it over the cut.

"Pebble usually hires help to oversee the night arrivals, so you'll be fine," he said soothingly. "I think Jarrod was going to call and tell them you were delayed but would be there within the hour. That way they won't worry about it."

She was having a hard time concentrating on his words. Awkward didn't begin to describe how she felt. And that, she reassured herself, was why her heart pounded and her pulse was behaving so erratically. "Good."

"Now, don't look down, whatever you do. I'm about to pull this rag away, and I don't want you seeing anything you shouldn't."

He had nice eyes. Blue like hers, but a deep, rich tone with endless depth like the waters of the ocean.

"And have you ever hurt yourself?"

"No," she said, as a band tightened around her heart.

He placed his hand on her shoulder and squeezed gently. "Are you okay?"

Abby sprang to her feet feeling as if she'd just been zapped by a live electric cord. "Could you take me to the motel now?" she asked in a rush, and saw surprise flare in his eyes. "It's been a really long day." The man probably thought she was a ninny or something, but she didn't care. She needed to leave. She needed sleep.

Needed to be alone.

"Sure." He carefully kept the rag out of sight as he took it to the sink.

It took everything Abby had to walk not run to the door. This was ridiculous. But looking at Bo Monahan swarmed her with sensations she hadn't ever expected to feel again and would rather not.

"You've been very helpful," she rattled off as she scurried out the door and made a beeline for his truck. Her insides were fluttering still . . . with unease, yes, unease, she tried to tell herself. She crossed the porch and beat him to the passenger door, which she wrenched open before he could get it for her.

Hoisting herself into the cab, she plopped onto the seat. She was being rude.

Weird would be a more accurate term.

She couldn't help it though. She needed to get to her room.

The way her insides fluttered when he came near was not welcome.

* * *

What had happened back there?

With him?

Bo had gotten all caught up in Abby's gaze. She'd been shaken up from the wreck and then the blood and he'd felt bad for her. But when he'd sat down, taken her chin in his hands, and touched her mouth with that cloth—he'd lost his absolute mind.

He'd managed to ask fairly coherent questions until that point, then he'd gotten so lost in her eyes that he'd scared her. Alarmed her. That had to be what was wrong because he'd seen the exact moment of change in those summer's-sky eyes.

His fingers tightened on the steering wheel as silence echoed inside the cab and the short few miles to town ticked slowly by.

She'd sensed his attraction and that had to be why she bolted up like that. It was the only explanation.

The woman was a beauty, and he'd been sitting there staring like some dumbstruck teenager. Which he wasn't. He was a twenty-eight-year-old man who'd seen his fair share of beautiful women and dated many of them.

Maybe she was affecting him like this because she was the first woman to have him thinking about dating again. Despite all his reasons for stepping back for a while.

He wondered again if she was one of the gals attracted to town because of Maggie's advice column where she had pretty much told the entire population of Houston that his little town was a ladies' playground. Not in so many words, maybe, but close enough since it started the day-tripping nonsense.

He was not *eye candy* . . . which he had specifically been called by a couple of women who'd stopped to watch him loading his truck up with feed at the feed store.

They'd stopped just short of catcalls . . . The ridiculous whole thing remained a little bit of a sore spot between him and Maggie.

He glanced over at Abby. She was staring out her window, but he saw her reflection in the darkness. Was she crying? He tensed and every other thought vanished. He yanked his eyes away, thinking fast . . . "I'm sorry, I hope I didn't upset you back there." He looked at her and saw her sit up straight then swipe at her cheek with her fingertips before turning her head and looking at him.

She didn't exactly look him in the eye. "No. I'm fine. It's just been a long day. And then having the wreck on top of that. Just a long day."

Bo paid attention to the road then shot her another look. No matter what she said, he'd seen the sheen of tears in that reflection. "Sorry about that. We should be there soon." That was the best he had to offer at the moment. But there was no stopping his mounting curiosity about her story. What had brought her to Wishing Springs?

She didn't look like a woman who would come here trying to hook a husband. Those female visitors, who were walking around town and even eating lunch at The Bull Barn, the local lunch spot on the outskirts of town, had overly bright, calculating eyes on the lookout for just the right cowboy.

Abby didn't fit that bill.

He found himself looking at his quiet rider again, and when she glanced his way and caught him staring, he yanked his gaze off of her and back onto the road.

"Thank you again for doing this. I know it was your cow and you feel responsible, but still, thank you and it's okay."

"Hey, you shouldn't have had to go through this in the first place. I can assure you that Jarrod will be out there with his ranch hands before daybreak looking for how that critter got loose. If he's not already out there searching by spotlight."

"Well, it's not like the cow was let loose on purpose. Oh—is that town?"

"Yup, the huge metropolis. Don't blink or you might miss it. We don't have any late-night stores, so all you see mostly are the motel lights and streetlights." The motel sign came into view a little way down the road. "You'll like Pebble's place. She keeps it immaculate and prides herself in making everyone's stay at the motel special."

"I'm looking forward to a couple of weeks there. Can you point out Doobie and Doonie Burke's real estate agency as well?"

He shot her a startled look. "You lookin' for property?"

"Mm-hmm. I am—at least I'm pretty sure I am."

Now that was interesting.

He pointed out Burke Brothers Realty and finally pulled into the motel half a block down the road. He insisted on going in to get the key and returned with the statement, "Pebble said for you to have a good night and that you could come by the office whenever you wanted to tomorrow."

"That was sure sweet of her."

He smiled. "Pebble's a real sweetheart. But, that's the way it's done around here. She knew you were tired, especially after all of this happened. I'm sure you'll find cookies and no telling what else in your room to greet you." He drove over to Bungalow Number Five, got out, and pulled her suitcases from the back of the truck. He met her at the door where she was inserting the key into the lock. Thankfully she looked more stable and less pale.

She smiled over her shoulder, her dark hair swinging, and his pulse did a sudden spin-kick right into the center of his solar plexus. He almost wheezed from the punch, it felt so real.

"The town's attitude is why I wanted to come to Wishing Springs. It just seemed like a very welcoming place. Kind of like Mayberry. As I was reading Maggie's column about the town I almost expected Andy Griffith and Aunt Bea to show up."

"You read Maggie's column?" His guard strengthened despite his instincts telling him she wasn't one of those husband hunters.

"I do and I'm serious," she said, pausing before pushing open the door. "Either Maggie is just a great writer or this town has a lot to offer in the hometown-charm department."

Manhunter or not, the woman was cute. "I think it's probably a little of both."

As if satisfied with that answer, she pushed open the door and the scent of fresh chocolate chip cookies swamped them.

"Told you."

She inhaled. "That smells wonderful." Hurrying inside he followed with her bags, watching as she lifted the foil from a plate piled high with soft cookies that he knew from experience would be perfect in every way.

"Cowboys have been known to fight over those cookies," he said.

A huge smile sprang across her face, lighting it up like Christmas. "Would you like some?"

He set her suitcase down. "I'll take a rain check, but you enjoy. And don't go bleeding or anything like that. When I come to take you to your car in a few hours, I don't want to walk in and find you on the floor."

She laughed then. The sound curled around something inside him, something that readily responded.

"I'll be careful."

He told his feet to move. They ignored him and stuck to the burgundy carpet like they were trapped in mud. The woman was probably starting to worry he wasn't going to leave.

He forced himself into motion. "I'll pick you up at

eight-thirty a.m. if that's not too early," he said, heading to the door.

"Thanks, that's perfect."

"See you then." The words rang with briskness as he strode out the door, gave her a tip of his hat, and got on the road toward home.

"*What*," he asked aloud, "was that all about?"

He felt like he'd just been blindsided by a bull. And no matter what he did, he could not get Abby Knightley off his mind as he drove back toward the Four of Hearts Ranch.

He hadn't been dating like he used to—the ranch he owned with his brothers had had rough times. After his parents had died in a plane crash, they'd found out his dad had very nearly gambled away the ranch his grandfather had worked so hard to build.

His contribution to paying the debt down became the successful stirrup business he'd created. He poured every moment he had into keeping up with the demand because they needed each and every sale. Especially the first year and a half when they didn't know if there was any way to keep the ranch despite all three of them working.

And then there was Pops. He and his brothers wished desperately that his Pops wasn't slipping away from them, but it was a hard fact that he was having to face. But for the most part he had a lot to smile about and that was what he tried to focus on.

And that smile was usually why he seemed to draw women's attention, which worked out well when he had the time. What he didn't like was that his new sister-in-law, Maggie, practically put a bull's-eye on his back with that article.

He'd gotten uncharacteristically mad over it. And for good reason.

Yes, he liked women and dating. On his timetable. Right now his plate was full.

But he sure was interested in knowing more about Abby and why she needed to find her very own Mayberry.

What had happened to put those shadows in her eyes and that need in her heart?

And then there was her reaction to the blood . . .

CHAPTER 3

A cup of warm green tea in hand from the small kitchenette of her motel room, Abby walked outside into the early morning light. It felt cooler this morning, a reminder that it was fall in Texas, but she knew that the day would warm again, as summer was never ready to leave without a fight. Breathing in the cooler, crisper air, she studied the Sweet Dreams Motel. It was darling—just like Maggie's column had described. With the individual bungalows, white exteriors, burgundy shutters and doors, and window boxes full of flowers, it was so welcoming. Add to that the colorful metal chairs outside each door and it provided the perfect small-town home away from home.

Despite all of that, Abby hadn't slept well. She hadn't slept well since she'd lost Landon. Her heart ached as it always did in the morning hours when her loss seemed closest—waking up without him lying next to her or sitting with her in the first light of morning drinking tea and coffee before starting their day. Oh, how she missed those early morning moments with Landon. The pain in her heart radiated through her now as she sank into a pink chair outside her bungalow's door. She took a sip of her tea . . . alone. She struggled as always to let the peace of the morning fill her. The grief pulled at her, but the relief of knowing she'd made a step forward surged, and despite all odds, excitement hummed inside of her.

She was really here.

And she was smiling. That was a rarity these days, but coming to Wishing Springs was the first step in making more smiles a possibility.

Though she didn't think she deserved it, she knew that she had to believe she did. Had to somehow fight to forgive herself and force herself to reach for a new start.

A new life. But when your old life had died—an early, tragic death—the thought of moving forward wrapped torture and need into one untidy, painful package.

Her hand shook as she took a long swig of the warm liquid. Pushing away the echo of guilt ringing at the end of that thought . . . knowing she was partly to blame. Her therapist had talked her off this ledge. Abby had to let it go . . .

She'd come here to find hope like Maggie was always urging readers to do in her columns.

Coming here was exactly what I needed.

"Yes, it was," she whispered decisively. But did she deserve a new start . . .

Release it, give it to God. She closed her eyes and handed it over one more time.

But, like always, it wasn't as easy to do as it was to verbalize. Guilt clung to her thoughts, determined to sabotage her. And feelings of unworthiness smothered her.

Landon would want her to move on, to find happiness again. He *would* and she'd even dreamed of him getting angry with her because she wasn't trying. She blinked away tears.

Stop using me as an excuse to give up on life. She could almost hear him speaking aloud despite only being in her heart. In her dreams . . .

A shudder moved through her. She stood. It was time to get moving.

She crossed to the office of the motel to officially check in and thank Ms. Hanover for her kindness last night. She needed to do it before Bo Monahan came to pick her up.

The dainty tinkle of a glass bell announced her arrival and the familiar, sweet aroma of freshly baked chocolate chip cookies welcomed her—Pebble must bake all the time. Bo had been right, the cookies in her room were divine.

A wisp of a woman with a gentle smile and soft eyes of blue rose from the pastel floral armchair in the corner. She placed her knitting project in the seat and came Abby's way.

"Good morning, you must be Abby," she said with warmth. "I'm Pebble Hanover."

"Yes, ma'am, I am. You were so kind last night. The cookies were fantastic. I'm sorry I got in so late—"

Pebble's smile widened. "You had a day of it, didn't you? Jarrod told me they were going to take you back to your car this morning. I hope it's not hurt too terribly much." She walked behind the counter.

"I'm really not sure about how bad, though it must

need some repair. Bo's coming to pick me up in a moment."

Pebble pushed the ledger forward. "You could sign in any time. I'm in no rush, but since you're here, why don't we take care of it? Was the room satisfactory? I put you in my favorite room—the one with the hummingbirds. Do you like it?"

Abby did love this, no computer, no technology, just a ledger and old-fashioned hospitality. "The room is perfect. I love the hummingbird pattern and the colors. It's very peaceful. I noticed you have a lot of hummingbird feeders around."

"Yes, I do love the pretty little things. My husband and I almost named the motel Hummingbird Cottages when we bought it way back when . . ." She sighed. "But they really aren't restful. They're so busy they'll keep you awake watching them if you're not careful, so we went with Sweet Dreams Motel instead. It does have a ring to it."

"Yes, ma'am, it does. I slept very well." She didn't mention that for her, sleeping well was equivalent to maybe four straight hours and then several restless hours fighting memories.

"That Bo is a very nice young man. Have you seen the stirrups he makes? They're works of art. Just beautiful."

"I've heard of them. I saw him holding a pair during that TV interview with Maggie Hope. I haven't seen them up close."

"Then you should have him show you where he makes them when he comes to pick you up."

Abby wasn't sure she wanted to spend any more time

with Bo than necessary. She heard a vehicle outside and glanced out the window. Her pulse did a somersault seeing him pull to a halt in front of the office. Her brows knitted at the reaction.

"There he is," Pebble told her, looking at Abby with expectation. "Aren't you going to go?"

Her feet felt glued to the floor all of a sudden. "Yes. I mean, I am. Did you need me for anything else?"

"You are free to go. I hope all is well with your car."

"Thank you." Abby didn't move, though.

"He won't bite, dear. At least I don't think so," Pebble added with a chuckle.

"No, I just hesitated because I wanted to ask you if I could have the recipe to those cookies when I get back?" Abby thought that was a pretty good save. However, the twinkle in Pebble's eyes told her the older woman knew exactly what she was doing.

"Of course you can. Come see me anytime and I'll print it for you." Abby forced a smile. Heading out the door, she paused when Pebble came around the counter. "Is there anything I can do for you?" Pebble asked.

The question had Abby turning back to find concern in Pebble's expression. "I may be a stranger, but I've been through some hard times and something tells me you have too. If you ever need to talk, I'm a good listener," Pebble continued.

Was it still so obvious to others that she'd had something go wrong in her life? Abby's heart thundered at the thought. Landon always had said all of her emotions were written on her face. "No. I'm fine."

"Well, good," Pebble said, though Abby could see

she wasn't convinced. To her relief, the sweet lady let it go. "About the cookies. I'm baking a lot tomorrow for Over the Rainbow. That's the home for unwed mothers on the outskirts of town. I take cookies out there and spend time with them on game night. You could help me bake them if you have any free time, and join me out there, if you'd like."

Abby hesitated, then pushed herself. "I need to get this car situation sorted out and see about finding a place to rent. But maybe . . . I'll talk to you later." She finally headed outside. Her stomach cartwheeled the instant she saw Bo. Unsettling on so many levels.

The man was here to pick her up because of her car. She'd go out there, get her car or at least deal with it for insurance, and then she would come back to the motel and head to the real estate office.

End of story.

• • •

"You're right on time." Abby was at the passenger door and inside before Bo had realized she was coming out of the office instead of the bungalow.

"Um, I try to be." Bo opened his door, climbed inside, and shot her a grin. To be honest, the grin showed up automatically. Looking at her just made him smile. "You sure are in a hurry this morning," he drawled, hoping today he didn't cause those pretty eyes to grow troubled.

"No. Just anxious to see my car." She buckled her seat-belt. "I mean, you know, to make sure everything's okay."

"Sure." He obliged by backing out, turning the rig

toward the exit. "We got it out of the ditch this morning, but that metal stake in the radiator means a trip to the shop for certain. Charlie can come out with his wrecker and take it in to his shop in town if that's agreeable to you. He's qualified."

"Oh." Her shoulders slumped. "Well, thank y'all. That's fine to call Charlie."

She was quiet as he pulled out onto the hardtop. Bo figured some women might have gotten mad about something like that. Or upset. But she didn't seem to be either, at least not after her initial disappointment. Was that the word? Or troubled? With the way the line between her eyes deepened into a fence post, he'd say troubled was the correct assumption.

He sure was—the woman had interrupted his sleep, she'd been on his mind so long. He'd tossed and turned and was up drinking his morning coffee long before the rooster crowed. Which wasn't abnormal, just he hadn't had a woman on his mind like this in a very long time.

There was something about her that hit him in the gut every time he looked at her. Heck, *every* time he thought of her.

Stealing a sidelong glance at her, he figured he could just stare at her all day. It was ridiculous. He was a grown man and not some pimple-faced teenager with his first crush. He didn't have time to sit stargazing and mooning over a female like a kid. Curiosity. That was part of the attraction. He was intrigued by her . . . there was something elusive there and he wanted to know more. That thought at least relieved him some, helping justify a little of his infatuation.

"So what has you thinking of movin' to Wishing Springs?" He tapped the steering wheel with his fingers. What if she said she was here to find a husband? She'd said she read Maggie's columns and now she was here. That didn't bode well.

She clasped her hands in her lap. "I needed a change of scenery."

"Scenery?" Relief surged through him. He just hadn't been able to see her as some woman-crazed man hunter. "Seems kinda drastic for scenery."

"I guess that's not exactly the right word. I'm here to make a fresh start. People do that, you know."

"Well, sure they do." He glanced at her. What did that statement mean?

That she's looking for a husband, what else?

So she *was* one of those gals hunting a husband after all.

Bo's opinion of her took a dive. There was only one kind of woman who would load up and move to a town to find a husband—

A desperate one.

One with problems or baggage so deep finding a husband the regular way was out of the question—that's what.

He was jumping to conclusions. She hadn't actually said she was looking for a husband.

"So, you own the ranch with your brothers?"

Her question came from natural curiosity, he told himself. She'd seen that TV special. Everyone knew they all owned the Four of Hearts Ranch. Wariness tightened like a steel band around his lungs and he kept his gaze focused on the road ahead of him. "Yes. With Jarrod and Tru."

"I thought that was *so* sweet how Maggie and Tru fell in love during that bet."

He shot her a glance, saw her eyes brighten almost dreamily as she smiled. He bit back a groan of disappointment and pinned his gaze once more to the road. A few silent moments later he spotted Jarrod standing beside Abby's car as they drew near.

Bo exited the truck the moment he pulled to a halt and rammed the shift into park. He wanted some distance and he wanted it now.

"Good morning," Jarrod said as they reached him. He tipped his hat at Abby and she smiled sweetly—again.

Bo studied that smile, trying to detect any fakeness to it. Trying to find any calculation or manipulation.

At least he wasn't looking at her like she was the first rain after a drought anymore. Which was a good thing, since his brother would have ribbed him to no end if he'd kept that up. Not that Jarrod did a lot of that these days. He was pretty wrapped up in keeping the ranch running. He'd grown pretty serious since they'd learned what their dad had done. But if he'd noticed too much in Bo's expression it would have happened. They were brothers after all.

Abby could have come here for more than just husband hunting. Maybe she had different reasons for coming. But he knew there was nothing else in this small town that would make a single woman suddenly up and relocate.

Least not that he saw.

It certainly hadn't ever happened before.

Get over it, Monahan, give it up.

"Hope you slept good last night. It was a late one," Jarrod continued while Bo was dug deep in thought.

"I did, thank you," said Abby. "And thank you both for worrying about my car. I understand we should call Charlie."

"Looks that way."

She stared at the stake sticking through her grill. "I'd hoped I'd dreamed this part and my car was just stuck."

"No, sorry. It's real. But Charlie will get you fixed up pretty quickly."

"Okay, that sounds good." She bit her lip and looked troubled.

"I called my insurance company," he said quickly, wanting, despite his disappointment, to relieve any concern she might have.

"Okay."

Jarrod looked concerned at her quietness. "I need to head over to the fire department for a meeting but wanted to make sure you were okay this morning. There are no breaks in the fence or weak sections. The steer must have walked the cattle guard. I just wanted to assure you that this didn't happen because of neglect."

"Oh, I never thought that." She sounded genuinely nice. "You're on the fire department?"

Bo rubbed the back of his neck, his thoughts working overtime. "Jarrod is the fire chief of our volunteer fire department," he told her, still trying to figure her out.

"That's wonderful. I respect firemen so much."

Jarrod held her serious gaze with his own. "Thank you, our volunteers are a great group of men. Bo's one of them—we do what we can." He tipped his hat. "If you need anything, let us know. We're sorry about the inconvenience. Bo's gonna make sure you have transportation in the meantime."

"Oh," emerged in almost a gasp and her gaze flew to his.

Dad-gum it, but she looked about as honest as they came. "That's right."

"I don't want to be a bother," she said a second time after Jarrod had left. He'd assured her it wasn't. Now Bo did it again.

"It's not any trouble and it's our responsibility."

Her expression only grew more worried. "Did he interrupt his plans for the morning just to come here and tell me that? I hope he's not late for the meeting."

"He changed the time so he could be here. I'll get the meeting details from him." Belatedly Bo realized he sounded like was looking for a little recognition himself.

"Oh, I'm sorry. I'm making you miss the meeting instead."

He felt bad for having mentioned it. "No, don't. It was only right for us both to make sure you were okay this morning. Like I said—it was our responsibility."

"That's considerate of you both, but I know that in cattle country, cows are going to get loose sometimes. And . . ." She stuffed her hands in her pockets only to pull them out quickly. ". . . and like he pointed out, it's not due to *intentional* neglect. This was just something that happened."

Bo studied her intently, hearing the unmistakable hard edge to her last words. What had caused that?

. . .

Abby noted the curiosity in Bo's gaze and knew he'd caught her tone. "There's no irresponsibility," she added, trying to sound more positive, focusing on the good and not . . . the wreck that had killed Landon. That they were firemen had her thinking even more of it—of the jaws of life and the firemen who'd responded . . . there had been nothing positive about that wreck. Other than that those firemen had tried to save both of them.

"You're right about that." Bo turned around abruptly and started back toward the truck and she followed. "Jarrod oversees the ranch and as you can tell, he's pretty detail-oriented. He personally rides or drives the fence lines of this ranch on a regular basis checking for weak spots. If there had been one, I can assure you it would have been dealt with immediately."

Had she upset him? "And I can tell that about him. You must be pretty detail-oriented yourself with your custom stirrups. I understand they are very popular."

He studied her as if trying to read her thoughts. Then he opened her door for her just as the rumble of the wrecker pulling in behind them gave him something else to focus on.

"There's Charlie," he said and strode away toward the older man as he got out of his truck.

"Looks like we got ourselves a humdinger of a problem,"

the grizzled older man said around the toothpick dangling at the edge of his lips.

"We do, Charlie, but we knew you could fix us up." Bo held out his hand and they shook. He introduced Abby and then they all walked back over to the car to discuss what Charlie would do.

"Shouldn't take more'n a couple of days. Got me a slow spot in the shop so I can get right on it—long as no unforeseen catastrophes happen round here."

"Do you have catastrophes often?" Abby asked, startled by the declaration.

Charlie chuckled, swiped his hat off his head, and scratched a bushy head of grey hair.

"Oh," Abby said, seeing the glint in his eyes. "You're teasing."

He chuckled again. "I do tend to do that. If I can get the insurance company to comply quickly, I can have this done probably in about two days since I ain't seein' any bodywork. You were very lucky on that end."

"Thanks, Charlie," Bo said, then told Abby, "Not much happens around here on a regular basis when it comes to collisions. Which is a good thing. But Charlie keeps all of the town's vehicles and tractors running at his repair shop. So I'm suspecting that he's about to bump your car into a priority spot in order to get it done. Am I right?" he asked Charlie.

"Well, that's right, but it ain't gonna be a big deal and you're new in town. We like to treat a guest right."

"But—you don't need to do that—" Abby felt bad, even though she did need her car.

"Nope, none of that. This car will be done as quick

as I can get it done. B'sides that, Pops is my old friend and has given me more'n my fair share of help through the years. Anyone who's a friend of his or his boys is goin' ta get first-rate service."

"That is awful nice of you. I really appreciate it." She glanced at Bo and thought she saw pride in his gaze. And he should have it. These were such nice words about him and his grandfather.

"Thanks, Charlie," he said. "That's real good of you to do that."

It didn't take but a few more minutes and Charlie had the car loaded up and headed off toward town.

"That was so nice of him," Abby said as she got back in the truck.

"Yeah, he's a great guy. A hard worker and as honest as they come." Bo slid into the driver's seat and glanced at the clock on the dash. "Hey, sorry, but I need to run up to the house and check on Pops before I take you back to town. Do you mind?"

Abby had relaxed a little during their talk with Charlie and she shook her head. "No, that's fine. I don't mind meeting Pops." She smiled. "From everything I've heard he must be a great man."

Sorrow flashed in Bo's eyes. "Yes, he is. I don't like to leave him alone too long and since I helped haul the cattle this morning, I'd feel better checking in on him."

"Is he ill?"

He hesitated, seeming to think over his words. "He's having some memory issues. He's in the mid-stages of Alzheimer's." She could see the sadness in his expression.

"I'm so sorry. I know that's got to be hard on all of you."

Their gazes locked. "Yeah, I hate it. It's taking my Pops away piece by piece. He's a great person—the greatest man I've ever known. It's disturbing to watch him struggle. My brothers feel the same way, but none of us are real good at verbalizing our emotions too much about it."

"That's the man in you," she offered before she could stop herself. Landon had been the same way.

He started driving. "Yeah, I guess so. The worst part is Pops knew what was happening to him. We started him on medicine immediately and it helped some. The doctors changed him to a new one now to find one that would help him have fewer disoriented days. But I can't tell if it's helping yet."

Abby's heart went out to Bo. He'd revealed so much to her. "I would think it would be so hard to watch."

"It's harder and harder to watch every day. Pops means the world to me. I cherish each day I wake up and Pops remembers who he is or who I am and can call me by name."

Abby heard the pain in his voice and knew that there was more than one way to lose a loved one.

"It makes me feel helpless—" he gritted, his jaw tense as his eyes shadowed.

Abby knew that emotion far, far too well. The almost overwhelming urge swept through her to lay her hand on Bo's to comfort him. She didn't. She didn't want to feel the connection pain and loss created between them. She looked away and hoped he hadn't seen her own pain.

"But we're taking care of him. Just like he's always done for us."

She almost felt relief at his words, knowing they confirmed that he hadn't felt the connection. And why would he? He didn't know her pain.

"I'm sure he knows." What else was there to say to that? She knew that sometimes there just weren't any words. Abby wasn't really sure she wanted to meet Bo's Pops now. Since Landon's death she'd found it easier not to get too close to people. She'd withdrawn from almost everyone she'd ever been close to and had stopped letting her emotions get involved in anything. Thus not watching the news. There was no room inside of her for other people's troubles.

But, you're here to make friends and to do just that.

She wanted to shoo the tiny voice in her head away, tell it to be silent, but it was true. She was here to develop relationships that would help her be more available emotionally.

She'd written in to Maggie's column a couple of times, anonymously, and Maggie had chosen her letter to answer in the column and also e-mailed her directly. Maggie had told her the same thing her therapist had, that she would help herself by developing relationships that required her to be in the moment, to be involved emotionally. Her therapist told Abby she needed to let herself *feel* again. That she needed to join in on life around her again. But give her worries over to the Lord.

None of that was easy.

And Maggie had confirmed the same. But as low as Abby had gotten, the depression she'd experienced, the withdrawal from everyone, she knew it was true . . . so that was why she'd come here.

Crazy, maybe, but once the idea formed that Wishing Springs was where she should be she hadn't been able to stop thinking about it. Reading Maggie's column, seeing the TV special with snippets of the town had put the idea in her thoughts. She wondered if Maggie might be at the ranch this morning.

"Does it help that all of you work at the ranch?" she blurted out, not wanting to ask about Maggie.

"Some. Tru's on the road a lot and he's not able to help as much as he'd like. He helps when he's home, though. Right now he's away with Maggie on their honeymoon."

"I saw the wedding announcement in the paper. I think it's great that they fell in love."

He glanced at her. "Yeah. Tru's happy."

"That's good." Hesitation filled her at the thought of telling him that she'd been inspired to come here because of the column. He was a man, he would probably not understand—and he'd probably ask why and she wasn't ready to answer that. Instead she scanned the ranch as they drove up the lane. Any true fan would have a natural curiosity about the place. Maggie had a way of giving advice as if you were sitting with her having coffee. While Abby hadn't been able to watch a news broadcast, she had been able to read the newspaper because Maggie always had hope in her column's words.

Abby had needed that during the last two years.

She owed Maggie a debt of gratitude. And she couldn't help being curious about the ranch she lived on. "The ranch is beautiful."

"We love it." She heard the pride in his voice and it

was well deserved. Not only was the place beautiful but they'd all worked hard to keep it alive.

Pops's house came into view—a pretty, white home with a wide front porch and a tree-lined yard.

As they drew closer, Bo leaned forward over the steering wheel. "What in the world? What is that?"

The front door of the house stood open. A tall, thin man was outside on the porch leaning over what looked like a portable playpen. Abby saw a tiny head sticking up over the edge.

"Is that what I think it is?" Bo asked, taking in the scene.

"I believe that's a baby. Do you have a baby?"

Alarm lit his expression. "No. What's a baby doing on the porch?"

There was no mistaking the complete bafflement in his words.

He pulled to a halt and was out of the truck in a blink. As he strode briskly across the yard, Abby followed him, not sure what was going on.

Pops, for this must be him, looked up. There was no missing the blank look on the older man's expression as he grinned at Bo.

She and Bo both stared down at the red-faced toddler with a thick head of brown hair curling about his face. He had a bottle in one hand and a pacifier in the other. He'd been crying and by the look of things, for a while. Tears had dried on his cheeks. Abby's heart clenched.

"Pops, what do you have here?" Bo asked.

Abby's gaze shifted back to Pops, who was looking at Bo as if he'd just asked the silliest question ever.

"Well, Bo, it's your baby."

CHAPTER 4

My baby." Bo took a step back. "No, Pops, not mine. What's he doing here?" He glanced around as the baby continued to wail.

"He's crying," Abby blurted, still hanging back from the porch. Bo thought she looked like she was fighting the urge to run back to the truck. Where had this baby come from? Who would have done this?

"I-I don't know what to do with a baby. I've never been around them. What do I do?"

She waved her hand at the baby. "Pick him up," she urged.

"Me?" He glared at her in horror. "How? It's not like he's a steer."

She glared right back at him and pointed. "Put your hands under his armpits and lift. It's easy. He's your baby."

"He's not my baby." The baby turned about as red as an over-ripe plum with his next holler. "How can something that little make a noise like that?" Bo stepped in and clumsily took hold of the baby just like Abby told him. He wrapped both his hands around the little fella's chest and hauled him out of the playpen.

"Now what?" As Bo held the boy in midair, the baby let out a piercing scream that brought Pops running to his side. Panic washed over Bo.

Pops looked distressed. "Don't cry, little baby, don't cry," he urged, then started pacing back and forth wringing his hands.

From inside the house Solomon, Pops's spoiled Basset Hound, joined in the ruckus and started wailing too.

Out of his element, Bo spun with the baby toward Abby and to his surprise she looked white as a sheet. "Help?" he asked, and hoped she wasn't about to pass out on him.

She blinked, visibly inhaled as if needing the air to keep from passing out. Bo's stomach sank. What would he do if she fell out and needed him? Finally, thankfully, she surged forward.

She scowled as she reached for the baby. "Let me have him." She scooped the little fellow into her arms, holding him close. "There, there sweet boy," she consoled him. "I've got you. No more crying. Calm down, sweetness, it's going to be okay." The more she cuddled him, the quieter he got, until with a squishy sound he plopped his pacifier into his mouth and looked up at Abby with wet, adoring eyes.

Confused by the entire situation, Bo could have picked Abby up and hugged her tight just for the blessed quietness. He'd thought Abby was upset or angry, but she sounded purely sweet as she spoke soothingly to the baby . . . but he had no time to really think more about that when he had no clue what this baby was doing here.

"Who would leave a baby?" Bo looked at Pops. "Pops, do you know who left the baby?"

Pops was clearly in a disoriented phase, but Bo had to try. This was important. Bo's mind scrolled through people he knew who might have a baby, but no one came to mind. There was the home for unwed mothers on the outskirts of town, but he didn't know any of those young ladies. Besides, this wasn't a newborn. This baby was older than that.

Pops got that confused look in his eyes that Bo had gotten used to seeing so much lately. He pointed at Abby and grinned. "Her."

"No, Pops. Abby was with me," he said, and then noticed a folded-up piece of paper sticking from beneath one of the legs of the playpen. Bending down, he freed it and then opened the note.

Dear Bo,

I'm sorry I've never told you about Levi, but I didn't think I wanted you to know, and I didn't think it would matter to you anyway. As I write this I'm not doing so well. I'm fighting cancer. And if you are reading this, then that means I'm gone and my friend has brought you our baby. I've made sure you are listed as the father and legal guardian on everything and as far as the courts or any social services would know, you've been involved in his life from day one. Take care of our son. His name is Levi. He likes cows and cuddling. I'm sorry I didn't tell you sooner. I wish things had been different between us but—anyway, take care of our baby.

Darla

The world around him slowed, sounds faded away. Bo stopped reading and focused on Levi. He sank to the porch railing.

"Bo, what does it say?" Abby asked.

He looked at her and struggled to speak. "According to this, he's mine. And his name is Levi."

. . .

"*Yours* and you didn't *know* it?" Abby asked, shock radiating through her. Color drained from her face—Bo was as shocked as she was. She didn't know what in the world she'd walked into, but it was a doozy. Bo looked like he'd just run into a brick wall. Her own heart beat erratically as she held the baby, Levi, close. She focused on Bo and not the struggle holding the baby was causing her.

Bo shook his head as the knowledge seemed to settle through him. "Darla Sims—a girl I dated for a little while over in the next county. She had him and didn't see fit to tell me."

His words trailed off and he looked lost. She could only imagine what he must be feeling. How could someone not have told him he had a son? Why would they keep something like that from him?

"She moved off and didn't leave a forwarding address, and now I know why. She didn't want me to know."

"Why is that?"

Bo raked a hand through his hair then rubbed the back of his neck, deep in thought. "She says she didn't think I'd want to know."

Abby couldn't help frowning. "And why would she think that?" Had he done something to make this woman believe he wouldn't be a good father—or want to be a good father?

"I don't know. Everyone knows I'm not looking to settle down any time soon. And we're pretty much a bachelor establishment here. Maybe that's why." He looked troubled as his gaze locked on the baby—at Levi. "She assumed I wouldn't want to take care of my responsibility."

So that was it. Abby instinctively cradled Levi closer and ignored the ache welling up in her heart. "Why did she just drop him off like this? It's very unorthodox." It was much more than that—for Abby it was incomprehensible.

The line between his brows deepened. "She's dead. Some friend of hers did this. She left this letter Darla wrote me and it says if I was reading it that she was dead. That she'd put everything in order so that I'm his parent on his birth certificate. I have no idea if this is real or not. I've never seen the baby. I had no idea I might have a child."

She stared at him; no words came. This was crazy.

"Hey, don't look at me like that. I'm sorry, I didn't know. It's not like I was told I had a kid and then I walked off and left him like some sorry son of a—" He clammed up, visibly reining in the flash of anger and frustration.

"I can't help it. This is a baby we're talking about." Abby had very strong feelings about who should and who shouldn't raise a baby—she didn't want to think about that. Didn't want to go there—couldn't go there. She shook her head, trying to clear the shadows creeping into her thoughts. "A baby takes commitment. Planning. The decision to have one shouldn't be taken lightly—" She hadn't taken it lightly. *Stop*—she screamed inside, not letting her thoughts turn inward. Her past had already ambushed her earlier and she could not let it spiral out of control.

Bo clamped his hands to his hips and thought for a moment. "Let's get this baby in the house. I need to call Jake Morgan, the sheriff, since I don't know what the procedure is in a situation like this, but he can help me figure out what to do."

Focus on a solution. "I agree completely," Abby said and they followed Bo inside. Pops trailed behind them.

A huge Bassett Hound lurked just inside the door, its long ears dragging on the floor as it took one look at her and the baby and galumphed off, toenails clacking on the hardwood floors. Its legs seemed to move in double time as it rounded the corner and disappeared from sight. Abby almost laughed, but the baby had begun wailing again and the dog immediately joined in from somewhere in the other room.

Abby felt the edge of the baby's diaper. Bingo. "This baby needs a diaper."

The blood drained from Bo's face. "Diaper, I don't have a diaper."

The man knew how to build a custom stirrup, but a baby was no-man's-land.

"Look around outside on the porch. Maybe this person who abandoned Levi thought to leave some supplies." If she could have snatched up the person who did this, Abby would not be responsible for her actions. The very idea, leaving a child on a porch like that!

"Yeah, sure. Of course. Babies need dry bottoms."

Abby found herself chuckling, despite everything else, as he ran for the door.

CHAPTER 5

Bo slid to a halt at the playpen. "Get a grip, Monahan. Get. A. Grip."

A father?

Was he a father? A dad . . .

He grabbed the porch rail with both hands and heaved in two deep gulps of air. He had to calm down, get his head on straight. Darla, dead? They had had a brief relationship that he'd regretted. It should have never happened as far as he was concerned because it had ended with Darla getting hurt—in more ways than he'd ever suspected.

The cry of the baby called him back to action and he scanned the porch and spotted the small bag on the porch beside the playpen. Relief surged through him. He snatched it up and yanked on the zipper. His fingers, normally so nimble with the intricate work he did with his stirrups, felt stiff and clumsy. As Bo tried to make the zipper work, Pops poked his head out the door and Solomon raced through the opening, looked up at him, and started wailing.

"Cut it out. I know." Bo glared at the dog. "I know we have a problem. And if you think you can do a better job, then come on, big boy, you go for it."

The dog tucked his tail and scurried back inside the house with Pops as if Bo had kicked him. Bo instantly felt like a slug, as if he hadn't already been feeling bad enough.

He hung his head, feeling every nerve sting with rawness as if completely exposed. What kind of man was a babbling basket case around a baby and yelled at dogs?

This day had held promise. He'd started out doing a good deed, helping out a female in need, and now he didn't know which way was up.

Spotting a couple of diapers inside the bag, he hurried inside. The kid was going to hurt himself if he kept this up. It was more than evident that he owed Abby Knightley a great debt. The woman was *his* knight in shining armor—and here he'd thought he was saving her.

That was almost laughable now. Bo had never been more out of his element. What would he have done if she hadn't been here?

. . .

"Got a bag. It's got two diapers in it—we've hit pay dirt," Bo said, racing back into the living room.

Abby noticed once more how appealing the man was even mussed and distressed—she yanked her gaze off of him and snatched the diaper.

He raked a hand through his hair. "Do you know how? Please tell me you do," he said.

Keeping her eyes off of him, she opened the diaper.

"Yes, thanks to many hours working at a day care during college," she assured him, and made quick work of getting a dry diaper on Levi. Her heart ached as she tended to the sweet baby—she'd been running on instinct when she'd taken the baby earlier. Instinct and survival mode . . . Landon had wanted babies so very much. And she'd put them off because of her career.

Abby dug around in the bag and found a can of formula and some jars of baby food. And finally a bottle. "That's a start. If you're calling the sheriff, maybe you'd better have him stop by and bring some diapers with him. I think he looks like maybe a size four—but I'm not sure how many pounds he weighs."

He looked like she'd just spoken gibberish. "Okay, I'm calling him now. Size four?"

She nodded. The man was all nerves. Abby didn't wait for him to say anything else. She walked into the kitchen and, holding the baby in one arm, she prepared a bottle of formula and then headed to the living room where she settled into a rocking chair in the corner. Levi was dry, eating, and happy at last—or at least for the moment.

Abby was about as far from happy as she could get, wanting even more now than ever to wring someone's neck. She had no patience for anyone who would abandon a child like this. Abby wasn't by nature a violent person, but right now she'd do some bodily harm to the "friend" who'd left Levi on the porch!

Yes, there could be reasons—mental illness, momentary insanity, whatever—but if there were any viable explanations to why this person had abandoned this baby on a porch without making certain there was someone there to take care of him, then Abby couldn't have cared less right now. Even if it was true and this baby's mother was dead, which was horribly sad, that didn't change the fact that she'd handled the baby's well-being carelessly. Not telling Bo. And then again, the so-called friend who'd left Levi on the porch. *What was wrong with that person*? Abby's head pounded— quite frankly she felt like she might explode, she was so steamed about it.

• • •

"I'll check into all of this for you," Jake Morgan said.

"Thanks," Bo was relieved to have Jake's help. He'd arrived within two hours after Bo called him, having stopped by the store and picked up some supplies for them. How many sheriffs would do that? Jake was one of the good guys.

He'd been the sheriff of Wishing Springs for several years. They'd all gone to school together and Jake had gone into law enforcement because it gave him the opportunity to protect and serve and ranch some at the same time. Jake had probably seen a lot of things in his years of law enforcement. Bo wondered how this ranked on the list.

"Strange that this woman's friend would leave the baby like this. Strange and wrong. But there are several reasons it could be. The person might have been scared you'd turn the kid away and they'd somehow think they were stuck with it."

"What?" Bo scowled at Jake.

"I'm not saying that's what would have happened. I'm saying that might be the impression this person had. Think about it. If the mom didn't believe you'd care to know about the baby, that's the impression her friend would have too."

"This is all just too crazy."

Jake slapped him on the back. "Yeah, but crazier things have happened."

Bo felt the heat of what—shame? Humiliation? Nothing good, he knew that for sure. Still he went there. "I tried to find numbers to call, but no luck."

"We'll take care of it. If you hear anything new, let us know."

Jake headed over to look at the baby as he slept in Abby's arms. When they'd first rung Jake, he'd been out on a call on the other side of the county and they'd had to wait. Abby hadn't mentioned leaving. Not that he'd asked. He'd needed her and he hadn't been shy about it. What was he supposed to do with a baby?

"Nice to meet you, Abby. If you need anything, you give me a call." He smiled, and Bo caught the interest in his gaze. Jake was a good man, so why did he want to tell him to step away from this particular single resident of Wishing Springs?

He walked Jake to the door and then turned and headed back into the living room. What would he have done if Abby hadn't been with him? He cringed at the very thought. Poor kid would have really been in a pickle.

Pops and Solomon had hovered near Abby and the

baby, completely curious about the tiny bundle, and Bo was just glad the baby and the dog had both quieted down. Again, he didn't know what he would have done if Abby hadn't been with him.

Jarrod came stalking through the back door. Though they were in the den, Bo knew instantly who was in the room.

"What's going on? I was in town and Clara Lyn said she'd heard through Madge the dispatcher that you had a baby out here. Asked me if I'd seen *your* baby yet. What's going on, Bo?"

Bo's shoulder muscles bunched into tighter knots. "When you figure it out, let me know. In the meantime, this is Levi. And, yes, he might be my son." He handed him the note off the table. "It's all there—what little we know, anyway. Someone left him on the porch with Pops."

Jarrod looked as stunned as Bo had felt. "On the porch with Pops," he said, taking the note and scanning it. "Is this true?"

Bo raked his hand down his face and let out a long sigh. "I don't know. It could be."

. . .

Abby left Bo and Jarrod and gently laid the sleeping child in the playpen that they'd brought inside. After pulling the baby blanket over him, she just stared at him for a moment, he was so sweet. Her heart ached . . . Pops, the sweet man, had trailed in behind her and he gently touched Levi's soft brown hair. "He's goin' ta be a cowboy."

Abby nodded. Trepidation consumed her looking into his twinkling eyes. When she'd filled the baby's bottle, she'd walked by a den on the way to the kitchen—a den full of Pops's life history. Truly a man's domain, the room was filled with bronze trophies, photos of a man on a cutting horse in several action shots, and an amazing pencil portrait. She'd thought it was Jarrod at first, but then after seeing all the championship photos with dates and names of Pops and his horses, she realized the pencil portrait was of Pops in his younger days. At Jarrod's age, midthirties, they'd been the spitting image of each other. And it was more than obvious that Pops had been a very talented man in his younger days.

She smiled at Pops. "Levi just might be a cowboy with all of you leading the way." She fought the urge to not form an attachment to Pops. Or to Levi. Or to the good-looking cowboy who very likely was a dad.

She wanted to go back to her hotel and disconnect—even though she'd come to Wishing Springs to do the opposite. But this was pressing a little too hard and fast at cuts that might never scab over.

But she was trying. She was here to force herself to take one day at a time and not compare it to the way it used to be—she was giving herself permission to have a good day.

Not that she'd had to have any permission since coming to Wishing Spings. A wreck with a cow and now, here she was taking care of this little boy, because if she hadn't what would have happened?

It made running for the hills impossible. She couldn't

run—not at the moment, even if she tried. She had no car and . . . she couldn't anyway, not yet.

Not like this.

"Hey, I hope you didn't need to be anywhere," Bo said, coming back inside from where he'd followed Jarrod to talk. "I don't know what I'd have done if you hadn't been here."

She placed a hand on her hip. "Bottom line, you're going to have to get comfortable with this baby. And you're going to have to do it soon. That means you're going to have to be able to pick him up without fear. You'll have to change his diaper, feed him, and talk to him."

He looked so panicked—like a forlorn puppy—that she almost smiled. Quite the opposite of the confident cowboy.

"I don't know what I'm doing."

"You'll learn, but the first thing is to get used to holding him. That was nice of the sheriff to bring out a car seat, by the way."

"He always keeps a couple handy because you never know when someone will need it."

"And now you definitely do. Let's go put Levi in it and find some more diapers and formula. He'll need both when he wakes up."

"Right. Sure. Let me stop Jarrod so he'll take Pops with him. He doesn't need to be left alone today. He's more confused because of the excitement. He does better when his routine isn't altered." He started back toward the door pulling his cell phone from his pocket at the same time. He spun back to her. "Wait, you're coming with me, right?"

Abby suddenly felt the heavy load sitting on Bo's shoulders. He had to work, keep watch on his Pops, and now he had a surprise baby on his hands. A sudden wave of compassion hit her. No wonder he was stressing out.

She closed her eyes and tried to calm the voice in her head telling her this was not her problem. "I'll go with you to the store and help you learn how to move about with a baby in tow—as best I can. I'm no expert. I worked at the day care and helped out with my cousin's baby a little while I was in college. But, Bo, believe me, you could probably find someone far more qualified—"

He'd stalked back to where she stood, and before she knew what he was doing, he'd grabbed her in a hard hug, stopping her rambling. Just pulled her into his arms and very nearly squeezed her in two.

"Thank you. Thank you! You have to know more than I do. We'll worry about the rest later."

Abby stared up into his bright eyes, completely shocked at finding herself in his strong arms, held tight against his solid chest. She could barely breathe, barely think . . . Pushing back, she moved away from him. Her knees wobbled as she did.

"Okay, good. Um, we should go. I-I need to get back to the motel soon." And away from this man and the unexpected and unwelcome emotions he had caused to rise up inside of her. She needed to get back on track with why she'd come to Wishing Springs. Finding a man had nothing whatsoever to do with it.

CHAPTER 6

Abby backed away from him like he had just made an outrageous pass at her. Bo wanted to kick himself—what had he been thinking to grab her up like that? He'd once again put her in an awkward situation. And even though he'd released her the moment she pushed against him he should have never grabbed her in the first place.

"Sorry about that," he said. "I was just so relieved to have your help."

"It's okay, I understand," she said quietly. "I'll get Levi ready and be right there. If you'll grab the diaper bag and the car seat I'll show you how it works when I get out there."

"Sure," he said, gathering up everything she'd told him to grab and heading outside to wait and kick himself a little bit more. A few minutes later she showed up with a bottle and the baby. She explained how to buckle a car seat in and then buckle Levi into it and then they headed out for the store.

Uncharted waters.

Driving toward town, his thoughts went to Darla. They had been going out for three weeks when things had gotten out of control with the beautiful woman. Bo had regretted it immediately. There were certain things he didn't take lightly. Sleeping around was one of those things. No, sadly that hadn't always been the case. He'd had his share of flings, but he'd recognized there was a void inside of him that ached for more, and so he began to draw the line at intimacy. He'd recognized that he wanted more from making love than immediate gratification. He wanted it to be special. To be right. He wanted it to mean something. And then there was the risk that always came that he could father a child. And that responsibility was definitely one he took seriously. At least he thought he did . . . With Darla he'd fallen short of his new convictions and she'd gotten hurt in the end and Levi, this innocent little boy, had almost paid for Bo's actions by being lost in the system, had it not been for Darla deciding to reach out to him in her last days.

Darla hadn't liked when he'd later drawn back from their relationship. But he'd known he didn't love her—he'd been wrong to let the physical relationship go so far. There was no going back; there was only ending it then, rather than later, before she got hurt any more. There hadn't been enough real meaning between them. Nothing to build a relationship on, nothing . . . of substance. He'd handled it all badly. He knew that more now than he had.

Was that why she'd kept Levi a secret—if in fact Levi was truly his?

He'd done fine until Darla, and now he was paying the consequences.

But worse, this little boy was paying them too.

He glanced at Abby sitting quietly in the seat next to him. This made how many uncomfortable trips in his truck? Man, what she must think of him.

The woman knew babies like she had two or three stashed somewhere—did that just come natural to women? But, despite her gentle care of Levi, she'd looked terrified a couple of times—especially when they'd first arrived at the ranch. He'd known Abby for less than thirteen hours and that entire time had been nothing but chaos.

Yeah, he thought with disgust. He thought she was great and she probably thought he was a loser.

· · ·

Abby stared out the window of Bo's truck and once again fought down the clawing need to run. Levi played with his toes in his car seat and Bo stared pensively forward as he drove into the parking lot of the discount store. He'd been a nervous wreck loading the baby into the truck.

Her lip stung from biting down on it in order not to tell Bo to drive more slowly, to look both ways at the stoplight, to watch for irresponsible drivers—for drunk drivers. All things that had played a role in the wreck that had stolen her . . . happiness, her world. Her—

No, she said nothing, not wanting to draw attention to her problem. He'd think she was crazy if she didn't explain why she was freaking out when he had been a very responsible driver so far. No, this was Abby's problem—one of a boatload she carried around with her—and she kept her mouth shut.

"Okay, here we are." Bo parked the truck and turned it off, but made no move to get out. "Abby, you okay?"

She glanced at him and nodded. "I'm fine. Just a lot on my mind. Let's go inside and stock up on some things. If you'll just get Levi, we'll head inside." Abby got out and walked around to his side of the truck and opened the rear door. He got out and stood beside her. "Okay, take him out."

Bo did as he was told, though he fumbled with the snaps and releases and she had to reach in and show him how to undo the buckle. Their fingers brushed and she yanked hers away instantly, but the electric sizzle tingled all the way through her . . .

Not good. Not good at all.

"You're doing fine," she said, tucking her fingers securely into her jeans pockets. She stared at his back, the muscles working as he lifted Levi from the seat and turned to her with a hesitant smile of triumph on his lips. Butterflies fluttered through her as if newly freed from their cocoons. It had only been two years since she'd lost Landon. She wasn't ready for butterflies—as shocking as it was that they were winging their way around her stomach.

"Bo," she said, determination in her tone, her mouth dry as grit. She needed out of this situation and she needed out fast. "I'm showing you how to do all of this and then you're going to have to drop me off at the hotel on the way home. You're going to be on your own."

His smile faded and the panic returned to his gorgeous

eyes. "Abby, hold on, please. I know you barely know me and you're probably wishing you'd never laid eyes on me, but we're going to be a mess without some more guidance. The poor little dude is gonna wail himself into a fit and break out in a large bumpy red rash or something—it won't be pretty. Heck, *I'll* probably do the same. All you need to do is name your price and you've got the job."

"No," Abby snapped, feeling as if an arctic wind had just blown through her, chilling her to her core. "I can't. I really can't," she said, more calmly now, but still firm. The man had awakened something inside of her she didn't want and it disturbed her beyond measure. "You'll be fine. You'll find someone if you need them, it's just not me." If Maggie were here she could help him. There were plenty of people in town who could help him.

This was not her problem. She'd just happened to be in the wrong place at the wrong time, and that was the only reason she was here now.

But she was done.

At least she was as soon as they were finished shopping.

. . .

Bo knew Abby was right. She needed to go home; this wasn't her problem. Following her into the store, he berated himself for having taken advantage of her this way. If he hadn't been desperate, he wouldn't have. But he had been desperate, and he still was. Staring down at the baby in his arms, he tried not to think about what he would do tonight when he got home and it was just the two of them—and Pops and maybe Jarrod. It was going to be a very long night. Of course he could call for help—maybe Peg Garwood, the nurse who ran Over the Rainbow. Or her daughter Lana. But Abby was here and for some unexplainable reason, her being here helped him.

Levi looked up at him and blew a spit bubble, then grinned. The kid was completely oblivious to the trauma that was happening around him. Bo was just thankful beyond measure that he wasn't crying.

He was glad the baby wasn't crying either.

. . .

"Hey there, Bo."

"Hi, Doonie?" Bo greeted, halting beside the shopping buggies.

"Doonie." The lanky man grinned, coming their way.

So this was Doonie Burke, town mayor and twin brother to Doobie. She'd learned about them through the columns she'd read. They owned the real estate agency in town and she hoped they would help her find a house.

"Is that the baby?" he asked, tickling Levi under the chin. He was in his late fifties or early sixties, and he had an easy manner about him. "I heard Madge on the scanner telling one of the deputies that you'd had a baby dropped off under suspicious circumstances."

Bo's eyes widened. "You heard that on the *scanner*?"

Doonie was grinning despite Bo's obvious displeasure at realizing he'd been the brunt of town gossip.

"You think he's yours?"

"I guess you heard that on the scanner too. Mayor, it seems to me you need to do something with your town employees. I bet Jake isn't going to like knowing his dispatch is using the police scanner to yammer about things she should be keeping to herself."

Doonie looked perplexed. "Well, Bo, Madge's been doing that for over twenty years. It'd kinda be hard to turn her off now. So is he yours?"

Bo glanced at Levi, indecision written all over his expression.

Abby frowned. Yes, there was a possibility that Levi wasn't his, but from all she'd heard and seen, the likelihood that he was Levi's dad was strong. It bothered her that he didn't acknowledge the possibility that Levi was his.

"An old girlfriend dropped him off," he hedged and shot Abby an uncertain glance.

Fighting off the unreasonable irritation she was feeling, she reminded herself that he didn't know if Levi was his. He'd just been surprised by all of this and thus he had reasons—good reasons—to hesitate. Still . . . she felt for the baby with no one to claim him. A baby should have someone claiming him.

"Well, why'd she drop him off at your place? That's downright odd if he's not yours. He sure is a cute little fella." Doonie grinned at the baby then directed his attention to her. "I'm sorry, little lady. I'm Doonie Burke, the mayor, and I don't believe we've met."

"I'm Abby Knightley. It's very nice to meet you." She was thrilled to have something else to focus on rather than the cowboy beside her.

"You're the little gal staying at the Sweet Dreams Motel. The one that hit the steer."

"I am. But I didn't hit the steer. I missed him." Goodness, news traveled fast.

"Well, that's not the way the story is going 'round. Heard you ran into him."

"She hit a fence to avoid the steer. So that should show you not to believe everything you hear," Bo grumbled.

Doonie grinned. "I agree. But that don't explain why your old girlfriend would drop a baby off if it wasn't yours. Don't you agree?" he asked Abby again.

"Actually, I do find that a bit odd." She narrowed her eyes at Bo.

"What's odd?" a man who looked identical to Doonie asked as he hurried from the crowd at a jaunty gait. There was no mistaking who he was.

Quick introductions were made between Doobie Burke and Abby. She was glad to have a moment to rein in her anger at Bo.

"So what's odd and whose baby is this?" Doobie asked again, tickling Levi under the chin and making the baby gurgle. Abby's heart tugged and she shut down the emotions she'd been fighting all morning.

She also realized they could spend all morning in the entrance of the store with the same question going round and round.

"That the mother of this baby just dropped the baby off at Bo's and he doesn't have a clue whose baby it is," Doonie informed him, and Doobie's mouth dropped.

"That's odd all right. Bo, why would she drop a baby off at your place if he isn't yours?"

All eyes turned to Bo.

"Fellas, I *told* you. I *don't* know who Levi belongs to. His mother is dead. She didn't drop him off—some friend of hers did. And *yes*, to be honest, there is a possibility he's mine. Jake's looking into it. I'm as confused as everyone, so could I get a break here?"

The twins looked at each other, and Doobie rubbed his long jaw. "Too bad about the kid's mother. That's sad."

"Terrible," Doonie said. He turned his attention to Abby. "What brings you to our little town?" he asked, effectively giving Bo the space he'd asked for.

"I'm moving here. And I'd planned to come to your real estate office today, so it's nice to meet the two of you."

They grinned with wide matching smiles. "Well, that's perfect," Doonie said.

"We'll be in, so come on by," Doobie added.

"I will, but it looks like it will be morning before I make it. I'm helping Bo this afternoon."

"Helpin'? Savin' his life is probably more accurate." Doonie chuckled.

"Ain't *that* for sure." Doobie shook his head, his brows hitched up comically.

Abby felt Bo's pain as he scowled at the twins.

He looked uneasy. "She's saving me all right and I admit it. I don't know anything about babies." That made the twins grin wider. And they were still grinning when they left a few minutes later after assuring her they could fix her up.

"They're a barrel of laughs," Bo grunted as the men headed into the parking lot.

Abby swung around. "You denied Levi even though you're pretty certain he's yours." She tried not to sound too accusing. Or too unreasonable simply because she was being unreasonable.

"Hey, whoa—I didn't deny him. Honestly."

"Well, you didn't acknowledge him possibly being yours."

"Because I don't *know* for certain if he's mine. And I hadn't exactly thought about being asked that question. It took me by surprise."

"I guess so, but it just seemed harsh." She studied Levi, hurting for him. He looked happy in Bo's arms—at least he seemed to be bonding with Bo, who was carrying him as if he were a football being protected in the crook of Bo's arm.

Bo scowled. "Can't you give me a break here? This came out of the blue today."

Abby raked her hand through her hair and stared at the ground for an instant, knowing she was being too hard on him. She knew she sometimes overreacted in high stress situations ever since the accident. She was being terribly unreasonable here. "I'm sorry." She sighed. "It's just me. I mean, the thought of this little boy having no one hurts my heart."

His eyes softened. "I understand that, it hurts mine too. I promise it's going to be fine."

Abby nodded. Suddenly unable to speak, she walked ahead of him, found the baby aisle, and headed into it despite the ache that throbbed through her with each step she took. This was the aisle she'd never had a reason to come down before now. She'd been too busy to think about a baby—despite how much Landon wanted one. And like Bo, she'd had no idea when she'd created a tiny life . . . she hadn't known until it had been too late. Swallowing hard, fighting off the lump of tears that suddenly clogged her throat, she brushed a tear aside and forced her thoughts back to the task at hand. This was about Bo and Levi. And she knew enough from day care and friends with babies to help him buy necessities. She just had to keep the door to her heart firmly shut and not think about her past. And she needed to lighten up on Bo.

She'd get this done and get back to her room. And she couldn't get there soon enough.

CHAPTER 7

Bo felt as if he were wading through a swamp with sinkholes, driving toward Abby's motel to drop her off. He could ride bucking broncs—had ridden plenty when he'd competed and even a few bulls in his teen years and it hadn't scared him any. The thought of being alone with Levi all night terrified him.

He'd never felt so inept in all of his life. He needed a woman to help—he needed Abby but he wouldn't beg. Okay, so there were a bunch of women, even nurses, in town who could help him, so why was he acting like Abby was his only hope?

Because she's the one you want. Levi's already comfortable with her.

Despite this, he cowboyed up and did not drop to the ground and throw his arms around her knees.

If only Tru and Maggie were home from their honeymoon trip, he'd be just fine. Maggie would know what to do—but she wasn't here.

And he couldn't hold Abby hostage any longer.

Hope that she'd offer to stay and help him had flown the coop back at the store. She'd lost all patience with him when he hadn't instantly acknowledged Levi as his son. She'd helped him, but she'd been withdrawn the rest of the time in the store.

"Thanks for everything, and I mean that," he said when they reached the motel. He held the panic back as she got out. He gave her a small smile when she looked at him. "Have a good night. It's time for you to get your life back. I never meant to hijack it today."

She nodded and shot an uneasy glance at Levi. "Bo, you'll do fine. You just have to get used to having Levi around and protecting him. Let your instincts kick in. You'll figure it all out."

The impact of her words seemed alien to him. "I'm still trying to get used to that. This morning I had no child and now, I'm supposedly a father. In an instant. It's just hard to have that thrown at you and for it to actually sink in."

She studied him for a long moment and he didn't know whether she was thinking he was a slug or trying to come up with some helpful words. "Don't get me wrong, I'm going to do right by him. And if I'd known about him when he was born, I'd have done right by him then."

She looked into the backseat at Levi who had fallen asleep almost the instant the truck started moving. "You know, there are some people who have it the other way around. They're a parent one minute, and then in the blink of an eye it's taken away and they have to adjust to that." His insides curled at that thought and the deep sadness that stole into her gaze. "I'd say looking at those two options, you have just received a beautiful gift."

He watched her walk to her bungalow and insert the key. He couldn't move until she was inside.

What was Abby's story? Something had happened to Abby Knightley and he was certain it went soul-deep.

.   .   .

The afternoon sun didn't penetrate the chill running through Abby as she walked away from man and baby. Entering her motel room, she closed the door and leaned her forehead against it. Her stomach felt sick and her heart cold. "They'll be fine. They will be," she whispered.

Spinning around she felt the hard wood against her back as she stared at the motel room. The silent room.

Abby's throat went dry.

She had come here to forget—not be reminded. She'd come here to move forward—not to be drawn backwards into memories, memories she desperately needed to learn how to live with. Feeling boxed in and unable to breathe, she yanked open the door and stepped back outside into the fall sunshine. She took a calming breath despite her racing pulse. She needed to do something else—it was time to check out the town.

Yes, a walk was what she needed.

She'd gotten off to an unusual start here in Wishing Springs. Fresh air, fresh attitude, check—she stepped purposefully down the street. Tomorrow she'd start jogging again. But today she'd walk, see everything, and figure out a good route. Today she'd grab a paper, look at For Sale ads tonight, and be ready to see Doonie and Doobie tomorrow.

A few minutes later she crossed several streets she could see were residential with sidewalks and green yards. She made herself tune in to the birds singing in the trees and to the peace within the shaded streets. She made herself not think about Bo Monahan and Levi. And she prayed Levi was smiling and not crying.

They'd be fine. There were plenty of people in town the man could call. She'd just gotten here—she was not the only person who could take care of a baby. She'd just happened to be the one with Bo when his world had gotten shaken up.

That's completely right, Abby.

"Right." There was no need for her to have to be around Bo. He just made her uncomfortable. And she didn't need or want uncomfortable.

She wanted peace . . . community. She wanted to smile more freely and feel okay doing it. Wanted to feel like she deserved to smile again. Again, Landon would want her to, but that didn't mean she could do it . . . not after the wreck. That would mean she had to forgive herself—she heaved in a deep breath and focused on the town square as she made it to the corner.

And she smiled as she got the full impact of Wishing Springs for the first time.

It wasn't really anything special to look at—a small town like so many across Texas, but she could feel the spirit of the place as she stood there . . . Maggie had described Wishing Springs through the people who lived there and that was the part that had drawn Abby to it. The community spirit. And as she walked from the motel several people had waved and greeted her. There was no courthouse in the center of the square, instead it was a wide grassy area planted with shrubs and flowers with a gazebo in the center. Brick walkways crisscrossed the grassy area and met at the old-fashioned white wooden gazebo surrounded by overflowing flower beds. Her spirits lifted. She sank onto a bench that faced the north side of the square. A huge old oak tree shaded the bench and a portion of the street in front of her, its limbs were so wide. The old song "Tie a Yellow Ribbon Round the Old Oak Tree" played in her mind. She half expected to see a yellow ribbon around the trunk as if it had been placed there for her.

The thought was nice.

Her heart tightened, ached with the ever present "alone" that echoed through her—never fully letting her forget that *she* was alone now.

When Landon had been alive, she'd felt strong. She'd felt strong prior to meeting him too. But since the wreck she'd lost more than just Landon. She'd lost who she'd been.

She had come here for many reasons, but at the heart of it was that she'd come here to find that strong woman she'd once been. Even if it was by force. And a constant kick in the rump. She inhaled the fresh scent of roses and focused on surveying the town from her spot—a dress store, a coffee shop, several antique stores, and the Cut Up and Roll hair salon met her eye.

She needed her hair done and it would be a great excuse to meet them—Clara Lyn Conway and Reba Moorsby, the two women who she'd seen on the TV special that had aired with Maggie and Tru. They'd looked like fun.

Suddenly the door opened and out came a short, slightly plump woman with styled gray hair, a colorful outfit, sparkly sandals, and huge jewelry Abby could see all the way from her seat.

She smiled. Clara Lyn just looked like a woman who enjoyed life—something Abby desperately needed to learn to do.

And in that moment she looked toward where Abby sat on the park bench. Then, to Abby's surprise, she hustled across the street and walked straight up to Abby.

"Hello, there—I bet you're Abby, aren't you?"

Abby laughed in surprise. "Yes, ma'am, how did you know that?"

"Awww." The spunky woman waved a hand, and a lively grin swamped her expression. "Pebble described you and, well, I'm nosey enough that when I saw someone that I didn't know, I came to investigate." She laughed at herself and that made Abby chuckle—it felt really good. "I have to tell you that we've had a lot of women visiting since Maggie did that show, but you're the first one we know of who has plans to move here. I am so tickled about that. I got to tell you, this town could use new blood to shake things up."

Abby wasn't sure how she felt about that statement. "I, well, I came for a fresh start. I was looking for a new place, my life needed a change, and through Maggie's column, this started to seem like a great small town." She hadn't really meant to say so much, but there was no taking it back now.

"Oh, it is. I've lived here my whole life and I won't leave for anything until the good Lord takes me home." She leaned in close and tapped Abby on the knee. "So, you've been out there with Bo. Doonie came by and told us he'd seen you at the store with Bo and his baby."

Abby hesitated, not really knowing how she should answer this question. "Yes, he has a baby." She'd been aggravated that he'd hedged on the answer when Doonie and Doobie had asked.

"Well, I know you've just gotten here, but I can tell you that is a good man. He and his brothers are working hard to carry on their granddaddy's legacy. I can't respect them enough. If that is his baby, he's born into a great family."

Abby found her loyalty touching. She almost revealed that he hadn't known about Levi, but she didn't. There was no doubt in her mind that everyone would know that piece of info soon enough and without any help from her. She was trying not to get pulled into that situation any more than she already had. "He seems to be a nice guy," was all she said. She had to say something.

"So, you read Maggie's advice column?"

"Yes, I do. She's really good."

Clara Lyn nodded. "That's the truth. She'll love meeting you when she and Tru get home from their honeymoon-slash-cutting-horse-exhibition."

"I would *love* to meet her." Abby tried to hold back her excitement at the thought of actually meeting Maggie. Abby had saved Maggie's advice in her heart—sometimes it took courage to make a change and take steps to become joyful and seek fulfillment again after tragedy. She was so right.

Those words had propelled Abby to step out and reach for happiness again. Not in the form of looking to fall in love again, Abby just couldn't do it again. Couldn't go through the heartache that love could bring. But she was stepping out, trying to find new meaning to her life—trying to figure out why she'd lived . . . trying to find some semblance of peace . . . like she'd seen others in her position do. But no, that didn't include looking for love again. She just couldn't risk that again.

She knew she had to find a way to live with the grief that was a constant and forever part of her now, but she had to go on. Like Maggie had told her, not living while she was living was doing no one any good. "Well, it's been so nice meeting you, Clara Lyn. I guess I better head back toward the motel. I have listings to go over before I meet with Doonie and Doobie tomorrow." She rose and so did Clara Lyn.

"How exciting. There are several places up for sale now—I'm sure you'll find the perfect spot." She paused, then opened her mouth to say more, but snapped her lips together.

"Were you going to ask me something else?" Abby was perplexed by the older woman's hesitancy to go on. It was obvious by the look in her eyes and the firm way she'd snapped her mouth shut that she had something on her mind.

"Yes, actually, I'm concerned. How do you think Bo is doing out there with that baby by himself tonight?"

The question rolled out in a rush then she kept on talking. "That boy hasn't been around a baby his entire life. I may have to grab up Reba soon as she finishes up her last manicure and drive out there and see if he needs anything. What do you think?"

Relief surged through Abby. "Oh, I think that would be a great idea. He could probably use the help. He was all thumbs today and nervous." She halted her rattling and felt her cheeks burn. "That would be nice of y'all."

Yes, she had just met the man and been thrown into his unusual situation completely by chance. They hardly knew each other. And he made her uncomfortable. But it wasn't his fault. It was nothing he did—it was her, not him . . . and that was what made her so uncomfortable. She could relax, though, because Levi would be taken care of if Reba and Clara went out there.

"Okay, well, I better head on back now. I tell you, these cowboys sometimes just won't reach out and ask for help when they need it," Clara Lyn said, but she halted before taking two steps. "Oh, before I go— would you like to join our committee and help with the picnic we're putting on next weekend? We can sure use some help, and we like making new folks feel at home, so we sure want to include you in the festivities. It's going to be a good old-fashioned dinner on the grounds. Everyone brings a basket with enough food in it for two."

The woman jumped around topics like popcorn in the microwave. Abby smiled again. "That sounds fun. What can I do?"

"We're going to be out here decorating on Friday, if

you'd like to help with that. It's our inaugural picnic for the shelter and we plan to continue them like they used to do. It'll be fun. There hasn't been a town picnic in a hundred years."

"Really, so they used to have them here?"

Clara Lyn's expression turned rapturous. "Oh, yes. Right here in this park. When I read about them I took it immediately to the town council and they all voted unanimously on it. It's always good to do things to bring new breath to a place. And we want to keep things rolling on a positive slant to take advantage of all the publicity we got from that TV show."

"It sounds like fun."

"Oh, it will be. I tell you, I've never seen so many women just come into town and walk around for a day. Of course some of the younger ones are wanting to see the cowboys Maggie wrote about." She chuckled.

"I'm curious, how does that go over with the cowboys? Are they thrilled about being the draw?" How did Bo feel about it, in other words?

"Some of them are tickled pink and give them some flirting. And there may have been a date or two come out of it, I don't really know for sure. It's hard to keep a finger on all of it. But me and Reba aren't shy about trying. Someone has to know what's making the town go round. But I can tell you that there are some of the fellas that aren't happy about the situation."

"It sounds like y'all have it under control." Abby found herself laughing at the woman's obvious delight in the matchmaking prospects of the situation. Then it dawned on her that if she were single and newly moved to town she very well could be targeted by their scheming. "Well, I better go. Talk to you later."

As she said good-bye and headed back toward the motel Abby's thoughts immediately went back to Bo . . . and Levi.

She couldn't help wondering if the baby was really his. And she was glad he was about to get some help—help that wasn't her.

CHAPTER 8

W hat do you mean, change his diaper?" Jarrod boomed, holding the baby away from him like he was a sack of potatoes gone rank. "He smells like the south end of a pole cat."

Bo glared at his older brother. The man worked with cows every day and had mucked out plenty of stalls—and so had he for that matter. But Bo needed a break. "Lay him down and take that atrocious thing off, then clean him up and strap on another one. It's like mucking out a stall."

"Hey, I did not sign on for this."

"*Uncle* Jarrod—uncles do this sort of thing all the time."

Jarrod glared at him with his piercing gunmetal eyes. "You do it. If I'm an uncle then it's not because of anything *I* did."

"I'm not the one holding him."

Jarrod crossed the living room and pushed the baby at Bo. "Take him."

"Aw, come on, Jarrod. Give me a break. I've changed him three times and you should see the stuff coming out of that kid. Maybe we should take him to the doc."

"I'm pretty sure what you're seeing is normal. I'm just not ready to deal with it myself. And that's why you don't see me with a wife or a baby."

Bo barely knew Abby Knightley, but he'd have given her a million dollars to have stayed here and helped him out.

Then came a knock on the door, and this time when Jarrod shoved Levi at Bo, he automatically grabbed him. Jarrod walked through the living room and out into the entrance hall. Bo met Levi's wide eyes, amazed the kid wasn't wailing. Resigned to the duty before him, he strode toward the couch where he had a towel laid out. He'd already learned when he changed a diaper everything in the immediate vicinity needed to be protected. Including himself. If he'd been smart he'd have bought a rain suit while he was at the store. The kid was dangerous. Bo had been given a shower the first time he'd undone the diaper.

The unmistakable voices of Clara Lyn and Reba drifted from the hallway. And the next thing he knew the cavalry rushed into the room. To the rescue, more accurately.

"Bo Monahan, you look like you could use a helping hand," Clara Lyn said, hustling across the living room with Reba right behind her.

He figured he probably looked like a starving man being offered a steak. "I wouldn't turn it down."

The ladies crowded round and started cooing and talking in weird voices to the boy. "Oh, look at the wittle fella. Aren't you just a sight for sore eyes? Yes, you are. Oh, yes, you are." Clara Lyn carried on as she shooed Bo out of the way and took his place on the couch. Levi gave her a grin while she continued her Elmer Fudd language.

"You are a stinky fella," Reba added, smoothing Levi's hair.

In the blink of an eye they had that diaper off and those wipes efficiently swiping. Within seconds there was a new diaper in place—actually on straight.

"There, he's all smelling nice again," Clara said, picking him up.

Reba turned to Bo and handed him the offensive diaper, all balled up and neatly taped together with the tabs. "You two can dispose of this, please."

Bo reached for it with two fingers and then took it to the back porch and stuffed it in the plastic bag with the others. When he entered the living room again Jarrod looked less stressed and the ladies were having the time of their lives entertaining the boy. His boy.

Bo had still not gotten used to the thought. Of course he knew there was a high likelihood that the boy wasn't his, but then there was that one time, that chance that he was. And until he knew otherwise, he would do what he needed to do to make it right for the little fella. He just wished those nasty diapers didn't come with the territory.

• • •

Abby jogged through a tree-lined neighborhood not far from the motel the next morning, enjoying the feel of energy that hummed through her with each stride she took. She'd always loved to run, but since the wreck she'd only gotten back to it in the recent months. Her extensive injuries had made it impossible until then, and even now she wasn't back up to speed, but she was grateful that she was doing it at all. It was one of those things she'd never take for granted again.

When she'd been confined to a wheelchair, she'd feared she'd never get the chance again. But though she wasn't running marathons yet, and it had taken more time than she wished, she'd finally started jogging a consistent two miles at a time.

Her phone rang and she thought about just letting the caller leave a voice mail, but she'd reached her jogging limit anyway. Her hip was starting to hurt. She slowed to a walk as she pulled her phone from her pocket and pushed the button.

"Moving to a town because of an advice column is just plain reckless," her mother said, repeating what had been her mantra since learning what Abby planned to do. "Come home, Abby." She hadn't even given Abby a chance to say hello—she just picked right up on the conversation they'd had the day Abby had planned to hit the road toward Wishing Springs. Her mother had basically blocked her path. This had become the only conversation they had.

Abby inhaled heavily. "Good morning to you too," she said, "and this conversation has grown very old, Mom."

"Good morning? I hope it's a good morning. But I haven't slept thinking about all this. You're my daughter and I love you. I know you needed a change. You had become a hermit. But this sits on the edge of crazy, and I'm worried about you even more now that you've actually done it."

Abby fought to keep her patience. Her mother's negative attitude had been one reason Abby had been shutting her out of her life. Since Landon's death she'd helped to cripple Abby with her continual attitude that Abby needed to give herself time to recover. It was almost as if she didn't think Abby could make a life without Landon. And that wasn't the kind of thinking Abby needed.

She'd written into the Gotta Have Hope column and asked Maggie for advice and Maggie had agreed with her. She needed positive thinking right now. And that meant limiting contact with people who couldn't give that to her. Of course Abby had basically limited contact with everyone. And that hadn't been good either.

"Maybe that's the whole point of this. I'm too cautious. Too fearful. I'm predictable and boring. Maybe I need to be a little crazy."

She could hear her mother's heavy sigh. Could envision the small worry frown that would etch her expression. Abby loved her mom despite recognizing that she exacerbated Abby's problem. "You know it's true."

"I know that, Abby, but you've only just lost your husband two years ago. Moving like this doesn't make sense."

"Stop. I'm here and so far it's not been exactly what I'd expected, but I'm staying."

"What do you mean not been what you expected?" her mom asked, ignoring the first part of Abby's declaration.

"I hit a cow—I mean a steer—and then found a baby on a doorstep—"

"What do you mean you hit a cow? And a baby— what baby? *Are you kidding me?*"

Abby cringed at her mother's shrill hysteria. "It's okay, I didn't mean that literally. What I meant was I almost hit a cow, but missed it and took out a fence, messing up my car. I made it through all of it. Bo Monahan came to my rescue with the cow and he and his brother Jarrod got the wrecker out there. The car is being repaired right now."

"But you're okay."

"Yes."

"But you said a baby on a doorstep. What do you mean? How did you find a baby on a doorstep? Whose baby?"

Abby told her everything, well, almost everything. She kept to herself the disturbing attraction she felt toward Bo. There would be no end to her mother's distress about that.

"So what are you going to do? Oh, Abby, a baby."

Abby rubbed her temple. "I don't know, Mom. I keep thinking about Levi, the baby. But I didn't come here to get tangled up with a cowboy and his mixed-up life." Guilt zinged her, because she sounded so callous. As if she were being too hard on Bo. But he had clearly been doing things that had major consequences. Things she just didn't believe in. When a man and a woman had a physical relationship, it was to be after they were married. She couldn't help how others viewed it—that was the way she believed.

She and Landon had waited, though it hadn't been easy, but Landon had respected her wishes and he'd liked them . . .

"Abby, I still can't believe you quit your job. Mr. Case called and asked me to tell you you can have it back any time you want it. You loved your career. It's not too late to come back. You could buy another house or better yet, get you a smaller condo. You won't have a yard to worry with and you'll be safe."

Abby cringed at the thought of going back to her marketing career. After the accident she'd taken an extended leave of absence with plans to go back, and her boss had been so patient and kind. But she knew part of that came from the fact that she'd been a relentless, dedicated employee who did an outstanding job for him. At the sacrifice of her home life. Abby had put far too much focus on her career, on moving up the corporate ladder and now, yes, she had money in the bank but an empty life . . . bile rose in her throat as weakness swept over her at the thought of even walking back into that building ever again.

And her mom saying that a condo in Houston was safer than this small town with a practically nonexistent crime rate would have been laughable in another conversation.

"I'll be fine. I can't go back to corporate life—it cost me too much. Mom, you have to stop this. I don't want my old career back." There, she was putting her foot down once more. But this time with a little more force. Maybe distance helped her disconnect from feeling as if she were betraying her mother by saying this. "I'm staying here and that's that. I committed to it and, well, I like it, despite the unusual beginnings. And I'm safe and you know it."

Her mother huffed. "Abby, I have done nothing but care about you. I loved Landon like he was my son. And he would not want you doing this. He would want you getting back to the life y'all had made here. With your friends that you've shut out and continue to shut out. Kim called me yesterday worried about you."

The exasperation and irritation of her mother's words struck her. And her friend Kim loved her, but had been pushing for Abby to do what *she* thought was best for Abby and finally Abby had to let go. At least for the time being. "That's just it. I only think about the way things were when I'm with all of you. And the continual talk of how it was, though it helped me cope at first, is now keeping me from making progress. And to be honest, I have to stop thinking about what Landon would want for me. Landon is gone. He's gone, Mom, and he's not coming back. And I have to come to terms with that. And so do you and everyone else. I have to make a new life for myself. Because . . ." Her heart pounded and blood was rushing through her veins so quickly it was making her dizzy. ". . . as bad as I hate it, I didn't die in that car crash. I was left here and whether I like it or not, that's what I have to live with."

Abby's stomach roiled. "I have to go." She hated this, hated the strain between them, but everything she'd said was true.

And that was why she'd had to leave. She hadn't died and she had to deal with that and find some way to live with that fact.

CHAPTER 9

Clara Lyn and Reba finally wore the baby out. They'd stayed and helped Bo with getting Levi settled for the night and some supper cooked for Pops. He'd enjoyed it and they'd acted as if having a baby in the house was an everyday occurrence. And that it was as easy as breathing. That would be laughable, if he'd been in a laughing mood.

Jarrod had gone home. And the ladies left—thinking like Bo that now that the little boy was asleep, everything would be great till morning. Boy, had that been a false assumption.

Not exactly the way it went. Exactly three hours after he went to sleep, all chaos broke out. Levi woke crying and wouldn't stop. Bo had picked him up and walked all over the house with him. There had been no consoling the kid. Morning's first light crept over Bo. He'd finally fallen asleep in the recliner with the exhausted baby asleep on his chest.

He awoke to find Pops standing at the end of the recliner trying to tug Bo's boots off.

That was Pops, even with his memory shot to pieces, he was still trying to take care of everyone.

Only problem was the tugging woke up the baby. And the wailing started again. And Bo suddenly felt something warm spreading over his chest and realized the kid's diaper was leaking.

"Great, just great," he grunted. "It's okay, Pops, I don't need my boots off just yet. Can you get me a diaper?"

"You got it, son."

Bo blinked at the familiar words. Then grinned. Whenever Pops had a good day his spirits lifted.

Stumbling groggily over to the couch where the towel was still spread out, he laid the wailing baby down and tried to soothe him as he stripped off the diaper and took the one Pops handed him. "Thanks, Pops," he said, his voice sounding gravelly with lack of sleep.

Pops beamed and sat on the edge of the coffee table. "Shh, little Bo, don't cry. It's gonna be okay, son."

Bo's gaze shot to his grandfather—did he think Bo was Pops's son, Bo's dad? He'd seemed so much more confused this month.

Bo still had a hard time thinking about his dad. The betrayal hit him hard. How did a man gamble so much that he hocked a ranch to the hilt—a ranch that his own dad had slaved over and built?

Pops had built the Four of Hearts up to the beauty it was with his own two hands. He'd buried three sons and now his fourth, counting Bo's dad, and he'd buried a dear wife and a daughter-in-law he'd loved like she was his own blood. He'd had only one other daughter-in-law and she'd remarried a long time ago and moved to Montana.

He'd lost so much. And before he'd lost his memory

to the extent that it was now, he'd known what his only living son had done before dying. Bo blamed his grandfather's advancing Alzheimer's on his dad. The strain had been too much.

And the situation seemed to be deteriorating. He hoped the medication kicked in soon and helped bring him back to them for a little longer.

It was hard to watch and getting harder, and Levi showing up wasn't helping the situation.

"Pops, we better find this baby something to eat, or he's going to cry himself sick."

Pops shot up from the coffee table and headed for the kitchen. Solomon, who had been lying on his back with his legs spread wide in a midmorning nap, grunted, then rolled laboriously to the side and hauled himself up to follow Pops. The creature was a one-man pooch, if useless.

Bo carried the baby on his shoulder and tried not to think about the caustic scent rising up from the wet area of his shirt. Boy, would he love a shower right now.

He pulled open the fridge and grabbed the formula that Clara Lyn had premade for him. He managed to get it in the many bottles that Abby had him buy and that the ladies had sterilized before they'd left. He got the formula poured into the bottle, splashing some over the edge when Levi moved around. He had to struggle to keep the kid from twisting out of his one arm. He'd estimated that if Levi was his, then he'd be about one year old. Bo didn't know anything about babies, but was learning quick that a person needed two sets of hands when dealing with one.

By the time he got the bottle warmed, Levi had a beet-red face and Pops was frantic. And Bo had no idea what to do. Jarrod had ranch work that had to be done today and Bo had stirrups to make. His guys could cover for him some, but there were certain things he took care of personally that were going to back up if he didn't figure something out.

Every custom stirrup carried the guarantee of Monahan hands on it in the process. He did the detailing and if nothing else, he always branded the logo on each one. He'd always taken that promise seriously . . .

But right now he had a baby to take care of.

And parenthood to figure out.

. . .

"So you want a small place?" Doonie Burke asked Abby after she arrived at his office. Abby had wasted no time after her conversation with her mom. She needed to rent or buy a place and she needed to do it soon. The sooner the better. She needed to make this official.

She had the money. She and Landon had had a very comfortable life with both of their incomes. She had a cushion from what they'd saved and put in the bank that had enabled her to walk away from her corporate job without worry. Then there was the other . . . the money from the accident. The money she didn't want to think about. She had no plans to live on that money. If she had needed it, then it would be a blessing in her life . . . but nothing about the accident was a blessing. Nothing. She had plans to use it for something good at some point, but hadn't had the heart to think about it.

And she still didn't. "Yes, not tiny, but not something I'd be rambling around in all by myself. And in town if possible. I'll be looking for a job and I'd like to be close to it." She didn't know yet what she was going to do but she knew working again was in her plans. She was still trying to figure that out, but she knew it wouldn't involve marketing reports, statistics, or cubicles. "I saw a cute little house over on Daisy Street. What do you know about that one?" She looked from Doonie to his brother Doobie—mirror images, if it weren't for the shirts they wore. Doonie had on a Hawaiian shirt and Doobie had on a striped western shirt.

"That belongs to Rand Radcliff, the editor of the newspaper. It was one of the ones we recommend you see. How about we load up in the SUV and head over to see it and two more we have a couple of quiet streets from here?"

The tingle of excitement at the prospect was welcomed. "I'd love that."

Within minutes they were back on Daisy Street beneath the big oak trees. With the well-kept yards, it felt welcoming.

"Now, this here is a rental , but Rand might be open to selling it to the right neighbor since he lives right beside the little place."

Abby felt drawn to it even more than she had been when she'd found it while jogging. A curving walkway bordered with a pale blue flowering bush drew her to the yellow house and its white-framed picture window. "I love it. I can't wait to see inside."

"Now, it's not been rented for some time. One of the school teachers rented it, but then moved off and it's been vacant since midterm last year."

She hurried out of the car and walked to the sidewalk, gazing at the place. Now that she was closer, she could see its age, but it was adorable. Doonie opened the front door and pushed it open for her.

Inside she stopped. The sunlight poured in from the front window and through the large window in the kitchen that she could see from where she was standing. Everything looked cheerful and sunny with the pale yellow walls and their cream accent. Abby's heart sighed. She inhaled slowly. She didn't even have to see any other part of the house. These two rooms alone and the outside called to her. "I'll take it."

"You will—you haven't even seen the rest," one of the brothers said, but she didn't look to see which one as she walked to the kitchen. Cream wooden cabinets and a cream door with a large paned window on which she could see gingham curtains. The house reminded her of peace.

And Abby craved peace for her restless soul.

She spun to the twins. "I want it. When can I move in?"

. . .

"She rented it on the spot."

"Really? Just like that?" Clara Lyn stared wide-eyed at Rand Radcliff across the aisle between their tables in The Bull Barn. Reba Ann and Clara Lyn happened to be sitting at their favorite booth, called "Tru

Monahan's table," since it had several photos of the local cutting horse champion. In fact, every kind of rodeo paraphernalia a person could find decorated the walls around them.

"Sure did," Rand said from his table. "She didn't look at everything before she snapped it up. I went over there and met her before she signed the papers. She seems like a very nice young woman. That house has been sitting vacant for over seven months, but she barely looked at it and just walked in and said she'd take it."

"Well, that's just great," Clara Lyn said.

"She's got good taste," Reba Ann offered. "I always did think it was a nice little place. But most people are looking for something bigger."

Clara Lyn smiled. "I guess it's just been sitting there waiting on her."

"It was meant to be," Reba agreed.

Rand looked up from studying his menu. "All I know is I'm happy to have it rented and she seems like she'll be a nice, quiet neighbor."

"How about you? You gonna be a good neighbor? No singin' off-key songs because you're tipping that lousy bottle?" Clara Lyn asked. She'd stopped beating around the bush long ago. She said what she meant and hoped it hit home when she said it. Right now, she watched as Rand stared at her.

"Yes, Clara Lyn, I'm fine. That was just a bad night. I've given drinking up."

That remained to be seen. "I sure hope so, because there was that incident in the grocery store last month."

Sadly, she suspected he needed a twelve-step program and to join a group. But as far as any of them knew, he hadn't done any such thing. "You decide one way or the other if you're going to get some help."

He laid his menu on the table. "Clara Lyn, I'm fine."

"That's good. But Rand, contrary to what you may have heard, singing Dolly Parton-slash-Whitney Houston songs to a woman are not the way to her heart."

Rand wasn't willing to accept that he had a drinking problem. He'd also gotten drunk at a wedding and mortified Pebble when he'd stumbled around and sang to her.

"Clara Lyn, you sure are stirring the pot. A man makes one mistake and no one ever lets him live it down. Would you drop it? I'm fine."

"I'm just asking out of concern, and you know it."

"I do, and that's why I'm not getting mad. But I'm fine and I think Pebble is coming around."

Clara Lyn wasn't so sure about that and she was worried about Rand. He'd loved Pebble back when they'd all been in school, but he'd been too rowdy for prim Pebble and she'd fallen in love with Cecil and they'd had a wonderful life until he'd died over ten years ago. Rand had been on the outside looking in all this time and now he was hoping to get another shot at winning her over. But embarrassing her in front of the whole town in a drunken spectacle was not the way to endear himself to Pebble. Not to mention the other not-so-high-profile incidents that had happened over the last few months such as walking to the grocery store so drunk he'd had to be driven home by the police.

But Clara couldn't fix that. He had to want to fix himself and he had to acknowledge that he had a problem.

"Well, I think it's great that she likes your little place," Reba broke in, trying to be the peacemaker.

Clara decided to let it go. "I am too." The twins walked in at that moment and made their way over to Rand's table.

"Yup, that's a sure nice little lady, isn't she, Doobie?" Doonie said soon as he sat and realized what they'd all been discussing.

"She sure is, and she was nice to help poor ol' Bo out with the baby yesterday," Doobie chuckled. "That boy looked scared to death when we spotted them in the store together."

"She told us y'all went out there last night," Doonie said, looking at Reba and Clara.

"We did," Reba said first. "Clara Lyn came up with the idea and she was right. He needed us in a bad way."

"I hope he's doing okay this morning." Clara Lyn had worried about them all night, but everyone had to get used to it when a new baby came into the world. "He's a capable man. I'm sure he figured it out."

"We gave him all the basics, and Abby had given him a boatload of help before us."

"You're right, Reba."

"Still," Doonie chuckled. "I'd hate to be in his shoes right now. When are Tru and Maggie supposed to be home from that honeymoon?"

"Next week," Clara said. "Maggie will also be a great help to him, I'm sure. Those cowboys have a lot on their plate right now. It's good they have a woman to help them navigate this." It just made her heart swell up thinking about it. Clara would be glad for them to get back. She was so happy for them. Tru'd been so road weary. He had a new happiness about him they were all thrilled to see.

As far as Clara Lyn was concerned, a young man needed a good woman. Her thoughts swung back to Abby Knightley. She and Reba had speculated about Bo's needing a wife all the way home from his house. And they hadn't missed that Abby had seemed genuinely concerned for Bo.

No, they hadn't missed that at all . . .

CHAPTER 10

A bby went straight to the office after signing the rental agreement. Her excitement shone in her voice when she spoke. "Pebble, I've found a place to move into."

Pebble looked up. "That's wonderful. Where?"

"Mr. Radcliff's place. It's just perfect for me. And I called and my furniture should be delivered on Monday."

Pebble looked troubled despite the smile she gave Abby. "That's a very nice place. Rand's grandmother lived there when we were all in school. He bought the place next door to it when he came back to town several years ago and he's kept it up. I think you'll be happy there."

Abby took a deep breath. "I plan to be. I'm very excited. I've needed this."

"I was just about to head over and have lunch with Clara Lyn and Reba at The Bull Barn. Would you like to go?"

"Yes, thanks, I've wanted to go and see it since arriving but with my car and everything, I didn't have a way over there."

"Well, now you do." She flipped the sign that said she'd be back at 1:15 p.m. and walked out the door.

Abby realized only then that Pebble had been standing there with her purse on her arm about to leave. Wasting no more time, Abby walked out behind her and followed her to a large Lincoln. They climbed in and Abby saw that, just as pristine as the older car was on the outside, it was as well-maintained on the interior. The car dwarfed Pebble—she actually had a pink chair cushion to sit on so she could see over the steering wheel more easily.

"Cecil ordered me this car straight from the dealer a few years before his accident. He picked out the color and everything special and insisted I drive it. It's huge, but it was for my protection, he said. He felt like having all this metal around me would help protect me if I ever had an accident." Her expression softened as she thought of her husband. "After he passed away I just haven't been able to let go of it. It's over twenty years old now."

At the mention of having a car accident Abby's heart began to thunder. She ran a hand over the soft leather and then Pebble's other words sank in—Pebble was a widow too.

She looked at Pebble. "Do you still miss him?"

Before driving onto the road, Pebble met her gaze with a knowing glint in her wise eyes. "Every single day. But it's eased up. I've moved on in most ways. I've made a good life for myself. Though I still own the motel we bought together and still drive this car, I have become my own person. I've made peace with everything that happened. And you—do you think of your husband every day?"

Abby gasped. "How?"

"I had my suspicions that you'd lost someone dear to you, but just now, I saw it in your eyes."

"It's been two years and I miss him every day. I'm learning to move on. Being here is part of that process."

Pebble placed a gentle hand on Abby's arm for just a moment then returned it to the steering wheel at the two o'clock position.

Abby felt a sense of deep comfort in that small gesture. Tears welled within her and she heaved a heavy breath and fought it down. "I'm here to move forward. I've been on standstill all this time and just knew I had to make a move in order to find happiness again. Does that make sense? Sometimes I think I may have lost my mind."

"Nothing of the sort. You've chosen well. We're a great community, and you do need to move forward, but grief has no timetable. You'll know when to push."

Abby felt the odd sense of relief wash over her as they drove away.

"I haven't really told anyone else."

"Is it a secret? Either way my lips are sealed."

"No . . . my friends were too protective of me and then with others—it was just different. Maybe it was because I was different, but nothing has been the same. I was suffocating in the pity and protection and . . ." Her words trailed off. There was so much about losing Landon that sparked things she hadn't told anyone and wouldn't still. Things that cut so soul-deep that if she voiced them she might break. In many ways, she was broken already. Abby shoved those emotions deeply back inside and locked the door. No one saw that—she couldn't even bear to see it. She was trying to let God help her deal with the issues, but right now she just couldn't think about them.

"I'm just trying to find me again. And not be labeled. At least for the moment."

Pebble wheeled the big car into The Bull Barn's parking lot and came to a halt in the first space she found. She turned to Abby. "I understand. Most people who've walked in our shoes understand. I'm here to talk and for support if you need me. Though I'll admit I changed, too, and haven't been able to go back to exactly the way I was. I'm comfortable in my skin. I have boundaries that I don't want to cross. And until I'm ready or willing, I don't plan to."

"Thank you for that, Pebble. I love my friends, but just couldn't deal. It's nice to be able to talk to someone."

"Friends push too hard sometimes because they want so badly to fix the heartache you're going through. They sometimes push for the wrong solutions and often pray for the wrong thing too. But, usually you'll learn it's because they just want to help and don't know how. When the time is right you'll let them back in. Or, you'll also find that some friendships, however close they might have been, were only here for a season in your life."

Abby let those words sink in. "I can understand that. For the most part."

"Thank you for sharing. I won't tell and I won't push you either, since I understand." A twinkle lit Pebble's eyes. "However, I'll warn you that Clara Lyn is very intuitive. And Reba also. They may figure it out. Being in the beauty business and hearing folks talk about their problems and heartaches seems to lend itself to reading between the lines. Please don't think I've told them if they pick up on it before you disclose it."

"I understand."

"Abby, you are a darling, darling young woman. You will be happy again. Now, enough of this seriousness— let's go into the craziness that is The Bull Barn and see what this town has been up to." She chuckled. "They've probably all been discussing your being here."

Abby followed Pebble inside to mouthwatering scents— baking bread, roasting meats. Such a mixture of savory aromas filled the air, as did the hum of conversation. This was definitely the place to be at lunch if you wanted company.

Abby would no longer be holed up or closed off here. With a town this small, she had a feeling trying to hide out wouldn't work. Folks would come by and bug a person enough till they finally did something. And that was exactly the motivation Abby needed.

.   .   .

Jarrod took Pops with him to check fence and then into town to the feed store. Pops loved getting out and they tried on his good days to do so. Sometimes on his bad days they took him riding in the pasture but that was all. He felt familiar and comfortable in the surroundings of the ranch.

Bo hadn't left the house since the day before when he'd gone to the store. Today he had decided he had to try and start taking control of his situation and stop letting having a baby in the house buck him out of the saddle. That meant he had to go back to work and to do that he had to figure out how to work and watch a baby at the same time. It had to be easier than changing a diaper.

While at the store Abby had placed a boxed-up baby swing in the buggy, and he decided it was time to put it together.

After loading the baby into his car seat in the truck, he put the playpen and swing into its bed then carted them all plus the baby supplies down to the shop.

Sergio, his only full-time employee, came out of the back with a curious expression as Bo brought Levi in and placed him in the playpen. Sergio'd been working for him for about a year now and was great with wood-work. He'd quickly learned the technique of building the stirrup that Bo had developed, and though he was only twenty he'd grown indispensable to Bo.

"So this is the little one? I heard him wailing from inside and felt pity for you. You don't know anything about babies, do you?"

"If you'd asked me that question forty-eight hours ago I'd have answered with an emphatic no. But now I know a lot more than I'm capable of processing. He's always surprising me with something new." He frowned in spite of himself.

Sergio bent over laughing then tickled Levi on the belly where he lay in the playpen cuddling a bottle.

"They teach you everything you need to know. That's what my mother says. And she should know—she has six kids."

"She's a brave woman." Bo was only half teasing. He set to work pulling parts from the box. To his surprise, he had it put together before hungry boy finished. "I've got to get this all figured out so I can get back to work. Thanks for working overtime the last two days."

"Anytime, boss. What's his name?"

"Levi. He's real cute, but man, what a surprise." He decided on the best place to set the swing where he could see Levi at all times, but Levi would be safe.

"My sister has one of those and her kid loves it."

"That's just what I need." Bo knew he was going to have to get this daddy business figured out soon or he was in trouble. He had orders overflowing for his stirrups.

Thankfully, the swing worked great. He tucked Levi in it and cranked the handle, and it started its back and forth motion. Levi grinned and cooed and decided his fingers were real interesting as he lifted them up and studied them while the swing rocked him back and forth. Bo backed away, slowly, not wanting to disturb the kid doing something so constructive. If Bo could find his fingers that enthralling, he'd never get anything done. But hey, it was working for the baby. That was a blessing sent straight from heaven . . . and at this point Bo was glad to get anything he could get.

. . .

Abby laughed as Big Shorty, the owner of The Bull Barn, brought out her club sandwich. The thing was a monster. It was built with thick Texas-sized toast rather than regular-sized bread and she could only imagine that the carb count was off the charts. And then the bacon—piles of thick slices topped with turkey, tomatoes, and lettuce. A work of art just begging to be eaten. "Well, it might not be healthy but I am overwhelmed with awe."

Big Shorty, and everyone within hearing, laughed at that. "I try to please. I can tell you that it's made from some of the best ingredients around, even the bacon—just take it in moderation. All those vegetables come straight from my wife's garden—nothin' alien on them."

Abby took a bite. She started nodding the instant the homemade bread touched her taste buds. "That's wonderful," she said when she'd finished her bite.

Big Shorty and everyone around Abby chuckled.

"That's just what I like to hear." He tipped his head and hustled over to lead none other than Doobie, Doonie, and Rand Radcliff to the table right next to them. Then he headed back to the kitchen, joking with several customers on the way.

"Nice to see you again," Rand said. She'd learned his soft-spoken nature yesterday when she'd met him while signing the rental agreement.

"Nice to see you again too. I can't wait to move into the house. Thank you again for renting it to me."

"My pleasure, indeed."

She talked for a moment with the brothers and her

new landlord. While his two friends were more outgo-ing and talkative, he was quieter, more reserved.

"So," Clara Lyn said, after everyone had taken a few bites of their lunch. "We went and saw the baby last night. Cute as a butter bean. And that Bo is in way over his head. Have you heard from him?"

"Me?" Abby wasn't at all certain why they were thinking she'd heard from Bo. It made her very uncomfortable. She'd been trying hard not to think of the cowboy and the baby he knew nothing about taking care of. But try as she might, worry crept in continu-ally. Clara Lyn was nodding at her with encouragement. Abby tried not to squirm in her chair. "Um, no," she said.

"No," Reba said, looking distressed. "Oh, I thought maybe he and you . . . well, you know."

"No," Abby coughed, choking on her water. "I just helped him out because I was with him when he found the baby." There, that was clarification—much needed since there seemed to be a lot of people in the diner paying attention to their conversation.

"Well, that boy needs your help," Doonie, she assumed, said. "He hardly knew which end was up yesterday."

Doobie grinned, eyes crinkling at the edges. "That baby is probably wearing a diaper on its head this morning."

That got chuckles from around the room.

Big Shorty was even grinning. "I'd sure feel for the man. But it's an odd bunch of tomatoes that the kid is just showing up out of the blue like he did. We were sorry to hear his mother had died. That's real tragic."

"Madge seemed to think she willed the baby to

Bo—you know, him being the daddy and all," a man from about four tables over offered.

Abby thought that sounded a little rude, but kept her mouth shut and found Rand watching her with an inquisitive gaze. Despite being the owner of the newspaper, he hadn't said anything, hadn't asked questions either, but he was observing and listening. Abby suddenly wondered, at the rate things were going, if Bo would find an announcement in the paper about Levi's arrival whenever the weekly issue came out.

She started worrying that maybe she should have helped Bo out more.

Lunch continued with more speculation about Bo and the baby. Somewhere in the middle of the meal and all the widespread nosiness she realized there was something going on between Rand and Pebble. The man couldn't keep his eyes off Pebble. Abby couldn't decide if Pebble liked the attention or not. She hardly looked at Rand and she didn't really say a lot during the meal, but when she did look at him, her skin flushed.

Interesting. Abby's curiosity was piqued. Pebble clearly had an admirer, but was she happy about it? On the drive over Pebble had said she'd made peace with her loss but did that include finding a place in her heart for another man? The idea made Abby uneasy . . . it was hard to imagine for herself.

Bo stirred up feelings that made her uncomfortable, but that was no reason to ignore that he needed help.

Abby's thoughts churned all the way back to the motel after lunch. She couldn't get Bo off her mind. She called the shop only to find her car was going to take another day to have ready. Something about a part having to be shipped in. The image of Bo trying to cope kept sliding across her vision and wouldn't stop. She headed over to the office and asked Pebble if she would mind if she borrowed her car. And just as she'd thought, Pebble handed the keys over without hesitation.

So here she was driving up the lane of the Four of Hearts Ranch with a fluttery stomach and a voice telling her she was making a big mistake.

I'm just checking in on them. No commitment.

"Right," she said loud and firm. She was simply being a good neighbor. Being a good neighbor just as he'd been when she had wrecked her car . . . true, it had been his cow's fault that she'd wrecked but still, he'd taken responsibility and she was certain he would have done anything to help her any way she needed.

And that bothered her because she hadn't been willing to do the same.

After the wreck, after losing . . . she'd stopped being that kind of person. She'd become focused completely on her own pain.

And that had to stop.

She passed a truck as she drove up the ranch drive. The young man driving waved.

When she got to the house, no one answered the door. Abby turned and stared down the lane toward the red barn that sat between the horse stables and Pops's house.

She could see Bo's truck there.

Abby decided to walk. As she came close to the red building, she saw that the sign on the building was the

Four of Hearts brand like the one on the entrance of the ranch, a large number four with a heart coming out of the straight side of the number, but this one had the word *stirrups* in capital letters beneath it. So this was where he worked.

Her determination faltered.

Through the open door she could see the baby swing sitting still as Bo bent over a workbench. She could see his profile—he was concentrating hard on whatever he was working on. Country western music played, Clint Black's gorgeous, raspy, melodic voice swayed through the room, and she could see Bo singing along, lost in his own world. Abby couldn't move. Her gaze strayed over him, instantly her pulse kicked up, and attraction, strong and interested, rose up from its dust-covered ruins inside of her.

Bo held something in his hand that looked like a small branding iron, but it had an electric cord coming out of it. As she watched, he grasped it with both hands and carefully held it to something she couldn't make out. She thought it looked like a piece of wood. Was it a stirrup?

Her heart pounded, threatening to come out of her chest. She took a step forward despite not wanting to feel the sensations coursing through her. She wasn't ready for this feeling of energy fueled by attraction. But she couldn't force herself to turn away and leave.

As if he heard her, he looked up and those blue eyes had her thinking . . . that she needed to get back in her car and drive away. Very, very fast.

What was wrong with her?

CHAPTER 11

A bby," Bo said, startled to find her there when he looked up from branding stirrups. His gaze collided with hers, and he swallowed hard. Despite how busy he'd been with Levi, she'd hovered at the edges of his thoughts.

"I-I came to see how you and Levi were doing."

Heart pounding, he laid the miniature electric brand on the workbench and stepped toward her. The air seemed to crackle between them and he knew it wasn't his imagination. He couldn't take his eyes off her and he was more than happy right then. *She had come to check on them.*

"I'm doin' all right. He's sleeping." She looked away from him and toward Levi. Her expression grew soft again.

He nodded as she came inside the building. Her sandals clicked lightly on the concrete.

She was beautiful. He was drawn to the smooth way she moved, the gentle sway of her hips, the graceful way she tipped her head as she looked almost shyly at him. There was something elusive about her. Something about her that stirred him in a way that confused him, grabbed his attention, and hadn't let go from the moment he first saw her.

"He looks content."

Bo caught the surprise in her eyes, as if she hadn't expected Levi to be content, quiet. Happy. It stung his pride, but then she'd seen Bo at his worst, so he shouldn't be surprised. There was no hiding his incompetence. She'd seen it all. He'd been a mess when they'd found Levi.

"It's not so bad," he hedged.

"That's good. Well, I just came to see if you needed anything. But you look like you've been doing this for years—you have it all under control. That's great."

She was backing toward the door . . . she was leaving.

"Hey, wait, slow down there. I didn't say I had it under control. I said things weren't so bad. People have called offering to help and I talked to the midwife from Over the Rainbow a little while ago and she made me feel a little more at ease. Said babies don't break, but they do take getting used to." He grinned, remembering Peg's words of wisdom. "But to be honest, I'm dying for some help. I'm not getting any work done and I've got a backload of orders that I need to get out the door quickly. At the rate I'm going the last two days, I won't fill all the orders I have for two, maybe three years."

"Oh." She halted, a tiny frown on her face. "That won't work."

"Look, I was wondering—I know you turned me down before. But you said you were going to look for work and maybe this isn't something you want to do all the time, but if you'd let me hire you for at least a short while, I'd sure appreciate it. Levi's comfortable with you. It would give me time to catch my breath and then I could look for someone to take your place."

She was the right one for the job and he knew it. There were others he could hire and he knew that, too, but something in his gut told him Abby was the one for this job. At least for as long as he could get her. She'd have everything running smoothly in no time—long as there was no blood. If this was an active toddler, he might worry about that part . . . he and his brothers had been terrors and there had been lots of cuts and scrapes.

Nope, this was good. This was perfect.

. . .

Could she do this? Abby looked from Bo to the sleeping baby. *Can I?*

From deep inside of her she felt an ache—it would be easier to deny his request. But she knew that Levi needed her.

Bo did too—but this was about a baby, a motherless baby boy. Surely there was someone else better than her who should—

"I'll do it," she heard herself say. "For a little while. Until you can find someone to help you full time. I'm not committing long term." She couldn't do that. But she could help get them going on the right track until Bo got his legs beneath him and had time to find not just someone to watch Levi but the right person to watch over him.

Instantly she was engulfed in Bo's arms. She gasped as he lifted her from the ground and spun her around. "*Yes!* Thank you."

Almost immediately he set her down and backed a step away. "Sorry. Was so blamed happy, I lost control again."

Abby smoothed hair from her forehead with the flat of her hand in a slow movement, taking the moment to try and compose the turmoil his sudden action had set loose inside of her. She was going to have to start being on the lookout for his out-of-nowhere bear hugs.

Her cheeks burned with heat. "It's fine," she mumbled just as Levi started crying. She reached for him automatically. Unclasping the safety belt, she pulled Levi into her arms. "Hey, little darling," she said gently as he curled against her heart as if digging a place for himself there. Abby's hands tightened protectively around him as her heart faltered and she wondered what she was doing. Her heart had been broken beyond repair when the drunk driver had driven into their lane—she'd come here to push herself to start feeling again, but committing to take care of this tiny angel scared her. Was this too much to ask of her broken and barren heart?

Bo moved to stand beside her. "He's probably hungry and wet. Let's head back to the house and fix all of that."

Abby pulled herself out of her inward battle. "Sure," she said, hearing the fear in her voice and hoping Bo didn't as she followed him out the door.

"And Abby." He paused to look at her. "I'm grateful to you. Thank you."

"You're welcome, and I'm doing it for Levi," she said, not knowing if it was for his benefit or her own.

"We'll come back for Pebble's car later." He showed her his dimple, grinning, and held the door of his truck open.

"Good plan." She let him help her settle into the seat with the baby in her arms.

The drive down the lane was over in a moment. Solomon was on the back porch lying on his back, his feet hanging limply at his side. He was snoring so loudly he didn't hear the truck pull up.

"He's not exactly the greatest guard dog . . ." Bo said dryly. "But he's sure entertainin' when he's sleeping and not barking."

The awkward way the rotund pooch was lying had Abby smiling, then suddenly his feet started churning in air. "He's having a dream."

"He's a heavy dreamer. If he were human, he'd be talking in his sleep about now."

Abby laughed again and felt the weight in her chest ease up. When Bo got out and slammed his truck door the old dog came alive. He woke howling, scrambling to his feet with startling agility, then immediately hid behind the planter by the door.

"Guard dog. See?" Bo laughed as he opened her door. Solomon followed them into the house then sat in the corner watching them with cocked head. But Abby's attention was drawn away from the dog to the room.

Down in Bo's workshop, everything had looked completely under control—not so in the house. It was a wreck. The first things she noticed were the cabinet doors standing open, baby bottles open on the counter, and though they were empty, they were not clean. Some were even on the floor. Formula powder trailed over the counter where Bo had filled bottles but not had time to clean up.

He hustled to the counter and pulled open the dishwasher. "It's a mess. If you'll change his diaper, I'll get him a bottle and some baby food and clean up while you feed him. How does that sound?"

She fought off a chuckle. "I think that'll work. See you in a minute." She headed into the living room and over to the couch. The dog followed, hovering close by, and Abby realized he was watching Levi. Within moments she had Levi all cleaned up and happy—though he was intent on getting down to crawl. She held onto him and he started squealing happily when she slipped him into his high chair and opened the jar of baby food.

"Look, you're having green peas. Mmm, I love green peas," Abby coaxed as he opened wide and basically inhaled the green goop then clapped his hands and grinned at Solomon who was sitting two feet away, clearly interested in everything the baby was doing.

"I am glad I'm older," Bo said from where he was using the bottle brush on the dirty bottles before loading them into the upper drawer of the dishwasher. "That stuff looks awful."

She laughed then. "It looks bad, but it's just pureed green peas, same as we eat."

"You have to admit it doesn't look appetizing at all."

"It does if you're a hungry baby."

He grinned. "Right. What was I thinking? It's all about perspective."

Abby gave Levi another small spoonful of peas and smiled tenderly at him. "That's a good boy," she encouraged and gave him another bite. "So, have you heard anything from the sheriff?"

"He called today." Bo paused and pulled soapy hands from the water to turn and look at her. "Everything checks out. He's just turned one. His birthday is August tenth, about a month ago, and I am legally Levi's father—according to all the paperwork. If I want I can do a paternity test to determine if I really am. You know, to make sure Darla didn't just put my name on the birth certificate."

"Do you think she might have done that?"

He grabbed a towel and wiped his drippy hands, then leaned against the counter. "She didn't strike me as someone who would do something like that. But in truth, I only knew her for about the span of four weeks. I hate to say that and for you to see that I have a son because of it. It doesn't really speak well for me or Darla, I guess."

He had the decency to look embarrassed.

Abby couldn't help asking, "What are you going to do?"

"I don't know. I don't think I'm going to do anything. I haven't had a chance to think about it long. Jake called about an hour before you got here. They found the friend of Darla's and she swears that Pops is the one who told her to put the baby on the porch in the playpen. She said she had no idea he was ill. Jake says the court will decide that, but it is a possibility she's telling the truth. Though since she left so little information behind, it could all be a lie. If so, she might be spending six months or longer in jail. That will be for the courts to decide. In the meantime, we now have baby records, health records, and so forth."

"That's good. This is all so bizarre."

"Yes, it is. I probably need to consult a lawyer, see if I'm missing something important. But the reality is I'm pretty sure I'm a dad. And I'm not sure I need verification other than my name on that certificate and her having declared me his legal guardian."

"But what if there is another man out there, and he's actually the dad?"

He looked troubled for only a moment, then his jaw tensed and his eyes seemed to darken. She liked that about him—that he seemed to take things in and think about them intensely. She liked that he wasn't taking Levi lightly.

"Then why isn't his name on the birth certificate?" he argued. "Think about it. If Darla didn't notify me that Levi was mine because she wasn't sure that she wanted me in his life, that says something about her. She cared for Levi and to be honest, she was angry with me when we parted ways. I hurt her." His brows dipped and a goal post formed between them. "I didn't mean to but I did, because it all happened so fast. She had deeper feelings than I did . . . and I'm not a man of commitment. I regret that she got hurt." He paused again and seemed lost in thought.

Abby remained silent, sensing he wasn't finished.

"The fact that she put my name on all the legal papers tells me I am the dad. I seriously believe that if there was another guy out there and he's the dad and she chose *not* to put his name on the papers, then he must be a real slug."

Abby could not help scowling herself. It made sense.

"I could be the only guy. And despite everything, I'm not a bad guy, Abby. And I don't think Darla was a bad gal, we just . . . got out of control and made a mistake . . . and she's the one who got hurt."

Abby didn't know what to say. She went back to feeding Levi and let everything turn over in her mind for a few moments. At last she spoke. "I'm not saying anything and I'm not judging. All I'm thinking about is Levi. What if you do a test and find out he *isn't* yours? What happens to Levi?"

"I don't know. I've been wondering the same thing." Bo looked troubled. He turned back to the sink, grabbed a rag and a bleach cleaner, and started wiping counters like they were filthy.

"And grandparents, are there no grandparents? No aunts or uncles? Where is Darla's family? Why is he alone—other than you?" Pulling her gaze from the tense set of Bo's shoulders as he worked, Abby stopped the endless list of questions and looked at Levi. Her heart knotted and ached with worry for the sweet bundle of joy.

* * *

Bo couldn't believe Abby had agreed to help him. His stress level had gone down knowing she would be showing up every day to help him. But then again, stress of an entirely different nature had skyrocketed off the charts. And that stress had everything to do with Abby and the way he felt when she was near.

Yes, she'd reminded him she was here for Levi and he was glad for that. That's what he needed. But he had a feeling he was going to have to keep reminding himself of that fact the longer he was around her. After Darla, he hadn't been dating as much. He'd found her declaration of love a swift, strong reminder that he wasn't ready to settle down. He'd hurt her and he was now afraid he might hurt someone else. He wasn't ready for commitment. It was just a fact.

And yet every time he looked at Abby or thought about her, his guard went down and he found himself forgetting this fact.

But right now, his thoughts were on the same thing she was wondering about: What would he do if he found out Levi wasn't his?

Just a few days ago he would have laughed if anyone had said a man could turn into a father in less than a week . . . but it was true. He had begun to get used to the idea of Levi being his son. The circumstances were getting in the way of it actually feeling real and true, but if a paternity test showed that he was then all that hesitance would disappear.

But what if he wasn't?

What if there was some other man out there who was really Levi's dad?

And what if that man was a jerk? Or what if he wasn't and deserved to know . . .

If he was a jerk and they were able to locate him, what would happen to Levi? Or if they couldn't find him, what would happen to Levi? The questions were endless. The only fact he knew was that he was listed. What was he going to do about it?

"Where's Pops today?" Abby asked, breaking into his thoughts.

He slowed attacking the counters with the rag and glanced over his shoulder. "He's with Jarrod. Jarrod had a lot of running around to do this afternoon—some fences to check and cattle to count and a few errands in town. Pops is having an alert day, so he took him. Pops has really been on a roller coaster over the last few weeks. That's why I'm staying with him right now. But getting out is good for Pops. And having him along is good for Jarrod too."

Tru was a year older than Bo and Jarrod was two years older than Tru, so Jarrod had really been the luckiest one of them, having had a longer relationship with Pops. Bo had Pops's sense of humor, though he wasn't feeling much of it these days. Tru got Pops's ability with a horse and Jarrod had his love of the land and all things cattle. Jarrod was one great cattleman. And while Bo and Tru had worked in their special fields to earn money to pay the debt owed on the ranch, Jarrod had done amazing things with the ranch and cattle to bring money in through several streams. Without Jarrod holding the actual ranch together, none of their efforts would have worked.

"I'm sure all of you struggle with him having Alzheimer's."

Bo knew it hurt Jarrod that Pops didn't really know everything he'd done—or if he knew it he didn't always remember. "Yeah, like a son-of-a-gun. Pops always looked a man straight in the eye and he taught us to do the same thing as we were growing up. When Pops would look us in the eye after work or a rodeo and say, "Well done, son," that meant something special to each of us. Those moments are few and far between these days." He had dropped his rag in the sink and walked over to sit in the chair at the table with Abby and Levi. The kid smiled at Bo through all the green stuff dripping off his lips. Bo had to chuckle.

"Funny kid," he said, smiling down at Levi. The boy grinned back and everything in the world just seemed better . . . it got Bo right in the heart.

Abby cleaned Levi's mouth with a baby wipe. "You just have to hang onto the good stuff about your grand-dad. He might be losing his memory, but y'all aren't."

"True. And that's what I'm trying every day to focus on." This conversation was getting way too depressing. "You know, there's room here if you wanted to move in," he said, instantly wanting to boot kick himself to the barn and back. What was she going to think about that?

"Room?" she asked, sharply.

"N-no. I didn't mean move in. I meant I know you are looking for a place and we have a cabin on the ranch that you could use. If you wanted it."

"Oh, I see. That's nice of you. Really. But I've found a place. I'm going to rent Rand Radcliff's house. And may buy it once I've settled in and like it as much as I think I'm going to."

"Really. The place that belonged to his grandmother?"

"That's the one. My things will be here on Monday. Well, I guess I need to head back to my room." She rose, gave Levi a gentle kiss on the forehead, and got a funny look in her eyes that he didn't miss—it was only there briefly before it vanished. But like everything about her, it had his attention.

"No need to rush off—but I understand. Thanks again for taking the job. You're a lifesaver."

She handed Levi to Bo, brushing him in the transition. The touch sent Bo's pulse into a tailspin. She didn't linger, though. She backed away and headed toward the door . . . and Bo found himself staring again. He was really going to have to get this under control or Abby might not hang around and he didn't want to ruin a good thing when it was just getting started.

. . .

"Oh!" Abby halted at the door as her muddled brain had a coherent realization. "I'm supposed to help with the decorating up at the park tomorrow." She really wished Bo would stop looking at her the way he was. It made her skin tingle. She focused on her job. "Charlie told me he'd have my car waiting for me in the morning, so if it's fine with you, I'll drive out and pick up Levi then we'll head to the park."

"You can do that with the baby?"

She laughed at the shock and awe in his voice. "Yes, and no. I won't be quite as useful as I might be if I didn't have him, but believe me, it can be managed.

I'll take along his portable carrier and that stroller I had you buy the other day, if you'll get it out of the box tonight. It will all work out. You'll see. And tomorrow you'll have a day to catch up on your work, if you can handle Pops."

"I can manage fine. Pops likes to come watch me work and he sweeps a lot. There's shavings in the back area where Sergio cuts and glues the layers of wood and Pops feels useful doing that. And he is."

"That's good. So I guess having Levi around messed up his schedule too."

"Pretty much. He walks back and forth from the shop to the house and enjoys being out. So far that's not been a problem. And when Tru is here, he's outside on his horses most of the time, so he keeps an eye out. They'll be back on Sunday or Monday for a week or two, which'll be great."

"Really?"

"Yeah, and you'll get to meet Maggie. She's cool. When she's not writing that the cowboys and the firemen are hunky."

Abby could not help the laughter that bubbled out of her at the disgust in his words. She had laughed so hard at the article about how the Wishing Springs volunteer fire department was made up exclusively of hunky cowboys. She'd actually envisioned a calendar of firemen and their cowboy hats. And then Maggie'd added that they were all single.

"I would love to meet Maggie! So I get it that you don't like to be called hunky?"

The look of complete disgust said what words couldn't.

The fact that he fit the title with five stars probably didn't merit pointing out.

But hunky and Bo Monahan were synonymous and that was a fact.

CHAPTER 12

Abby was still reeling from her unexpected decision the next morning.

She'd hired on as Levi's nanny.

She and Bo had clarified the hours and schedule she'd be working and he'd demanded to pay her a wage that was more than fair. And now, it was official.

That scenario had never entered her mind when she'd decided to move to Wishing Springs and start a new life. She had her deep reservations about it—the fear of falling in love with this baby and then losing him was at the top of the list . . . but it was done.

Temporary nanny, she reminded herself. If she began to get too close she could pull away. She'd made no permanent commitment.

She peeked out her window before getting dressed and was thrilled to find her car waiting outside her motel just like Charlie the mechanic had said it would be. Once dressed she drove out to pick up Levi before heading to the center of town to help Clara Lyn and the other ladies with the decorating of the town square park.

As fearful and uncertain as she'd been, anticipation filled her as she drove along the country road. Her fingers tapped the steering wheel in time with the radio and for the first time in what seemed like forever, she was looking forward to her day.

"I didn't have to dodge a single cow on my way out here," she told Bo when he walked out onto the porch to greet her. He looked tired but happy to see her and she was glad she'd come.

Within minutes he had strapped the car seat into the back of her car then loaded the playpen and stroller in her trunk while she got Levi ready for the day. There was nothing sweeter than the welcoming smile of a baby.

Pops and Solomon came into the living room to watch and this time the dog came closer.

"Mornin'," Pops said, grinning at her. "You're still pretty as a peach."

His compliment was unexpected both in that he had said it and that he seemed like a different man than she'd met the first time.

"Why, thank you." She finished pulling a tiny red shirt over Levi's fresh, baby-scented head. She hugged him and let herself enjoy the feel of him in her arms and against her heart . . . an ache throbbed deep in her heart as if to break through the barrier keeping the sorrow in. Pulling away, she thrust the barrier back in place and smiled at the innocent baby. She'd given him a quick bath in the sink and he'd loved it.

"Just look at you. All dressed for the day, looking so handsome and smelling simply irresistible, little man."

Abby could still not completely grasp the situation she was in since arriving in Wishing Springs. Not at all what she'd envisioned. She hadn't expected there to be a baby involved. But there was. And she hadn't expected there to be a man involved either. But there was.

She was completely out of her comfort zone with both.

She was willing to force herself to adapt with Levi, simply because Levi needed her.

But that was that.

She wasn't sure how she felt yet about the way Bo affected her. These emotions she felt when he was around were so unexpected she just wasn't sure what she wanted to do about them.

Nothing.

Her inner voice warned. And it was the part of her that was talking sense.

She and Levi arrived on the square about nine o'clock with action already taking place. Why, the twins were hustling around carrying colorful banners that proclaimed "An Old-Fashioned Picnic in the Park" and women swarmed everywhere. She'd heard several single-ladies groups were checking into the motel today and staying the night just for the picnic. What was Bo thinking about all of that? Day-trippers, as he called them, had come back to town.

Doobie (or was it Doonie) ambled over and helped her pull the stroller from the trunk.

"Hey there, little fella," he said. "He reminds me of my grandsons."

"Oh, how many grandsons do you have? Are you Doobie or Doonie?" she had to ask.

He grinned. "Doobie. I've got ten. And not a grand-daughter in the bunch. Me and my wife had three sons and they were all productive." He chuckled as he opened up the stroller like he'd done it a time or two. "Nothing like my little wild bunch to keep a man young."

Abby smiled. "Spoken like a grandparent. You can always send them home."

He hooted. "You got that right. If you have them too long, then it's a completely different scenario. Having those little boys for long stretches of time would have this old man worn and haggard. You carry that baby like it was second nature."

"Working at a day care while going through college will do that for you," she explained, enjoying the feel of Levi in her arms. "I have a brother, but he's not married yet." She placed the plump tot in the stroller.

"Ahh, well, you look just like a little mama. I'll let you get over to where the ladies are because they're going to flock over this kiddo like seagulls." He pointed to where the ladies were huddled up.

Abby's heart clutched at the "little mama" comment but she forced a smile and headed across the park. It was a beautiful morning with a slightly cool breeze.

Clara Lyn waved her over, the many bracelets on her arm jingling as merrily in welcome as her smile.

"Whoo-hoo! You've got Levi."

Abby's cheeks warmed. "Yes, Bo needed help and I needed a job, so I'm now Levi's temporary nanny."

"That is just wonderful! Goodness, you're all set— got a job, got a house, and soon some furniture. You've just jumped in with both feet."

"We like that," Reba called from where she was sorting through greenery that Abby assumed would decorate the gazebo they were standing in front of.

"All these other women that have come to town are just lookers, you know, coming for the curiosity and moving on. Which is okay, but we really love it when someone new moves to Wishing Springs because they want to be a part of our community."

Pebble was separating ribbons. "I think it's a lovely compliment the way you wanted to move here. But I wasn't sure you meant it until now. And you are here just in time to come to Bo's rescue."

"Isn't that the most unusual coincidence?" Clara Lyn added. "Of course I don't necessarily believe in coincidence. Everything happens for a reason. Everything."

Abby forced a weak smile thinking back to the wreck that took Landon and . . . "Maybe so. I just wasn't prepared for it is all." She swallowed the lump in her throat.

"And that is the fun of life. The unexpected." Clara Lyn stood and moved to the gazebo and started winding greenery around the post.

"Is there anything I can do?" She really needed something to do. "I brought Levi's playpen so I can set it up. Let him play and watch us." She saw the eight-foot ladder and assumed there would be decoration needed there. "Maybe I can climb up on the ladder and put ribbons around the beam right there."

"That would be perfect," Clara Lyn agreed. "And we're going to decorate some of the trees, too, but some of our firemen are going to do that for us."

Within a few minutes, with Pebble watching Levi, Abby went and pulled the playpen from the car. Mr. Radcliff came across the road as soon as he saw what she was doing.

"Here, let me do that for you." He reached for the small fold-up playpen that was compact enough to be easily carried by anyone.

"Thank you," she said.

"My pleasure." He tipped his jaunty hat then walked beside her toward the gazebo.

Pebble looked up from singing "Pattycakes" to Levi just as they came to a halt, and Abby thought she felt an arc of tension as Pebble looked at Rand. There was definitely something up between them.

"Hello, Pebble," he said gently, removing his hat and bowing a touch. "You're looking lovely as usual today. You looked just as lovely at lunch yesterday."

Pebble looked down at Levi, her cheeks slightly pink when she raised her eyes back to the man who clearly had a thing for her.

"Hello, Rand, you are looking well yourself."

"Thank you. I expect we will have a large crowd of out-of-towners coming in tomorrow—it should be a good piece for the paper."

"I think you're right," Pebble said with stiffness.

Abby was getting mixed signals from Pebble, but there was absolutely no mistaking the very distinguished newspaperman's interest. His boyish good looks contrasted with his silver hair. There wasn't a stitch out of place, from the creased khaki pants he wore to the starched oxford shirt tucked perfectly at his trim waist. Add the hat and he appeared to be the perfect gentleman. A perfect match, Abby thought, for the trim and delicate motel owner who also didn't have a hair out of place.

"I'll just set this up for you." Rand went to work on the playpen. Abby knew from experience exactly how to unfold the playpen, but she let him show off his skills in front of Pebble. Though he had to pull his glasses from his pocket and read the instructions on the side.

After a moment he had it open without a hitch.

"Thank you so much, Mr. Radcliff."

"Any time. And once you're in the house next door, if you need anything, you just ask me and I'll fix it for you."

With that he tipped his hat at her then turned to Pebble. Abby was certain there was something going on.

"You have a nice afternoon. And the same goes for you at the motel. Call if you need anything."

He tipped his hat and headed off toward where Doonie and Doobie were clearly arguing over something that had to do with one of the banners.

"I do believe you have an admirer."

Pebble blushed scalding pink. "Please don't think for one moment that I'm happy about that," she said. Her expression troubled, she stared after Rand and her eyes grew sad. She gave Abby a small shake of her head and walked away.

Abby watched the petite widow leaving. Did this have to do with losing her husband ten years ago or was there more? Abby thought of Bo and knew from the attraction she felt toward him that being drawn to someone after losing the love of your life was uncomfortable to say the least.

. . .

Bo was standing at the entrance of the stable when Abby drove into the yard that afternoon. She'd taken Levi to town for the decorating. His gut bucked as she got out of her car and eased her door closed.

She left her hand on the door handle. "Levi's sleeping, so I've left the air running and will take him on up to the house in a minute. I just wanted to let you know we had a great day."

"Great." Bo had thought about her all day.

"He just played with anyone who would give him some attention and that was everyone. The ladies are all so nice."

He liked the way her eyes lit up with happiness. "I'm glad they've taken you under their wing." Bo set down the feed bucket he was holding. He'd done the feeding today instead of the ranch hands. It had felt good to get around and back to his usual schedule, though he'd been working at high speed all day trying to make up for lost time. There was something about walking inside the hay-scented building to the soft nickers of the horses as they greeted him that just pulled all his worries aside for a little bit. Riding was even better, but he'd not had time to even think about that in the last few days. But standing here beside Abby brought a whole new energy into the building and he wasn't thinking about a horse or feed or riding as he fought off the need to touch her.

"They are just as I'd pictured them from Maggie's description," Abby said with a sigh. "I'm so glad I came here, Bo. This is just what I needed." She walked over to a stall where one of the new arrivals had craned his neck over the gate and was beckoning her with his snorts. "He's gorgeous."

Bo went to stand beside her, not ready to let her get too far away. The soft scent of her hair tickled his senses. He stepped a little closer. "He's new. He arrived just the other day and is waiting for Tru to train him."

"Does Tru work with a lot of other people's horses?"

"He does. He trains them, and then he competes on them for a fee. It works well for him. It keeps him on the road a lot, though I know he's really starting to wish he could be here more. But it'll be at least another year, maybe two, before he can do that. With Maggie's writing, she can pack her computer and travel with him. It's a real blessing that he's found someone who can ease the road weariness he's feeling."

She touched the horse's neck, unafraid of the animal at all, like many people might be—including Maggie when she'd first come to the ranch. No, Abby looked at Bo over her shoulder as if she'd been around animals all her life. "I can see where that would be terrible if your heart was now longing to be at home."

He had to think about what she was saying and remind himself they were talking about Tru. "Oh, yeah. I think that describes it very well," he said, almost mesmerized. "His heart is longing for more. A family, to be specific."

He couldn't stop staring at her. She swallowed hard and held his gaze.

"You are beautiful," he laughed. "I can't seem to stop looking at you." It was the truth, but he could see by the flicker of diminishing light in her eyes that saying so was a mistake.

"Your cowboy is showing in that statement."

"What does that mean?"

She gave a small laugh. "Cowboys are flirts, didn't you know?"

Okay, so he knew he shouldn't, but his mouth was overriding his brain. "Yeah, that may be true, but they are also not blind. And honey, your beauty is not all in the outer layer, either. When you laugh and that twinkle comes into your eyes, it's just downright attractive."

She stared at him as if she didn't know what to make of his boldness. He sure didn't know what to make of it. The woman had just started working for him—was he trying to run her off?

"I appreciate your opinion, but I'm not looking for a boyfriend. I'm here to work."

"There you go. I'm not looking for a girlfriend. I just need someone to work for me. I'll keep my opinions to myself from here on out. How's that sound?"

The tension hummed like a buzz saw between them as they stared at each other.

He hoped he hadn't just made the mistake of a lifetime.

"Fair enough," she said. "So, moving on, is there something between Mr. Radcliff and Pebble?"

Relief slapped him—*remember to tow the line like you would with a skittish colt.* Abby Knightley had walls up around her that screamed no trespassing. He wasn't going to tell her this, but he knew that there was no way he was going to be able to stay on this side. Trespass or not, he wanted to know why that wall was there. He'd just need to be patient.

"Well, let's just say Rand would like there to be." Boy, did Bo understand that feeling. "But so far he's not making any headway." Ditto with a capital D . . . but Rand had made some pretty big and stupid mistakes where Pebble was concerned. Bo hoped he hadn't just done the same with Abby. The woman was skittish enough without him opening his mouth and running her off.

CHAPTER 13

Abby, Abby, Abby—stop overreacting.

Abby tried to tell herself to calm down. Bo had knocked her feet out from under her with his blatant compliment earlier. She deflected it as best she could. The last thing she wanted to do was lead him on when she had no intention of dating or building a relationship with a man.

Thankfully he was letting the awkward conversation go and moving on to another topic as she'd prompted. "I suspected something was going on," she said. Her gaze strayed to his broad shoulders. His thick biceps. Those were powerful arms—and she remembered the feel of those strong arms holding her. Her mouth went dry and her mind shifted to thoughts she was alarmed about. She turned back to pet the horse again and fought to calm the galloping of her heart and the rushing of blood crashing through her. It was suddenly far too hot and suffocating in the airy stable. "I need to check on Levi," she said, and it was true . . . hurrying to the car, she peered through the cracked window. The kid was practically snoring, he was so contentedly sleeping.

Bo leaned over her shoulder. "He's sleeping like a baby."

She smiled and tried to ignore his nearness. "They don't always, do they?"

"That's a big affirmative. He likes to wake up in the middle of the night and play."

"Not good for you. He was very entertained today by everyone playing with him. But you might want me to wake him up or he might not sleep tonight."

He grinned at her. "You can do whatever you want. You're the expert, I certainly am not. I'm so thankful you had all that day care experience with babies."

"Me too." Abby's heart tugged with the desperate wish to have had experience with her own sweet child. Regret flooded her mind and heart at the loss of her baby. She forced a smile and focused on Levi. "I think I better wake him. It's almost five o'clock anyway. Are you going to be able to keep him soon?"

"Yeah, sure. I'm finishing up here now and can follow you up to the house and take him. Pops is already there. Jarrod dropped him off a little while ago."

They were back on stable ground. At least for the moment. "Sounds good. I need to go do some stuff at my house. I think I'm going to spend the night there tonight." She headed around the car. "See you in a minute."

"Yeah, sure."

She didn't wait, but got into the car and headed straight to the house. She found Pops taking a nap in the recliner in the den. Solomon trotted out to meet her and the baby, even wagged his tail. It appeared the animal was not just a one-man dog—he had now become a two-man dog: Pops and Levi.

Abby didn't waste any time leaving as soon as Bo

showed up. He told her that he was going to take Levi to the picnic and they'd make a day of it. So she shouldn't worry about working. It was Saturday after all, he'd said. She'd been fine with that. Maybe not being around him for the weekend would help her get these unwanted vibes between them under control.

Her head knew that her heart couldn't handle chancing a relationship. But Bo was causing havoc on the laws of attraction.

After leaving the ranch, she went to the store in town and found an air mattress to sleep on until her things arrived on Monday. She enjoyed the motel, but she was ready to get settled into her own place. She needed the grounding, the sense of permanence that it would hopefully give her. Having a place of her own meant this wasn't temporary.

Mattress, coffeepot, a coffee mug, and a glass for water along with a few other necessities piled into the car, she went back to the motel and found Pebble to check out. Then she loaded up the rest of her things and headed toward her new home.

Rand had kept the utilities turned on, so she could move in when she wanted to. That was now.

The place looked sparkling clean, but Abby started cleaning again the minute she walked in. Cleaning kept her hands and mind busy, and it just made her feel as if this place was really hers.

But it didn't work. The things that had been straining to occupy her thoughts kept breaking past her defenses—she reached for her earphones and turned up the radio, singing loudly along with Lady Antebellum as she wiped down cabinets.

This was all Bo's fault.

If he hadn't gotten her hormones in an uproar or suddenly become the daddy of a precious baby boy, then Abby's emotions and memories would have stayed locked safely away and not be banging to get out and cause her anguish.

Yup, it was Bo's fault and she gave him what-for as she cleaned.

And tonight, if she couldn't sleep, she'd take a sleeping pill like the doctor'd ordered, though she seldom did. She only took them when she needed nothingness . . .

Needed to totally and completely shut her mind down.

She couldn't remember what a normal peaceful sleep felt like. She'd been a good sleeper before the wreck. But not since. Not since losing . . .

Abby sang louder and forced herself to think about how she would decorate the house when her things arrived. The place was going to be darling. She'd make it all her own—fresh, new, and she would be happy here. Completely happy.

She'd have a sweet baby to keep during the day, one that could satisfy the hole in her heart . . . almost.

She'd have a handsome man with whom she would just build a friendship. Nothing more. She'd laid it out plain and simple for him. Things would be fine. She wasn't interested in anything more and neither was he. His plate was full. Her heart was full. They were the perfect match.

Yes, she had a plan. She was thinking positive.

Glancing out the window, she saw the lights on at Rand's and she decided she might need to say hi and let him know she'd moved in.

That would be neighborly and also a distraction. After all, she'd come to Wishing Springs to force herself to get involved.

She let herself out the front door and walked across the grass to the front door of his pretty brick home. He didn't answer. So she walked around to the back and entered the gate. And there, on the back patio, sat Rand. He had his arm on the table and had slumped forward, with his head on his arm. Something wasn't right. Abby stepped forward, then stopped—there was a bottle of alcohol sitting on the table next to his elbow. No glass, just the open bottle of clear liquid. She was close enough now to see the large letters. It was an open half-empty bottle of vodka.

She had never pictured this distinguished-looking gentleman as a drinker. Abby knew more than she cared to about heavy drinkers. Drunks.

Drinking and driving . . .

Abby knew that not everyone was an alcoholic and she had no business instantly jumping to conclusions. Despite the look of things.

This wasn't her business. She should just back away and leave. No one would know she'd even been there. But she forced herself to step forward into the light of the porch. "Mr. Radcliff. Are you okay?"

He lifted his head and she knew this was no normal situation.

"Fine. I'm fine . . . wha-ya-want?" he said gruffly, his words slurred.

Abby cringed. *He's sitting in his own backyard. It's none of your business, Abby.*

None of my business.

It was true. He wasn't on the road. He was harming no one. "I came to let you know I went ahead and moved in. Okay, then, I'll see you later." She started toward the gate.

"Fine. Sounds peeerrr-fit . . ." He plopped his elbow onto the table and dropped his forehead into his palm. "She hates me," he whined. "Never going to love me." He looked up through bloodshot eyes. "You know how hard it is to luf someone and not haf that luf returned?" He slapped his heart and hiccupped. "She-wan-gif-me-the-time-of-day," he slurred, his bleary eyes digging into Abby.

She felt sick to her stomach. She needed to turn around and leave. "I know how it hurts to love someone and not to be able to be near them. To have them taken away—" She knew that pain all too well. How empty her arms were and the hole that penetrated not only her heart but her soul.

"That's just terrible. I try. I try and try to make amends. But she won' hear me."

She'd wondered what the strain was between them, and now she was pretty certain she understood Pebble's attitude. She reminded herself that she didn't know Rand Radcliff. Not really. He was now her landlord and she needed to keep her mouth shut.

Walk away, Abby. Just walk away.

She turned and took two steps toward the gate, then stopped, closed her eyes as the anger mounted and intensified. She turned back. This wasn't going to be good.

Crossing to the table, she stared down at Rand with zero sympathy. He leaned his head back as if it weighed fifty pounds and tried to focus up at her.

"Mr. Radcliff, do you do this often? Drink till you can't think straight?" She couldn't stop the anger in her voice.

"Nooo."

"Oh *really*? I think that right there says you have a problem. I don't think you realize that or you would have had a different answer for me. I'm not going to talk to you now, because it won't do any good. But I think you need to set this aside tonight." She reached for his bottle and walked toward his house. *What in the dickens are you doing, Abby?*

She was trying to save a life.

If not his, some other poor innocent family he could very easily kill with one bad driving choice. Her knees weakened and she shoved thoughts away and kept on going. She opened the patio door to his house, walked in, and heard him stumbling along behind her.

"Hey, gimme back that. I'm not through." He grabbed the door frame for support.

"You are tonight." She emptied the large bottle into the sink. It was more than half empty so it didn't take too long.

"Hey, hey!" he hollered and propelled himself toward her, not anything like the sweet man she'd seen today. Tonight he was pathetic. He glared at her and grabbed the counter to keep from falling. "Ya got no right ta do that."

"So sue me." She took the bottle to the trash and lifted the lid—there was another empty bottle inside. Her stomach lurched. She dropped the bottle inside and spun. "You need to go to bed, Mr. Radcliff." She needed out of here.

He looked suddenly drained and he swayed.

Abby was at his side in an instant and grabbed his arm. Dragging it across her shoulder she almost passed out herself from the scent of him. Hanging onto his hand at her shoulder, she wrapped her other arm around his waist. "Okay, where's your bedroom?" she demanded and started walking him out of the kitchen. He just mumbled and slowed down. She knew she didn't have long before he was going to pass out and drop to the floor. If he did she'd just leave him there and go call his twin buddies. She had to wonder if they drank with him.

A door stood open down the hall and she headed that way. Bingo: a bed. She didn't care if it was his or not. She had to hoist him up a little because he was becoming heavier with each step. Once they made it to the bed and she tried to ease him down, he dropped like a rock across the mattress, landing on his face.

Abby stared down at him and her heart hardened. "What a waste."

Turning, she walked back down the hall and out the back door. He wouldn't wake till sometime tomorrow. But for tonight he seemed safe enough. Safer than he'd been sitting on the porch getting ready to drink more.

She crossed to her house, got inside, and her knees gave way. Her hand splayed across her abdomen, she sank to the floor and with her back against the door . . . covered her face with her hands and wept.

The screeching of tires, the glare of the semi's lights, and the sound of splitting metal . . . and the blood. So, so much blood.

CHAPTER 14

What was that smell? Bo popped an eye open to find Solomon sitting on his chest, his wet snout stuck in his face, Solomon's awful breath wrapped around him as the dog's thick tail whacked him in the chest. Bo was awake in an instant—the same one the dog started yowling in.

"What are you doing?" Bo growled, shoving the heavy lump off his chest. Solomon hopped from the bed and looked back at him, howling. Normally the crazy dog would run from the room, but he didn't. He stopped at the door and howled. Then he ran back to Bo and howled again as he trotted impatiently back to the door. Bo plopped his feet to the floor and yawned. "What is wrong with you?"

Solomon barked and it hit Bo's sleep-deprived brain that the dog was trying to tell him something. Then he heard Pops's mumbling voice over the baby monitor sitting on his night stand. Abby had helped him buy it and now he was glad he had followed her advice. Bo shot up, fully awake. Instantly the dog spun and raced out the door and Bo followed.

Bo's heart thundered as he followed Solomon. He rounded the corner of Levi's room and stopped.

"Pops?" His grandfather was bent over the baby's bed, and when he turned to Bo, he was a mess. Literally. Pops had tried to change Levi's diaper.

And it was not good.

"Oh, Pops," he groaned. It was bad.

Really, really bad. *It* was everywhere.

. . .

Bo spent the next thirty minutes cleaning up Levi, Pops, and . . . everything else. When he was done, he finally stopped long enough to take a breath. Pops sat in the chair in the living room, and when Bo brought the baby into the room, his grandfather started laughing. As stressful as the last few minutes had been for him, Bo started laughing too.

"That was bad, Pops," he said, collapsing onto the couch beside Pops.

"It was. Stunk too."

Bo chuckled more and Levi, who was sitting on Bo's lap, looked from him to Pops with a grin on his cute little face. The kid hadn't cried through the whole incident. He'd found it quite entertaining, in fact.

Bo's heart clutched looking at his son and he pulled him close and gave him a cuddle. "We're a trio, aren't we?" he said out loud, more for his own benefit than anyone, but unexpectedly Pops hiked a bushy brow.

"Yup. Taking care of a baby is somethin'. But you're a good'un."

Bo realized his grandfather was looking him straight in the eyes. And Pops's eyes were clear. A lump slammed into Bo's throat and his eyes burned. "Thanks, Pops. You're a good'un too."

Moments came unexpectedly. Moments that shot straight to his and his brothers' hearts. Moments when they saw their Pops and he saw them and they knew it was a gift they needed to hold onto with all their might. This was one of those moments and it zapped him hard.

"Hey, where is everyone?" Jarrod called from the kitchen. Only then did Bo realize it was six a.m. Bo usually already had coffee going by the time Jarrod arrived from his house. Not today.

His older brother came into the living room. "Hey, is everything all right? It's still dark in the kitchen." A sure sign something was up.

"It's all right," Pops said. "Takin' care of the baby."

Jarrod's eyes widened slightly. "Oh really. That's good, Pops. Your help is much appreciated, I'm sure."

Bo almost laughed. His expression was comical, he was certain. "Oh, definitely an unforgettable morning, hasn't it been, Pops?"

"Kind of messy," Pops said, grinning, and Bo hooted. He'd figured it was better to laugh than cry.

"What?" Jarrod asked, obviously feeling left out from the inside joke.

Bo rose and handed Levi to Jarrod. "Here you go, uncle. I gotta make some coffee *then* I'll let you in on the joke."

. . .

By eleven o'clock the festivities had gotten underway, though Abby still hadn't shown up. Different sections of the park had horseshoes or a bean bag toss and a few other old-fashioned games. People were everywhere.

After Jarrod had had a really good laugh at Bo's expense, they'd decided they'd bring Pops and the baby to the picnic. Jarrod would stay glued to Pops while Bo would have Levi.

They'd settled their basket of sandwiches on the blanket, and Bo had Levi in the stroller. A week ago he'd have been here as a single guy just enjoying the day, but today he was here as a father and it felt more alien to him than anything he'd ever experienced. Though he was getting used to the idea, it still seemed surreal in many ways.

He had to admit that he had gotten attached to the little fella. He was a pretty happy dude and he loved his stroller. It was as if he knew something life-changing was happening when he first arrived and so he had cried all the time, but now he was settling in. Abby had helped with that. She'd helped Bo calm down some around the boy and that was helping. But she also found things that gave Levi comfort. One of those was being rolled around in the stroller. The kid grinned at everyone—obviously a born flirt.

Bo kept disengaging from each flock of women so he could look for Abby.

Where was she?

Scanning the park, he finally spotted her at about eleven-thirty. She was walking across the street carrying a small blanket and a basket he assumed held her picnic lunch. Even from the distance he thought she looked pale.

He reached her about the time she made it across the street and to the park.

"Abby, hey, we've been watching for you. Everything okay?" He was beginning to sound like a broken record. How many times had he asked her that? She was probably going to tell him to mind his own business or something. Instead she nodded.

"Everything is fine. It's a lovely day for a picnic, don't you think?"

"Yes. Do you want to join us? I have a spot saved with a blanket laid out and everything."

She hesitated, then smiled. "Sure, I guess, for a moment. But I'm running late and I promised Clara Lyn I'd help with some auction she was working up."

"Sure." He studied the new hollowness to her eyes and he wanted again to ask her if she was okay, but he didn't.

"Have you seen Mr. Radcliff this morning?" she asked as they walked through the crowd toward his spot on the grass.

"No. Not that I can recall." Not that he'd been looking for Rand. "He's usually hanging out with Doobie and Doonie. You know he's on the city council—they're a part of all of these new things the town is doing."

"He's on the city council?"

"Yeah, has been for several years now."

"Oh."

"Hey, maybe you know the answer. What is it with women and babies? There have been women almost tackling poor Levi this morning."

Abby looked at him and suddenly some life flickered

in her eyes. He liked that he'd put it there. He didn't have a clue why she suddenly looked as if she was going to bust out laughing, but whatever the reason it was a whole lot better than the lack of emotion that had been there before.

"Bo, you seriously don't understand why Levi is attracting hordes of women?"

"Well, he is cute and all. And the kid knows how to flirt."

"Bo, have you looked in a mirror lately?"

He gave her a baffled look. "What does that mean?"

She gaped at him. "You cannot be this clueless. They are using Levi to get to you. A baby or a puppy are great icebreakers. Great excuses for mingling . . . get it?"

He felt like a total fool. "You mean it's not about Levi?"

"Bingo, Einstein."

He laughed now. "Wow, what has gotten into you? Where did the quiet gal go and who is this person who has taken over?"

She looked embarrassed. "Funny. But seriously, you had to know they're trying to get to you."

"Honestly, no, I was—" He stopped himself before he blurted out that there was only one woman on his mind. "That's just weird," he said instead.

She laughed again, with a gentle melody that played havoc on his insides. "Not weird—reality. You need to get used to this. You've probably never had a problem meeting women, but I have a feeling that now, being a single good-looking guy carrying around a baby, you're going to really be a magnet."

"Like I said, that's just weird," he said again, but was

distracted by her just saying that she thought he was good-looking.

"I've known men who borrow their nieces or nephews strictly as pickup tools. It's kind of disgusting if you think of it. But before I got marrie—" She stopped talking and it hit Bo between the eyes. Abby had been married once.

"Before I got married," she continued, slower, "I had men pushing strollers come up to me and pretend to need some advice about something so they could talk to me. Anyway, it's the same thing."

Abby had been married. And it seemed to be a tender subject. How long had she been divorced? Or was it something else? Was she a widow? She was too young to be a widow. She couldn't be more than twenty-six, twenty-seven at the most. There was no way she was older than him and he'd just turned twenty-eight.

"There's Clara Lyn, I need to go see her and I'll come join you after I see what she needs me to do. She's probably wondering what happened to me."

"What did happen to you? I was starting to get worried."

She was already gone, though, and didn't turn back to answer his question when he was almost certain she'd heard him.

He watched her go, the soft skirt swirling about her gold-sandaled feet. Her dark hair hanging loose about her shoulders swayed as she moved smoothly and with grace. He couldn't pull his gaze off of her. He was beginning to think he could look at her all day, every day. And that was saying something for a guy who usually lost interest in a woman pretty quickly. But Abby was different. Way different, and she was becoming almost like an obsession. Like his love for chocolate, only better . . . she was on his mind all the time.

CHAPTER 15

Clara Lyn and Reba hovered by the entrance to the gazebo as she approached. Apparently Abby had already missed the welcome by Mayor Doonie Burke. They'd said sometimes they suspected Doobie stood in for him, but she had a feeling that today it was really Doonie. Besides, she'd already talked with Doobie earlier.

"Abby, so glad you're here. I thought you'd decided not to come or something," Clara Lyn said, looking relieved to see Abby.

"You had us worried there for a few minutes." Reba wrote Abby's name on a piece of paper and dropped it in a basket.

"What's that?"

"Oh, it's just for the auction I was telling you about earlier. We've been collecting names—see the sign-up?" Clara waved a hand at the sign on the front of the gazebo that hadn't been there yesterday. It called for all single women to sign in for a chance to be in the auction.

Abby looked from Reba to Clara. "So, what's the auction?"

Clara Lyn grinned as if she could barely contain her

excitement. "You'll see. I think it's going to be so fun. You will have a blast and meet some new folks. Just stand there. It's getting close to time to start. Doonie's about to get things rolling."

Abby looked around, confused, but did as she was told. She'd had a horrible night and had to really give herself what-for this morning. She was sick and tired of feeling like a victim. Sick of everything that happened making her feel like she was slogging through muddy mire. She had to face her life. Stop looking back—she had to. And seeing Rand last night, drunk like he'd been, had sent her spiraling into despair.

She crumbled into a crying, grieving mess once she'd made it back to her new kitchen and had only dragged herself out of her grieving when she'd heard Landon, as real as if he'd been standing in front of her, lose patience with her. *"Get up, Abby. It's time to stop crying. Start fighting."*

She'd felt him. Heard him. Even saw him in her mind's eye, so very dear to her heart, with the kindest eyes she'd ever known that were now blazing with impatience. "Be that strong independent woman I loved. Stop using your grief as a crutch."

The thought had felt like a two-by-four between the eyes. She had a right to her grief. A right to be a crybaby if she wanted . . . but had she let her grief turn into a crutch? Had she let her love become a tool to hold her back despite her brave front of coming to Wishing Springs?

Had she really thought just making a change of scenery would be all that was needed?

She had been awake most of the night.

And mad at Rand despite what she was experiencing emotionally. The man had a crutch too. His just happened to be the same one that had been responsible for her husband and . . . her child's death. The last echoed softly from the depths of her soul. It was too unbearable to think of . . .

She'd buried the private information in her heart and soul. Very few people knew everything that wreck had cost her—God, her, a nurse, and a doctor—no one else knew that she'd miscarried after the drunk had crashed into them.

And that was why she hated alcohol with a passion.

Now, standing here in front of the gazebo, her heart pounded like beating drums thinking about what the drunk had stolen from her. Cost her. She blinked through the sudden surge of tears and forced herself to push the thoughts away or else she'd slide back into the treacherous waters of her past.

She eased in a steady, purposeful breath. Willed herself to calm down—truly she thought she was losing her mind.

But she was here.

She'd made herself listen to Landon, knowing that God was using his memory—his essence—to give her a hard shove.

Despite much preferring to hide in her house, she'd picked herself up this morning, driven to the store and grabbed a bunch of fruit, some croissants, and some chicken salad from the deli, and rushed home to make up her basket. And here she was despite now having a very odd sense that something unexpected was coming.

Something causing a new kind of unease to roll through her.

What were these ladies up to?

Doonie made his way toward the steps and smiled at her. "Morning, Abby, aren't you lookin' lovely today."

"Thank you, it looks like you've got a hit on your hands."

He beamed. "I do believe we do. But we're about to put the real fun into the mix." He winked and moved up the stairs.

Odd . . . matter of fact, Abby decided everything felt odd. Looking around, she felt a little self-conscious standing alone at the bottom of the steps. She started to move aside, but Clara Lyn hissed. "No. Stay there. Right there."

Abby halted. Okay, what was going on? Something wasn't right.

"Ladies and gentlemen," Doonie boomed over the crackling loudspeaker. Abby jumped forward, since the speaker was right behind her ear. "We're delighted you've all come out today for our inaugural Picnic in the Park. A special welcome to all the visitors from out of town. We're happy you've come to join us today. And now, we want to get the picnic started. We're asking all you ladies who signed up for the auction to make your way up to the gazebo to stand beside this pretty little gal." He pointed at Abby.

Butterflies erupted in her stomach.

"And if you're single and newly arrived and haven't signed up, come on up and Reba Ann and Clara Lyn will put your name into the pot. Oh, and bring your basket."

Abby watched as women came from the crowd. Eager ladies with much more excitement on their faces than she felt. She tried to smile, thinking she probably looked like a prune standing there. For goodness sake, they were about to have some fun and she was standing here worrying herself to death. That right there was the kind of thinking she was about to stop. She inhaled and sent a smile toward the approaching ladies. Abby counted ten ladies beside her.

"Okey-dokey, here we go. Now, in the early nineteen-hundreds they'd have a festive picnic like this and the single gentlemen in the crowd would bid on the single ladies' baskets *and* the opportunity to share lunch with the lady who prepared it."

Abby gasped.

"So, a few of us got together and decided that today we would add this to the picnic as a bit of fun and excitement. We want to thank each of these lovely ladies for participating. Now, let's begin."

Abby figured if someone had poured a cooler of ice-cold water over her, she wouldn't have been as surprised. She swung toward Doonie and then toward Clara Lyn and Reba. The sneaks were beaming like Cheshire cats. They gave her a thumbs up and winked like this was about the best thing since ice cream.

Abby started to walk off and then Doonie called her name. She spun back to him. What was going on? She shook her head and gritted a quiet, "No," trying to withdraw without attracting too much more attention.

"Now, Abby, don't worry about being the first one up. It's a good thing. The money will go to Over the

Rainbow. So who will give me a bid on this basket? Abby, I forgot to ask what you have in that basket."

Abby could feel every eye on her. She swallowed hard and croaked, "Chicken salad and fruit."

"Fantastic. Who will give the first bid on this chicken salad and fruit basket and a chance to eat with the *lovely* new *resident* of Wishing Springs, Miss Abby Knightley? We're starting all bids at fifteen dollars."

Abby bristled at being called Miss, she was and always would consider herself a Mrs. . . . but before she could think much about it, someone in the crowd shouted, "I'll give fifty."

Abby's mouth dropped open and she swung around to the crowd. *Who would bid fifty dollars? Were they delusional?*

. . .

Bo couldn't believe his ears. He had not known what was happening when Doonie first started speaking. He couldn't believe their little scheme. So this was what they'd been up to. Had Abby known about this? Before the thought was fully out, Abby swung around and the shock on her face clearly said no. She was as shocked as he was.

He felt bad for her.

He glanced over at the herd of cowboys that had enthusiastically jumped into the fray. By the time he'd recovered from his shock the bid had already gotten to eighty-five dollars.

"Who'll give me ninety?"

Slick Jones had been the first to bid and now the rowdy cowboy yelled out, "I'll up it another fifty."

"That's a good one," Doonie yelled. "Who'll make it one hundred fifty?"

Abby had a "deer in the headlights" expression he couldn't take. And besides that, he wanted to eat lunch with her. "Two hundred," he yelled.

Someone squealed—probably Clara Lyn if Bo had to make a guess.

Abby's mouth fell open. Her gaze found his as if pleading for help.

"We have us a bid of two hundred," Doonie boomed. "Who'll make it two hundred twenty?"

Abby swung around to stare up at Doonie and Bo's gaze narrowed. This was not happening.

"Two hundred twenty," yelled Slick, and everyone else remained quiet.

"Two hundred forty," Bo barked, and pushed the baby carriage a step closer. *Nope, not happening on his watch.*

Slick shot him a glare and yelled, "Two hundred sixty."

"Three hundred," Bo barked again. No way was he letting Abby have lunch with the womanizing, slick-talking lover boy. He saw Slick blanch and knew he had him.

"Three hundred ten," Slick said, lacking conviction as Bo held his glare with his own.

"Three hundred fifty," Bo added, upping it to get this disaster ended.

Slick said something under his breath, shook his head. His gaze immediately scanned the other grinning ladies in the line.

Bo's adrenalin didn't slow down at all, even as satisfaction set in.

"Going once. Going twice. Sold. We have our first picnic couple. Mr. Bo Monahan and Abby Knightley, enjoy your lunch."

. . .

Abby stalked from the group and came his way. Her cheeks flamed red and he wasn't at all sure if it was embarrassment or anger. He'd be hot, too, if he'd been the one stuck up there.

"Did you know about this?" she hissed under her breath as she reached him.

She was hot all right. No doubt about it.

"I was as surprised as you. And about as happy about it as you—this is the scheming coming from that article of Maggie's. They're trying to turn my town into one of those come-marry-our-cowboy towns. And I, for one, am not a pawn."

Abby gaped at him, in shock at his outburst probably, then she burst into laughter. "Oh my, and here I thought it was *me* who was the one being manipulated. You poor fella. What will you do when some woman comes to town with a shotgun and makes you marry her?"

"Funny, real funny. So, yeah, it's ridiculous. No one can make me marry them. But still, you know what I mean."

She was biting her lip to hold in her laughter.

He chuckled. "I feel so cheap."

She shook her head and grinned. "Well, you definitely paid a lot for chicken salad and fruit."

"And the pleasure of your company."

"Oh, yeah, there is that. I think at this point I'll head home."

"See'n as I saved you from the lecherous paws of Slick there, you kinda owe me a pleasant lunch—no strings attached. Other than helping me ward off the babymongers. I'd sure appreciate your help keeping them away. What do you say? Just a friendly lunch that protects us both from the crowd."

"Fine," she said, with a quick nod as if putting a period on the end of the decision. "That sounds like a fair plan of action."

He couldn't help the smile that instantly flashed across his face as his spirits did a high five. This day had started with Solomon's heavy breathing in his face. Then there was the moment with Pops that he wouldn't have had if not for the bad beginning—that had certainly been God taking a really bad situation and using it for good. Bo didn't know how the man upstairs did it sometimes. But that was why He was God and he was Bo.

And then there was Levi and Abby. Looking at her he couldn't help wonder where this was going . . . he was just glad lunch was on the agenda.

CHAPTER 16

Abby felt much better now. She was grateful that Bo had helped her out and still couldn't believe he'd paid three hundred fifty dollars to have lunch with her.

She couldn't deny being very grateful that she did not have to have lunch with Slick. The guy looked like he lived hard and partied harder. If he'd won the auction, there would have been no hesitation on her part—she'd have handed the man his lunch and kept right on walking to her house. There were just some things she would not do. No matter whose feelings got hurt.

Clara Lyn and Reba Ann were going to get a good piece of her mind. The sneaks.

She followed Bo to the quilt he'd set up and sank to the ground. "I'll get Levi out of this." She unstrapped the happy baby from the stroller. He was so excited he squealed and cranked his arms up and down in his excitement at being set free. She set him in front of her and let him balance with the help of her hands. "I think he liked the show just now."

Bo wheeled the stroller out of the way then took a spot on the blanket and reached over to tickle Levi's belly. "I believe you're right. He's also glad I won us the honor of lunch with you. He wasn't interested in any of the other gals who've been flirting with him. They squeezed his cheeks too tight." He laughed. "And besides, a baby knows when he's being used, even if his daddy is clueless."

Abby cocked her head and looked at Bo. "Do you realize that's the first time I've heard you say you were his daddy?"

"Yeah, well, it was a little shock. And I'm not going to lie, I planned to have the test tomorrow, but I can't do it. I've been thinking about it and thinking about it ever since Jake called. I'm listed as his dad, and he looks enough like a Monahan that I believe he's mine. I"—he looked at Levi thoughtfully and ran a gentle hand over the baby's soft dark hair—"I just can't risk what would happen if the test showed something different."

Abby stared at him, unable to look away—her shock and admiration were so great. That he was taking responsibility like that slammed her right in the heart. After all that they'd discussed about the risk of Levi belonging to someone else and that person being a jerk, she understood where Bo was coming from on this decision. She just hadn't expected it.

Wouldn't most single men in his situation want to know? It was a great responsibility to take on when there could be a question mark at the end.

The fact that he was stepping up before he had confirmation said a lot for him—at least it did to Abby.

Bo Monahan was much more than the handsome love-them-and-leave-them cowboy she'd feared him to be . . . and that made him all the more dangerous to her peace of mind.

She glanced away from him and back to Doonie, looking about as proud as a peacock standing up at the podium as the excited cowboys joined the fun and the bidding continued.

"Were we the only ones who were surprised about this or thought it was a little odd?" Abby asked, playing with the gurgling Levi. Bo set the food they'd each brought out on the quilt. "I think we were the only two who didn't think it was fun."

Bo grinned at her. "Hey, it's growing on me now that I have you sitting on my blanket."

Butterflies erupted inside her chest again, but this time they felt good, unlike a few moments ago at the gazebo. Meeting his teasing gaze and seeing the dimple appear beside his smile, excitement jumbled the butterflies about. Her mouth went dry realizing the situation—she was having lunch with the most handsome cowboy around. And he'd wanted her company.

Abby let the good feeling settle inside her and this time tried not to feel wrong that she found Bo so attractive. Landon was gone. He wasn't coming home. She deserved a second chance—at least that was what her therapist had tried to help her realize. She just couldn't make herself believe it. Hadn't had the desire to challenge her qualms . . . until now.

"Thank you. That's nice of you to say," she ventured, trying to adjust to the thought that had just stunned her. Could she possibly be thinking . . .

"It's a win-win situation, if you ask me." He winked.

Abby focused on Levi. Win-win. She'd saved Bo and he'd saved her and that was it.

Win. Win.

Her heart thundered, her skin turned clammy—if it was win-win then why did she suddenly feel like she was having the panic attack of all time?

Jarrod and Pops walked up then. Jarrod had this look about him that Abby figured left women falling in piles as they spun to watch him walk on by. She envisioned some of them swooning at the very sight of him.

The man was perfect. A combination of power mixed with a calm assurance—completely undeniable. Dark good looks so amazing absolutely nothing could be done to improve upon the man . . . however, Abby felt no attraction to the handsome cowboy in the least.

She looked from Jarrod to Bo and instantly compared the two brothers. Jarrod had an intensity to him that almost formed a barrier, while Bo had a more approachable air. Bo seemed ready to smile, when he wasn't upset about women trying to tie him up and force him to marry them. Thinking about the cute expression that had lit his face when talking about that made her smile to herself.

"It's a great day," Pops said. There was no mistaking he was having a good time. He crouched down, despite his age, and grinned at the baby. "Cute fella."

It took him a minute to get the two simple words to form with his misbehaving mind, but he got them.

"He is. And he likes you." Abby smiled at him.

Levi reached for Pops. The old man took the child's

tiny hand in his aged one and shook it gently. "Hi, nice to meet you."

Levi squealed in delight.

"I was going to head on back with Pops. He's had a good morning. I have some hay sales calls to make," said Jarrod.

"Okay, if you're sure," Bo said.

"I'm sure. You have fun. This was nice, but it's not really my thing."

Bo laughed. "You need to loosen up, big brother. Have a little fun. Bid on a lunch date."

The look Jarrod shot his teasing brother said it all. Bidding on a date was not on his bucket list.

"You ready to head to the ranch, Pops?" he asked, and Pops stood up.

"Yup. I've got horses to train."

Abby watched Bo's gaze soften looking at his Pops. "Watch out for the bay. She's been actin' a little contrary this morning."

"I got it," Pops said, and then went with Jarrod through the crowd.

Bo's shoulders slumped. "It gets me right here in the heart when he reverts back to the man he was up until a little over three years ago. The progression has been slow. Only in the last year have we really had to take over his care and watch him close."

"It's sad, but he's happy."

"Yeah, he lives in his own little world and it's different every day."

"I think it's great how much you and your brothers take care of him."

"He took care of us growing up. I mean, we had our mom and dad, but he was always there. He was so chock-full of wisdom, solid, strong wisdom. I don't know . . . do you think it's bad of me to say I miss him? I mean, he's still right here in front of us, but so seldom is he really with us."

"I understand. And no, I don't think it's wrong at all."

"So, Abby, you have me buffaloed." He gave her a small smile as he reached for a bottle of water.

"I'm so sorry you're confused." Abby knew a change of subject when she heard it. "Why so?"

"I can't figure you out. How long were you married—if you don't mind me asking?"

"Five years. I got married when I was twenty. And I lost Landon two years ago."

He stared at her. "Then you're a widow? Aw, man, that had to be hard. I'm so sorry."

She looked down, her insides churning. She didn't want to see pity in Bo's eyes. She'd grown so tired of all of her relationships with friends and acquaintances who knew about the tragic night. And sitting in the middle of a park with people everywhere was not the place to talk about this. "Bo, I'd really rather not discuss it here."

"Sure. I mean, I'm sorry. I shouldn't have brought it up—"

"It's okay, Bo. Really. You did nothing wrong."

His blue eyes bore into hers, searching . . . "If you say so. That had to have been tough, though."

"Yes, it was."

That was all she said, and all she planned to say on the subject right now. She gave him what she hoped was a reassuring smile. "Let's get this lunch on the go. My stomach is about to leap out of me."

He took her cue and smiled back, but this time it didn't quite reach his eyes. They were still concerned and full of pity. She hated the pity. "Mine, too, let's dig in. These sandwiches you made look great."

"Oh, they're not homemade, but they should be pretty good."

"You haven't eaten my food yet. If you had then you'd understand my enthusiasm for your cooking."

Abby chuckled at that, and the look of pity grew more distant as they relaxed a bit. Maybe this would be all right.

· · ·

Bo had enjoyed the day more than he could say. Winning the bid on Abby's lunch and getting to know her better had been worth every penny and more. He was still in shock that she'd lost her husband. He hoped he hadn't made her too uncomfortable, but he was glad he was aware of it now. Maybe he could be of help to her in some way. His feelings of protectiveness had been there from the moment he'd met her and now they'd grown even stronger. He told himself it was understandable. Especially after how she'd been helping him with Levi.

It had been a nice afternoon and though Bo wished it could last a little longer, he knew it was time to get

Levi home. He and Levi walked Abby to her car and he was putting her empty basket in her trunk when he saw Abby's expression tense. He turned to see what had caused the look on her face and saw Rand approaching.

"Hey, Rand, how's it going?" He hadn't seen the man all afternoon and Bo noticed he looked a little ragged around the edges. *Was Rand drinking again?* He hated that was the first thing that came to mind but lately Rand had been having some trouble. And looking at him now his skin was grayish and he had his sunshades on, but Bo was pretty sure there would be proof in the red eyes behind them.

"Bo, Abby," Rand said, glancing at Abby.

"I hope you're feeling good today," Abby said, looking stiff and uncomfortable.

Bo was certain he was sensing an uncomfortable vibe between the two. Why?

Rand frowned at her, almost scowled—which was unusual for the older man. "I'm just fine," he grunted, then walked away toward the park.

Definitely something going on here. "He seemed to be acting strange." Bo studied Abby.

She said nothing. Instead she bent to adjust sleeping Levi's light blanket. Bo waited, completely baffled by this. After fidgeting with the covers for a moment, she straightened up and looked conflicted.

"I have something to ask and I'm not certain how to ask it, but I feel I need to."

"Okay, shoot." He was more than ready to hear what was going on.

"Do you know he drinks? A lot?"

"Ah." Bo grimaced. "Yeah, I do. I think he's been trying to deal with it. Get it under control. Why?"

"Why? The man was totally wasted last night."

"And how do you know that?" Bo frowned, not liking this.

"Because I went over there last night to tell him I was staying at my house and he was sloshed to the hilt. I put him to bed—"

"*You what*—put him to bed? What in tar—you should have called me." Every protective instinct he had raged forward at the thought of Abby having to deal with Rand's drunkenness all by herself.

She looked shocked at his outburst. "Hey, I took care of it. I just helped him get to his room then left him sprawled across his bed passed out. I didn't like it. But I dealt with it."

"You shouldn't have done that. It wasn't your responsibility."

Her eyes narrowed. "I was there, I couldn't just ignore it. If I turned a blind eye—"

"Abby, you have *got* to be kidding me. There is no reason that you should have had to deal with his problem. You could have gotten into a bad situation."

"I just told you I couldn't turn around and ignore it. I was there . . . I seem to be in the wrong place at the *wrong* time ever since I drove into town."

He halted at her declaration. "Wow," he said quietly. "Direct hit." She was right though—the reality of her words slapped him across the face.

Abby looked down and rubbed her forehead before meeting his gaze. "I didn't mean that."

"No. I think you did and you're absolutely right. Man, Abby, I know that since you arrived my problems have somehow become yours to deal with. I apologize for that."

"There's no need to—"

"No, really. Look, this arrangement was temporary, and now that I look at it, you had plans when you came here and I've barged right into the middle of that with my unusual situation. I've managed to monopolize your time, and I'm not going to do that any longer. I'll find someone to help me. Okay?"

"But—"

He shook his head. "You've been great, really. But me and Levi—we'll be fine." Man, he was a jerk. She must think he was the most inept man alive. "Thanks." He started to walk away, but could not let the Rand thing go. "Look, it's bad enough you had to try and deal with my problems. But I got to tell you straight up to leave Rand's troubles to him. The man gets himself into these situations—just like me and my stupid, reckless behavior. It's not right for you to have to walk in and clean up his mess. Just like it's not right for you to have to clean up mine. You didn't come all the way out here to deal with a drunk. Or a cowboy in a pickle."

"This is ridiculous." She glared at him. "I don't need you telling me how to deal with stuff. And you are seriously telling me you don't want my help?"

They stared at each other.

"Yeah, I'll manage. You need to do your thing—take care of your agenda, not anyone else's. It's a good thing, Abby."

"But you need me."

The woman was unreasonable. About everything, it seemed. "I don't need you. I was a capable, responsible man before you or Levi showed up—maybe not as responsible as I should have been, but I'll take it from here." He tipped his hat. He was cutting her loose. She should be running while she had the chance. "But thanks. We'll see you around town."

Her mouth went slack. Maybe he was being a jerk—who knew? All he did know was that he was embarrassed beyond words over the whole situation. He pushed Levi down the street toward his truck and resisted the urge to turn around and see if she was still in shock—or angry.

Man, he'd acted like an idiot.

Bo scolded himself all the way down the street. He'd gotten himself into this wreck and he'd get himself out of it. And if his stirrups didn't get made in the meantime, so be it.

Abby had said she felt like she'd been in the wrong place at the wrong time ever since arriving in town and yet she'd come out yesterday and offered to work for him. And he knew it had to be because she was a kind person and felt bad for him . . . or obligated or something, because she felt really sorry for Levi and was worried Bo couldn't deal with the situation.

And he'd taken advantage of that. Not any longer. The woman had problems of her own she was trying to handle. She didn't need his too. Or Rand's—the man needed to straighten up his life before it got out of hand.

• • •

How dare he treat her that way! Abby watched Bo walk away and then turned and yanked open her car door. Her insides had shaken like gelatin as he took Levi away from her. Two days ago, against her fear of both falling for and losing the baby, her instincts had taken over and she'd committed to being his nanny. And before the end of forty-eight hours Levi was already being taken away.

Scalding fury poured through Abby, and she had to clasp her elbows and hang on tight in order to keep from trembling out of control.

Yes, she should have thought before making that remark. Of course he'd jumped to conclusions because he felt guilty. Of course he was going to pull back and close himself off and that was fine. Her fault for bad word choice.

But his attitude about her helping Rand was unacceptable. Someone needed to before the man killed someone.

She wanted to march after Bo and demand that he not renege on their agreement. She would have to think about what to do about that, but if Bo thought she took orders from him where her personal life was concerned, well, he could think again. She shouldn't have asked him about Rand. She should have waited to approach Rand later when he was back home and sober.

One thing she would not do was sweep drinking under the table, even if being involved ripped her heart out.

CHAPTER 17

I tell you, Abby was upset." Reba had been fretting over the auction ambush for three days and now, over tea in Pebble's kitchen, she had to voice her opinion once more.

"I know," Clara Lyn finally agreed, for the first time since Saturday. "I've been denying it, but it just never dawned on me that we'd upset her. But, well, y'all know she seemed fine after she sat down on the blanket with Bo. Didn't you think so?"

"Yes, it appeared to be so," Pebble said. "But she certainly looked shocked about being auctioned off. You know I never thought this was a good idea, and I told you both it wasn't."

"Pebble, stop your worrying. We know you said that. I keep thinking she was all right in the end, but then she's just disappeared. I kept thinking we'd see her out and about." Clara Lyn couldn't believe the mess she'd made of things. She'd thought nothing of surprising the poor girl with the auction.

"She might have her reasons for not dating." Pebble looked worried again. "Have you ever thought of that, Clara Lyn?"

Clara studied Pebble. "Do you know something we don't know? You *do* know something."

Pebble had never been good at hiding things. She might not tell a secret she was holding for someone, but she had no poker face. Clara Lyn could see right through her.

Reba gasped. "Pebble, what do you know?"

"She confided in me and you know I can't tell. But y'all are heading in the right direction. I didn't say anything to you about stopping this absurd idea Clara had because there is a chance that a push is what she needs."

Reba Ann looked worried now. "But what if we've caused her to slip back into whatever trouble it is?" She studied Pebble intently and Clara Lyn joined her.

"Has she gone through a horrible divorce?" she asked, but Pebble said nothing. Clara Lyn pressed on. "Lost someone?" Pebble looked down and fidgeted in her chair and Clara Lyn knew she'd hit the right trail. "Oh no, you can't tell me she's a widow. She's too young. Far too young."

Pebble's blue eyes widened. "I didn't tell you anything."

"No," Reba said. "You didn't, so rest easy, but I'm glad we know finally. How utterly sad."

They all sat silent for a moment thinking about Abby.

"We might need to go check on her," Reba said.

"I went by after church the day after the picnic and she was home, but she said she was fine. She really didn't seem like she wanted company."

Clara Lyn frowned. "I don't like the sound of this. I'm the one who came up with this meddlesome plan. I should have gone straight there and checked on her, but she seemed happy sitting on that blanket with Bo and Levi. And then y'all saw Jarrod and his grandfather come up. Everything appeared to be just fine. Do you think something happened after she left?"

"I agree," Reba said. "As far as I could tell, after the initial shock wore off and Bo bid so high, she looked happy. But I'm worried now."

"I wouldn't have done it if I'd known it might make things worse for her." Clara Lyn was feeling more worried with every second.

"Maybe I should have told you. But I knew you would figure it out on your own. I even warned Abby that you would. With Cecil's loss, it was almost as if I sensed it."

Reba sighed. "I wish I would ever find someone with half Cecil's love for you. Then maybe I would consider marrying again."

Clara gave her a skeptical look. "At this late date. Not me. I'm enjoying doing some matchmaking, but I'd never marry again. Speaking of, Pebble, that Rand is sure still sweet on you. His face was as long as a hound dog Saturday."

"Now, Clara Lyn, you know how I feel. I loved Cecil. I—"

"That doesn't mean you can't love someone else. But Rand—"

"I have told you before I don't want to discuss Rand."

Pebble was about the sweetest, softest-spoken woman Clara knew, but she had a stubborn streak.

"That's what's nice. We all can have our own life choices. I think Abby needs to just move forward, and

Clara, you may be helping her do that. We all know that change isn't easy. Sometimes we need a shove even if we don't like it."

Clara hadn't meant to cause anyone to feel bad. "Maybe y'all have a good point. Maybe she does need us to stop by and check on her."

. . .

By the time Tru and Maggie arrived at the ranch mid-week, Bo's stress level had risen and so had Jarrod's as they'd put together a schedule around Levi and Pops. Bo had an ad running in the paper on Tuesday, but it was going to take time to find the right person.

He didn't know how Tru and Maggie would react to the news that there was now a baby in the family mix. Especially when Tru had recently learned he couldn't father children because of the chemo treatments he'd had when he was a kid.

With them on their honeymoon, Bo had held off sharing the news. So there was no way of knowing how they would react to Levi. He hoped it wasn't too hard on them.

Bo had already made a wreck out of things with Abby—he'd thought about her every day and even almost gone to see her several times, but he'd forced himself to leave her alone. She needed time to settle in without him and his problems lurking around the corner.

Besides, he didn't have time to pursue anything with Abby.

He'd known it before and it was the truth.

And then there was the fact that he'd felt the need to jump off into her business. Where in the heck did he come off telling her to leave Rand alone? But the thought of her over there carting the drunk, lovesick councilman off to bed before he collapsed made him crazy. But was it any of his business? She was right.

And she'd had no problem letting him know it either.

And what had he done? Acted odd.

Real odd. Who was he kidding? Abby was probably saying good riddance to the cowboy with the crazy life.

Standing in the drive watching his brother park the truck, he pushed the thoughts aside—which was a good thing since he was feeling like he was heading too deep into woe-is-me territory.

"Welcome home, newlyweds," he called, really glad in that moment that Tru had Maggie.

Tru smiled and laid his arm across Maggie's shoulders and pulled her close. "We're glad to be home."

Maggie looked up at him with an expression so loving that Bo couldn't help hiking a brow at his brother. "Looks like she still loves you."

"Oh, I do. No doubt about that ever."

"Glad to hear it." Tru grinned, then gave her a brief kiss on the forehead before looking back at Bo.

He looked more relaxed than Bo could remember in years. Maggie was good for him.

"So, what's been going on?" Tru asked. "It was as quiet from y'alls end as I've ever known it."

"You were on your honeymoon," Bo hedged. "We weren't going to pester you with our business while you had better things to concentrate on." He glanced toward the house. He'd left Levi in the playpen inside while he stepped out onto the porch to greet them. He figured it'd be better to give them the news out here before they walked inside and saw the baby. Their nephew.

"Well, I appreciate it." Tru laughed. "Is Pops doing good?"

"He's doing okay, about the same." Bo took a deep breath. "I do need to let y'all in on a little bit of news."

Tru's eyes narrowed just a touch as he picked up on the edge in Bo's tone. His brother's ability to read signs was one reason he was a champion quarter horse trainer and a rider too.

"What?" he asked. "Is something wrong, Bo? You said Pops was okay, right?"

"Yeah, Pops is fine. It's—well, there is just no other way to say this. I became a father while y'all were gone."

They just stared at him. As if having trouble understanding what he was saying.

Bo raked a hand through his hair. "I mean, I was already one, I just didn't know it," he said before they could respond.

"Like a father with a baby?" Tru finally said, as if confused that Bo might have suddenly become a priest or something.

"Yeah, a baby. A boy. He's twelve months old and I didn't know about him until a week ago Monday morning when he showed up on the porch."

"On the porch?" Tru prompted.

"Yes. His mother is Darla. You met her when I was dating her. She died of cancer and before the courts could notify me, some friend of hers left him in a play-pen on the front porch with Pops."

"I remember her." Tru's jaw tensed and his eyes narrowed. "That didn't last long—and she's dead? This is bad."

Bo knew all the things running through his brother's mind. He was disappointed in Bo and feeling bad for Darla and wondering about the baby all at once.

"Left him. Alone?" Maggie said, skipping over everything except the baby's well-being.

Tru frowned. "You're joking about that, right? Because this is really not funny."

"I'm well aware how not funny this is," Bo snapped, fully aware he'd caused this through carelessness but still not liking feeling incompetent. "That's just the way it went down. I came home from town and the baby was in a playpen on the front porch with Pops." He continued on trying to iron out any misunderstandings his first explanation might have made.

"I'm really sorry about his mother," Maggie said, "but I'm glad you finally know the truth. You deserve to know your son. Can we see him?" She glanced at Tru who hadn't said anything else.

"Sure. He's inside. I wanted to prepare you before you just walked in and found out."

To Bo's relief, Tru didn't look upset. That serious expression Bo knew so well crept over into Tru's eyes and his bronzed skin crinkled at their edges. "Thanks for the warning. It would have been a shocker."

Bo held the door open. "Believe me, I know about shock. If Abby hadn't been with me, I don't know what I'd have done."

"Abby?" Maggie said as she stepped into the kitchen.

Bo explained quickly how he'd come to meet Abby, lest they think she was involved in a different way. "She's helped out a lot."

Tru followed Maggie into the house and Bo thought he looked a little troubled. Maggie had always wanted kids. Bo hadn't really thought about what this was going to do to Maggie, but he wondered if Tru was concerned about that.

Levi had heard them coming and stood up watching as they walked into the room. Pops was grinning from where he stood behind the playpen holding a stuffed toy. Levi had probably thrown it out of the playpen, having learned over the last couple of days that whatever he threw, Pops would retrieve. The kid loved the game and so did Pops, and it kept them both occupied.

Maggie gasped the instant she saw him. Her hand went to her heart and she shot Bo a look of pure emotion. "Oh, Bo." Her voice cracked just a little. "He's adorable. Can I hold him?"

"Maggie, you can do whatever you'd like. I'm certain he would love you cuddling with him."

For the first time since they'd driven up, Bo felt real relief. Maggie had a deep capacity for caring for others. It was evident in everything she did—though he'd been really hard on her about the article she'd written about him and the other single men of Wishing Springs. Now, he felt guilty watching her expression soften as she lifted his son into her arms.

"Hello, sugar. I'm your Aunt Maggie. We are going to have the best time getting to know each other."

With that she hugged him tightly and met Tru's gaze with the biggest smile Bo had ever seen. Her eyes glistened. "He is so precious. Come see him, Uncle Tru," she urged, and Tru moved to join her. Bo hadn't even thought about this part of the equation—that they'd be happy about a baby around. All he'd thought was that the baby might cause them pain.

Maybe things were going to be all right.

CHAPTER 18

Abby woke on Sunday morning yearning to go to church, but also with no desire to see anyone. It was a familiar feeling that she'd succumbed to over and over and over again in Houston. She'd spent the night frustrated, tossing and turning, worried about her landlord trying to give her the boot despite her six-month lease. But mostly she'd spent the night worried about how angry Bo Monahan could make her.

She hadn't gone to church despite being drawn to do so; instead she'd driven around the country roads thinking, but nothing eased the turmoil inside of her. Nor caused her to stop thinking of Bo.

After a few hours she sat at the crossroads thinking about what she should do. *Drive out there and tell him he'd had no right to go back on their agreement.*

She realized now that she hadn't helped the situation with her horrible statement. He'd felt guilty for causing her plans to be so mixed up.

But he needed her despite telling her he didn't.

And she knew it too.

And you need them . . . The four words whispered in the back of her heart.

She didn't need them. She wanted to help them—but need them . . . Abby's baby was gone.

The truth hurt her every time she let the thought escape from her broken and grief-torn soul.

Her tiny rosebud of a baby.

Her baby that Abby hadn't even known existed until she woke, bleeding in the emergency room, and the nurse told her she'd lost the baby.

Lost the baby.

And she'd lost Landon too.

And she'd known in that instant, in that excruciating blink of time, that it was her fault.

They'd been fighting over when to start their family when the wreck happened . . .

Even now, two years later as her guard dropped and the wound gaped open, Abby still couldn't believe what had happened. Still couldn't believe . . . She'd lost her baby and her husband.

And it was as much her fault as it was the drunk who'd plowed into them.

How she relived that night day after day . . . if she'd not been angry at her husband, if she'd just kept her mouth shut . . . Landon would have had his eyes on the road and not her. He would have seen that the oncoming truck wasn't acting right. He would have been able to react.

Instead he'd been glaring at her in disbelief, unable to believe she'd just told him she wasn't sure she wanted children after all.

And now Abby lived with the knowledge that this was as much her fault as it was the drunk driver's. Sunday was never a good day. She'd hoped, been determined, that coming to Wishing Springs somehow would help, but it had been a disaster from the beginning.

The wreck, meeting Bo, and feeling the strong flutters of attraction had thrown her off balance, but then finding Levi . . . the precious boy had wrapped his little fingers around her heart and now she was at risk of losing another baby. Just as she'd worried the moment she'd seen him standing in his playpen red in the face from crying that first morning.

Looking down the road, her heart beating dully in her chest, she turned her car toward Wishing Springs instead of Bo's ranch. Her spirits heavy, she knew she had no right to feel the joy that she'd felt in the last couple of days.

Abby was thankful on Monday when the moving truck drove up at eight a.m. She'd never been so relieved to see her things in all her life.

She needed this. Needed the unpacking, needed something to help her out of the funk she was in.

By Wednesday she had made some progress in the unpacking and she'd talked herself off the ledge. And had climbed out of the feel-sorry-for-me hole she'd fallen into. She was functioning at least.

Maybe one day she'd actually be living again.

The knock on the door Wednesday startled her.

Her heart lurched into her throat . . . she pulled open the door and realized as she did that despite everything, she was hoping it was Bo.

"Abby, we are sorry and finally had to come say so," Clara Lyn said, busting into the room the instant the door was cracked. "We came to apologize for making your life hard. If there is any blame to be had, it's mine."

"I'm responsible too," Reba declared, filing past her into the house with Clara Lyn. "I should have kept Clara Lyn in line, but I didn't. And for that I'm truly, deeply sorry."

Clara Lyn shot her friend a glare. "You keep me in line? Ha."

"Girls, there is no need to fuss. You were both responsible," Pebble said, looking primly at Abby as she stood on the threshold beside her. "They just jump in with both feet sometimes. So, if you are still upset with them, it is completely understandable. Completely."

Abby stared from one to the other and then she inhaled and her heart started beating again. "I didn't mean to be a bad sport. It ended up being fine. Really. I was upset at being ambushed and auctioned off. But in the end it was a very enjoyable day." She didn't add *until Bo got all huffy and strutted off after firing me.*

Clara Lyn's forehead crinkled. "Really? But if you're not mad, then why have you been holed up here all week?"

Abby rubbed the tension from between her eyes. Getting pushed from hiding was a good thing, she reminded herself. These ladies were part of why she'd come.

"Did you have a fight with Bo?" Clara Lyn asked.

"How did you know that?"

The older lady waved her hand, and the colorful rock bracelet rattled against the gold bangles. "Bah, if you've been around people as much as I have, you get a sense. But I sure missed it where the auction was concerned." She glanced at Pebble. "I only just figured out that you had been through a heartbreak that might make you not want to be matched up with a fella. I'm so sorry."

Abby shifted her gaze to Pebble. Had she told them?

Pebble's gaze softened and she gave a slight shake of her head. "She figured it out on her own."

"It's okay," Abby sighed. "It's not something I meant to hide."

"You're too young to be a widow." Reba shook her head, too, and Abby wanted to shake hers along with her.

"I am. But I guess that's not something anyone gets to choose." She wanted the conversation to end. "It could be anyone and it was me." Abby knew it was true. Why not her? But deep down she knew it was so much more than losing her sweet husband and lifelong best friend. "Really, I'm fine." It was her tried and true answer.

They all studied her quietly for a moment, then Clara Lyn took over. "Well, we hope so. We came by to abduct you this time instead of ambushing you. We're going to lunch. Getting you out of this house."

Unable to resist, she'd let them sweep her off to lunch and when they arrived back at her house almost two hours later her nosey friends had cheered her up some despite their prodding and pulling trying to get info from her. They'd barely driven off before to her surprise Bo rolled into her driveway.

Her pulse kicked in—and those stinking butterflies began winging their way around inside of her as he sauntered up the drive from where he left his truck at the curb. He snapped his Stetson from his head. Her heart—drat it—was thumping erratically when he halted in front of her.

She'd missed him.

"Hi, Abby."

"Bo," she said. Her mouth went dry and her heart jumped in her chest. And there it was, the knowledge that denying she'd missed him was useless. Even if he had been out of line at the picnic the distance they'd had for the last few days at least had kept her from having these unwanted feelings. She wanted distance.

She didn't want to feel this attraction that he stirred inside of her, the heat that hummed through her just looking at him.

Didn't want thoughts of him elbowing their way into her thoughts day and . . . night.

"I came to apologize."

"Bo, I don't need you trying to tell me how to run my life. I barely know you."

He stiffened. "Abby, I'm apologizing for acting like a jerk. But I'm not apologizing for being upset that you were over there dealing with Rand when you should have called me. That was irresponsible, dealing with something like that all by yourself."

Irresponsible. Her mouth dropped open and the heat turned explosive. True, the most reasonable plan of action might have been to call in help, and where alcohol was concerned, she wasn't reasonable. But to call her irresponsible—"I did what needed to be done. What I felt was the right thing to do."

His jaw tensed. Abby figured he was probably about to break his molars gritting down on them so hard.

"You're driving me crazy—you know that, don't you?"

"You're driving me crazy." Abby hiked her chin and glared at him. "You might as well go ahead and leave if you think I'm going to apologize for not meeting your requirement for saneness." She turned away from him and inserted her key into her lock. Her fingers trembled.

"Abby, wait." His hand on her arm sent a shiver of awareness crashing through her.

She bit down on her lip and tried to still the erratic pounding in her heart.

"I was just concerned for you," he said, his tone as smooth as butter. She felt him as he moved closer and gently turned her to face him. She was unable to stop herself from following his lead. Great—she could snap all she wanted but with him this close . . . and suddenly finding him looking into her eyes from only a breath away—Abby trembled. Shame washed over her at these feelings, but she was unable to stop them . . .

Breathless. *Irrational.*

He lifted his hand to her face and gently, ever so slowly, he traced the line of her jaw with the backs of his fingertips. His blue eyes raged with emotion like swirling seas as his hand slipped from her jaw to gently cup the back of her neck. The warmth of his fingers sent heat spiraling through her, the need that suddenly curled inside of her as she realized he was going to kiss her.

"No," she said, shaking her head with horror at her

reaction to him. How could she? "Don't," she ground out, as remorse swamped her. "This isn't right." It was oh so very wrong. Landon had only been gone two years. Her heart was his. Always would be . . . dear Lord, how could she let these kinds of feelings affect her?

"Why?"

It was a simple enough question—a single word, and no way could she explain what was going on inside her thoughts. "Because I'm not ready to have a relationship. And, and because we wouldn't be a match even if I was."

He'd stepped back giving her room but the small distance wasn't helping her thoughts unmuddle.

"Abby, didn't you say it's been two years?"

"So now you're putting a time limit on my *emotions*?"

"No. Not at all, that came out sounding callous. That's not what I meant. Didn't you tell me you came to Wishing Springs to move forward?"

"Yes. But Bo, I'm never getting remarried, so there is no reason for me to . . . to do this."

"This?"

"This, this—" She impatiently dangled a finger from him to her. He knew what she was talking about, saw it dawn in his eyes. "I have no desire to have a relationship, to kiss a man. I-I love Landon. If you think there will be more, you're wrong. I was just helping you out with Levi. I'm here to try and move on with my life, but I can't do—this." There she'd said it. Her heart was irrevocably wounded, like a crater burned deep and wide from a meteorite and now empty because the meteorite had disintegrated. Her heart couldn't take losing anyone she loved ever again or it would turn to dust . . . and even if it could, she didn't have the will to test it. These emotions and feelings swamping her were merely because she missed Landon's touch so very, very much.

Yes, that was it. That was exactly it. Relief calmed the guilt threatening to swallow her.

When you missed someone as much as she missed Landon, then it would be easy to be vulnerable . . . it would.

. . . .

Call him a jerk, but Bo didn't like knowing Abby was writing herself off ever loving again. It was wrong— that emotion grabbed him around the heart.

He'd almost kissed her and it had taken everything he had not to. The only reason he hadn't was because she'd let him know she didn't want to kiss him.

A little over a week ago he wasn't interested in any-thing to do with a serious relationship. But now, staring at Abby, he knew things had changed for him. No one had ever affected him like Abby did. The thought of her never loving again just didn't sit well with him. "Abby, there is nothing wrong with deciding marriage isn't for you again. That's your business. But to just give up—I can't stand the idea that you're closing the door to your heart."

Her front porch didn't feel like the right place to have this conversation, however Bo wasn't letting her go until they'd made some progress. Since he'd met Abby in the dark on the road in front of his ranch things had changed for him at the speed of light. Abby had drawn him from the first moment. Sure she was beautiful, but there was something about her that pulled him in. Drew him like a bee to pollen. And he knew absolutely that he wasn't ready for "this," as she'd called it, to end. He wanted to explore it slowly, take care with it, and see where it could go. He wasn't walking away again.

He didn't plan on using her to babysit again either. He'd learned that he could survive with Levi in the last few days, so he wasn't desperate any longer. He'd reached out to Peg and Lana at Over the Rainbow and run into Clara Lyn at the grocery store. He'd had plenty of offers of help and advice. But he wasn't giving up on Abby. He wanted to see inside that beautiful head of hers and know what made her tick. What made her smile. And he wanted to do whatever it took to see more of those smiles. They were unbelievable. He knew that she'd been through tragedy and was surviving and he knew that she had a heart that was kind and good and nothing he did could get her off his mind.

Looking at her now though, she wasn't smiling. She looked distant and looked as if she'd stepped behind an invisible barrier.

"Bo, sometimes it's the only choice to make. I need to go in."

"So you're not going to invite me in." He gave her a smile, determined not to be so easily sent away. He did not want to walk away right now.

"Under the circumstances I don't think it's a good idea."

To resist the need to reach for her, he crossed his

arms. "Let's start over, Abby. No way to get around it, I like you. You're a good, kind, and compassionate woman. And despite the fact that we have differing views I'm not willing to let go of our budding friendship. I don't know, maybe it has nothing to do with "this" as you've called it. But I know I value your friendship and I hate thinking that you're going to push me away because there is a possibility that there could be something more between us."

She moistened her lips. He could read indecision in her expression. He'd just muddled this more.

"We'll probably just fight again," she said, a hint of a smile turning up the corners of her lips.

"Makes friendship interesting. Friends don't need to agree on everything." Bo's gut turned over thinking she might still tell him to hit the road. He wasn't above using every card in his deck to stop that from happening.

"Maggie's watching Levi while she's home and loving it. And that's another reason I came by. I wanted to invite you to dinner on Friday." He didn't want to let her close the door between them and he knew she would want to meet his sister-in-law. "Maggie and Tru are home and they'd love to meet you. And Pops has been asking about you and Levi would be overjoyed to see you."

"Bo—"

"You know you want to meet Maggie. Her column is why you uprooted your life." He saw the truth in her eyes and knew she wanted to. He grinned and felt his dimple show up and for the first time in his adult life, he hoped his dimpled grin softened her up.

"Okay. I'd love to come to dinner at your house with

you and your family. If it's not too much trouble. But Bo, this is not a date. It's me coming to dinner to meet Maggie. And that's that."

"Great. I'll come pick you up—but it's not a date. Got that."

"I have a car—"

"Yes, you do, but it'll be dark after you leave and I'll just not feel right about you getting home safe. I'll pick you up."

"Okay, fine. Thank you."

He gave her an easy smile, holding back his enthusiasm so as not to push her away again. But he didn't care what she called it. He called it success by baby steps. He'd kept the door open and if he got his way, Friday night he'd open it a little wider. It wasn't just about the fact that he wanted to get to know her better. He felt with every fiber of his being that Abby needed help herself. And he planned to give it to her.

One step at a time.

CHAPTER 19

"Mom, things are fine. Stop worrying."

When Abby's phone rang she'd been sitting outside the newspaper office thinking about going in and applying for the job there, but she hadn't been able to. For one, Rand would probably have asked her to leave—or slammed the door in her face. And then there was Levi. Who was taking care of Levi?

Now she was sitting in her car listening to the worry in her mother's voice and wishing she could get her point across. "You've got to let me move on. And that means stop pushing for me to revert to the way things were. They aren't and never will be the same." It was the same old thing from the moment her mother had started talking.

"I just thought given a few days, you'd come to your senses."

What was it lately with people telling her she didn't know what she was doing? "Mom, stop. I have not lost my senses. I lost Landon. And Landon is not coming back. And if you continue on with this, this negative attitude, I'm going to have to draw away from you."

Abby hated to say this. But she was determined to

either fix this between them or distance herself. She couldn't continue with the attitude. It was as if her mother had ignored their previous conversation altogether.

"Abby, I'm just doing what any mother who cares about her child would do. I care about you. I love you—"

"I know you care for me. But if you love me then wish me the best in this new life I'm being forced to navigate. Pray for me to find happiness here in the midst of change. Change that isn't easy for me. It's not easy for you either as my mom and I recognize that. But I can't keep having you insult my decisions."

"Abby, I can't believe you're saying this. I just believe you're wrong and that being here would be better for you."

"Mom," Abby sighed, rubbing her temple and feeling suddenly weary. "If I was getting into drugs, or drinking too much, or going off the deep end where men were concerned, I'd get that you should be trying to stop me. I'd want you to stick to your guns and try and shake some sense into me. But I'm doing none of that. I'm just trying to simplify my life. To find a place that makes sense to me and as much as you hate the thought of that, I'm the only one who can figure this part out, Mom." Abby just wanted her mother and her friends to accept that things were never going to be like they were.

"I was only trying to help."

Abby heard hesitancy in her mother's voice and hope flared inside of her. Was she going to let it go? "I know. But now you could help by letting it go. Just be my friend right now, Mom. Support me and tell my friends to support my decision."

She would have loved to have been able to call and tell about the unexpected events of her first week in Wishing Springs—about the wreck, about Levi . . . about Bo. No, not about Bo. Her mother had been through a lot in her life and Abby loved and respected her very much.

There was silence on the other end of the line.

Then her mother asked, "So, what are you doing right now?"

Abby's eyes misted with the hope that they'd just taken a step in the right direction. She smiled, trying to form the next words. "I'm about to go to the grocery store." No need telling her she'd almost gone into the newspaper office and applied for a reception job. She wasn't going to, so she just moved on to the next item on her agenda.

"I guess mundane tasks continue wherever we are," her mom said, and the sound of her trying to do as Abby asked felt so good.

"You know I don't do change very well in my own life. I really didn't mean to hurt you."

Abby's heart clenched. "I know."

"I'm here if you need me."

Abby's spirits lifted. "That means the world to me." They spoke a little longer, like old times, and then hung up. Abby started to back out and head to the grocery store. It was probably better this way. She hadn't seen Rand since the picnic when he'd barely spoken to her. But he was her landlord, whom she'd seen at his worst.

She also knew that if she were to have any kind of influence on Rand then they had to have a relationship of some sort. But she'd decided a working relationship might be pushing it.

She was about to put her car in reverse when the door opened and a pretty woman with long blond hair walked outside carrying Levi.

Abby's heart jerked and an instant smile burst to her lips at seeing the baby. She'd missed him in the five days since she'd seen him on Saturday.

And that was Maggie carrying him. Abby recognized her from the picture on her column and the TV interview between her and Tru. Abby was out of the car in a flash.

"Hi," she called, and Maggie stopped on the curb.

"Hi," Maggie said brightly as Levi gave Abby a huge smile and leaned forward for her to take him. 'I believe Levi knows you. Are you *the* Abby?"

Abby laughed. "Yes I am. Abby Knightley. I helped take care of Levi for a couple of days. And you're Maggie."

"I *am*. Oh, our Levi likes you."

"The feeling's mutual. I adore him." Levi grabbed her finger and grinned at her. Abby's heart swelled with tenderness.

Maggie laughed, too, and had to hold on tight when he lunged at her. "Oh," Maggie gasped. "He's strong. We are so thrilled to have him in our lives. I was actually coming to see you after I left here. I wanted to come thank you for all your help. You've been a huge blessing to Bo."

Heat crawled up Abby's neck. This was the woman whose advice had given her hope when she'd been in dark places. This was the woman whose advice, even when it had nothing to do with anything going on in Abby's life, inspired her nonetheless, because it was stated with such care and warmth. It was hard to believe that Maggie was in her twenties like Abby. Abby certainly couldn't give the kind of advice this beautiful woman gave. It was, in no uncertain terms, a gift.

Abby finally found her voice. "He would have been okay without me—"

"Are you kidding me? He wouldn't have made it without you. Period. He told us you were amazing. And though you had your own plans, you felt sorry for the poor baby and helped him. He said you had an extremely kind heart."

Abby got caught speechless for the moment. He'd actually said that about her. "I volunteered because I wanted to help. It wasn't that I felt sorry for them." Abby was disturbed that Maggie might think it was all because of pity.

Hearing the unhappy tone in Abby's voice Maggie's expression changed slightly, concern entering her eyes. "Unfortunately, right or wrong, this is how Bo felt. You have to remember he's a cowboy who believes he's capable of anything. To be brought to his knees by a tiny baby—must be a little unsettling to his male ego." Levi lunged at her again and Maggie let him transfer into Abby's arms.

"I understand that. It's just he's so touchy." She grimaced thinking about it. Levi grabbed a fistful of her hair and grinned. She cuddled him close, inhaling his sweet scent, but her thoughts were on that moment standing beside her car with Bo.

Maggie continued. "Capable is a cowboy's middle name and they can do so much you don't even expect. I was amazed at what I saw when I came here and participated in the infamous bet with Tru. For Bo to have accepted your help showed just how out of his comfort zone he was with Levi."

No wonder her words at the picnic had affected him so—saying she'd been at the wrong place at the wrong time ever since coming to town had hit him hard. He'd already felt bad about what he was doing and then she'd said that.

That he'd taken advantage of her. She knew that wasn't entirely true. She'd been the one to offer her help. He hadn't come to her, but like he'd said when he apologized to her, he really believed she'd only offered because she was worried about Levi and maybe felt obligated . . . that's how it sounded to Abby.

"You always have such insights, I'm amazed. I have to tell you that I'm a big reader of your column. Your advice has helped me very much." Abby wasn't sure if people in Maggie's position were bothered when fans came up to them but one way or the other Abby had to express her gratitude. A warm, wide smile spread across Maggie's face.

"Thank you, Abby. It means a great deal to me when I can help someone. To tell you the truth, sometimes I have to make myself say what I'm thinking and pray the Lord is leading my words. I can be pretty blunt and

I worry it might hurt someone's feelings, but sometimes the truth hurts."

Abby knew that was so. "Like me, sometimes people need a wake-up call. A little kick in the pants to get them thinking straight. Or to make them take courage and move forward. Your advice is always sound. I'm trying to implement it in my life . . . because I know I need to."

Maggie studied her, cocked her head slightly. "This is really hard for you, I can see that. If I can help in any way, I want to help." She smiled. "You remind me of someone I love so much. My friend Jenna made hard choices too. Forced herself to make them, actually."

Abby sobered, knowing by the intensity of Maggie's words that this meant a lot to her too. "And how is that working out for your friend?"

Maggie sighed. "She's making it, and she holds fast to the belief that she made the right choice despite how tough and heartbreaking it was for her to give her baby up for adoption. Abby, I hope I didn't mislead you in any way. Change isn't always easy. And it doesn't always turn out the way you think it will or want it to."

"I know. Believe me, I know. And you didn't mislead me. I came here to force myself to move forward and knowing it could be a good move or a bad move . . . but at least it's a move and that is more than I was making sitting in my home. I wasn't doing anyone any good there."

Maggie smiled. "You're a kindred spirit, I believe. We'll talk more, but I need to get this little fella home for his nap. Are you planning to come to dinner at the ranch tomorrow night? Bo was coming by to see you and I'm hoping you accepted his invite. We really want to have the whole family together to officially welcome you to town and to thank you for your help. We'd do it tonight, but Jarrod is tied up on the road and we want him there too."

"I'm coming. I told Bo I would. As long as I'm not intruding."

"Intruding? Are you kidding? I'm the only female out there. I would love some female company and that little fella right there obviously wants you to come."

"It sounds like fun, I can't wait."

As Abby drove home, she knew it was true. Friday couldn't arrive soon enough . . . she just hoped Bo didn't read too much into the evening.

CHAPTER 20

Bo snatched his hat from his head and knocked on Abby's door. He'd half expected her to cancel but Maggie had told him she'd also invited her and Abby had agreed.

The door opened and all he could say was, "Hey." She was gorgeous, maybe not in a magazine-cover way, but Bo knew that wasn't important. She was real, and her eyes sparkled with anticipation. Her thick dark hair was tucked behind her ears but that didn't stop his fingers from itching to lose themselves in it. To feel the silky texture and draw it close so he could smell that familiar soft scent of spring that always clung to her hair and skin. He'd tried to hold down his anticipation, but he'd thought about her all the time.

"Hey, yourself," she said with a gentle laugh.

He swallowed hard. Like always, her laughter reverberated through him like music "You look per—" He cleared his throat and started over. He was trying not to run her off. "You look like you're ready to make one little boy extremely happy tonight. And you'll get to see his new game." Good, Monahan. Keep the focus off the energy that radiated between them.

"No happier than me," she said without hesitation. "I can't wait to see him again. And Pops. I've missed them both."

And Bo'd missed her.

So much that the realization of it shook him up. Had she missed him?

She didn't waste any time conversing on the doorstep today. Instead she hurried to his truck and he kept pace beside her, reaching to open her door.

It was quiet as he backed out of the driveway a few seconds later and nothing was said as they drove down the tree-lined street. Rand came out of his house and got in his car as they were leaving, but Bo didn't say a word about him. Neither did Abby. Bo was instantly reminded of their argument over Rand. He hoped he was doing well and made a note to himself to drop in and see him soon.

"I met Maggie, did she tell you?" Abby said, breaking the silence.

"Yeah, she did. She's looking forward to seeing you again."

"How's Pops doing today? She said he'd been having some good days."

He liked that she asked after him. "He's doing great. You'll see. He'll probably even hold a conversation with you. I mean, it's not like it used to be, but we celebrate every day that resembles the way he used to be."

"That's a good way to look at it, Bo," she ventured after a pause.

Bo shrugged. "It is what it is. After a while you can't be in denial about it. You have no choice about whether to accept it or not. You just have to do what you have to do."

Abby looked thoughtful. "I think that applies to a lot of situations."

"Yeah, and that's the thing . . . everyone has something." She nodded, and he knew she was probably thinking of her own loss. "How are you doing?"

"I-I'm doing good," she said, her gaze sliding away from his to stare at the passing pastures. It seemed they'd traveled this road a lot in the short time they'd known each other. He watched the road too . . . but he glanced back at her, studied her profile, and didn't believe her.

They didn't say much more on the final leg of the trip. At the house, he led the way inside to Pops's study and Abby didn't hesitate to hug Pops and reach out to Levi the moment she saw them.

Bo grinned watching her as she bounced his son on her hip and looked his Pops in the eye and asked him how his day was going.

"Not bad," Pops said, his eyes as clear as Bo had seen them in weeks. And now his eyes twinkled even more vibrantly looking at Abby. "I've got a great-grandson I need to teach . . ." He hesitated, his eyes unfocused momentarily and Bo's heart dipped as he watched the man he respected more than anyone falter somewhere in the fog that was inside his own head.

"To ride?" Abby added for him with an encouraging smile.

"Yup. He'll like it. I've got a show this weekend, feels like a good weekend to win."

Bo grinned and glanced over to see Tru and Jarrod grin, too, at their Pops's favorite saying most of their lives.

Maggie's eyes twinkled like Pops's. "Okay, fellas, y'all have to keep yourselves entertained for a few minutes. Abby, do you want to help me with the salad?"

"I sure do. Pops, maybe you can teach me to ride sometime," Abby said as she stood up.

"Nope. Bo can teach you."

Abby's mouth fell open slightly and Bo didn't blame her. Pops might not be able to remember who any of them were in the morning, but tonight nothing was getting by him.

"So what's going on between you and Abby?" Tru asked Bo the moment Maggie swept her to the kitchen.

"Nothing. What makes you ask that?" Bo was leaning against the bookshelf and all eyes turned to him.

Jarrod gave a slow smile, obviously finding humor in the moment.

Tru grinned. "Give us some credit, that smile on your face is not because of us."

"Nope," Pops agreed, looking as if he never had a problem with his memory.

"Okay, okay, so I think she's great. But there is more to it than that. It's complicated."

"Complicated? Sounds serious," Tru chuckled. "Like I don't know complicated—believe me, complicated is good. So spill."

"Hey, not happening. And that's all I'm saying on the subject right now." He knew by their expressions that he'd said plenty. One thing his brothers weren't was dumb.

• • •

"I have to tell you that Tru and I were shocked and over-joyed to find out Bo had a son," Maggie confessed not long after they reached the kitchen away from the men. "We knew going into our marriage that we couldn't have any of our own—it was a very hard thing for us to accept. There were some things to work through, but our love is strong and we've accepted it." She looked thoughtful, as if thinking back to something then she smiled happily at Abby. "There are plenty of babies out there that need good homes. But to have a nephew right now has thrilled us both. I love babies. It's just an unexpected blessing—though I'm terribly sorry for his mother."

Abby started chopping a tomato on the cutting board. "I feel bad for her too. But she made the right choice when she let Bo know he had a son and chose our family to love Levi after she was gone." Even if Abby hadn't already picked up on that in Maggie's column, she'd have known it the moment she saw Maggie with Levi that he would be loved by his aunt.

Maggie turned to look fully at her. "I still can't believe you moved here because of my column."

"Does that make me weird?"

Maggie laughed as she pulled enchiladas from the oven. "No. I knew there was a possibility someone would move here. Wishing Springs is wonderful and there are all these cowboys, but you're the first one."

Abby finished chopping the tomatoes for the salad and tried to calm the nerves that had been steadily rising from the moment Bo picked her up. "I have to admit that all of my friends thought I'd lost my mind."

"Nope. Not at all. I'm glad you're here. And, I hope that it's as good for you as it's been for me." Maggie smiled warmly and Abby topped the salad off with the cheese. "There—the masterpiece is finished."

"It looks good enough to eat," Abby said, a smile in her voice.

While Maggie set the tea on the table, Abby went to let everyone know dinner was ready. As she entered the den she grew still, overwhelmed by the array of trophies and various awards that Pops had won through the years.

"Dinner's ready," she announced. Levi threw his stuffed giraffe out of the playpen and giggled. Pops instantly went to pick it up.

Bo came to stand beside her. "I'll round Pops and Levi up," he said as Jarrod and Tru rose.

"Sounds good," Tru said, grinning. "Good luck breaking up that party."

Levi giggled again and Abby saw Jarrod smile on his way out of the room.

"Looks like they're having fun."

Bo crossed his arms and smiled. "Levi and Pops's new game. The baby throws his toys out of the playpen and Pops retrieves them. They love it."

Abby's heart swelled with emotion watching the two and their new game. "Levi is good for him." She glanced at Bo and her heart thudded with awareness. "I would have thought Solomon might be a little jealous," she added quickly. "But he seems to enjoy lounging under the table and watching."

"I know. I hate to say it, but that is the strangest dog."

She agreed. "He's like a stealth bomber or something. You never know from where he's going to appear and he's silent as a whisper until he gets his tail in an uproar and then he'll scare the daylights out of you with that wail he does."

"Levi likes him," Bo said, sounding distracted as he held her gaze.

"Yes. He does," Abby agreed, enjoying the conversation. She found herself leaning toward Bo and her pulse raced when he leaned toward her, his deep eyes drawing her. He was going to kiss her. And she . . . Abby jerked back. "Dinner. Dinner is ready. I'll get Levi."

She practically ran across the room, not feeling steady until she'd lifted Levi into her arms and held him close. Without looking at Bo again, she carried Levi into the kitchen. What had she been thinking?

That kissing Bo sounded . . . perfect.

• • •

The minute dinner was over Bo asked Maggie if she'd watch Levi and then he asked Abby if she'd take a walk with him.

"Just a walk," he assured her after Jarrod had headed home and Tru and Pops had headed back into the den to watch tapes from Tru's latest competition. Something Pops loved to do and even with his Alzheimer's he was still able to point out some small thing that could have improved the ride.

"Okay, sure." Abby didn't sound completely sure she

wanted to be alone with him and he deserved that, after that near kiss before dinner that sent her running.

The sun had lowered in the sky as they started down the lane toward the barns, and though he found himself wanting to reach for her hand he kept his hands to himself. They didn't say anything for a few yards, just listened to the crickets and frogs. When they got within hearing distance of the stable, the soft neighs and whickers could be heard.

"You have a great family, Bo."

"Yeah, I think so."

"And this ranch, what I've seen of it, is amazing. I can only imagine how lucky you were to have this beauty around you growing up. Levi is going to love it. It's so peaceful," Abby said.

"Yeah, I love it. After my parents died in the plane crash, we were faced with the strong possibility that we would lose the place. It nearly tore me up." He tucked his fingers in his jeans pockets and gave her a sidelong look. "But then, you're no stranger to loss, to grief."

"No. But I'm sorry that happened to you. I had no idea you almost lost the ranch."

He kicked a rock with his boot. "Yeah, my dad had a really, really bad gambling habit. This ranch was in hock to the hilt and twice over."

"But—" Abby had stopped walking and turned in a circle looking out across the pastures. "Bo, I'm not sure how many acres you have here, but even I know a ranch this size is worth several million. How?"

"Yeah, we asked the same question. Turns out if you know the right people you can borrow until you bury yourself in debt at interest rates that would make your skin crawl. But you can only keep borrowing up to a point. My dad had reached that point."

"I am so sorry."

Bo started walking again and Abby fell into step beside him.

"Are you still angry with him?"

He glanced at her as if startled. "You could tell?"

"It's totally understandable that you would be."

"I'm not angry, not anymore. I let it go."

Abby walked over to the arena and stared through the metal pipes at the pair of horses on the far side. Bo hadn't ever talked to anyone about his dad except for Tru and Jarrod. And even then they never said a lot. He stepped up to the pen and rested his arms on the railing watching the horses too.

"I don't believe you," Abby said suddenly, turning so she was facing him. "How do you get over a betrayal like that?"

"I chose to." Her eyes dug into his as if trying to figure out what was hiding there. "Okay, come with me. Enough of this. You look entirely too serious all the time." He reached for her hand and tugged her into the barn.

"Wait, what are you doing?"

"I'm taking you riding."

"But I don't ride."

He shot her a grin and felt his dimples flash. "You do tonight."

"But—"

"Just stand right there." He placed both hands on

her shoulders and moved her to a safe spot away from any accidentally flying hooves. "I'll saddle the horse."

"But—"

"Nope, three of those is too many. I'm not listening." He went into his horse's stall and Midnight immediately came over to him, always ready for a ride. "Hey, buddy, got a pretty lady for you to show off for."

He made quick work of getting Midnight saddled and then led him out into the arena. "Come on," he said, and was glad when Abby went with him. Though the way her brows were nearly meeting in the middle worried him a little.

"Okay, halt. Bo, I don't want to say 'but' again, but really, I haven't been on a horse in years and then I was a kid and didn't know what I was doing."

"I never took you for a chicken, Knightley."

Abby's jaw tightened. "I'm not. I'm just stating facts." He'd thought he saw fire flare in her eyes, but her response was lacking.

"Well, stop stating those facts. I'm going to take care of you."

Abby stiffened. "I don't need you to take care of me."

Something told him she did. Maybe not in the way he wanted to, but . . . maybe it was just wishful thinking on his part since it took every ounce of self-control not to kiss her.

He managed not to. The trick was keeping it that way.

CHAPTER 21

Abby stared at Bo, mesmerized by the teasing light in his eyes. It should be against the law to be so captivating with charm.

Of course his irritating moments balanced his overall appeal out, so that was a help.

She'd watched him saddle Midnight and wondered which horse he would saddle for her. She hoped it was one a little less powerful looking, but after glancing around she realized that in this stable, powerful seemed to be a prerequisite. That included Bo himself.

Now, after following him and his horse out into the evening light, she wasn't sure exactly what his plan was. But her plan didn't include riding the horse while he led it around on a rope.

As she stood there trying to figure it out, Bo stuck his boot into the stirrup, a beautiful handcrafted Four of Hearts ranch stirrup with that special carved logo on the side. She couldn't help noticing it as Bo rose up and settled into the saddle. Her breath caught in her throat as he grinned down at her.

"Just take my hand and put your foot in the stirrup and I'll help you up."

He intended for her to ride with him. Abby's mouth went dry. That would mean she would be very near him. Instinct told her to shake her head and back away but before she could do that she lifted her hand and slipped it into his. *What?*

He smiled down at her. "I've pulled my boot from the stirrup, so just place your foot in there and I'll do the rest."

She didn't hesitate; instead she lifted her foot and placed it in the stirrup without question. One minute she was on solid ground and the next he pulled her up, took her by the waist, and settled her in the saddle in front of him. He scooted back to make room for her. Abby's head spun, and her pulse pounded erratically at his nearness. She went still as he wrapped his arms around her, holding the reins in one hand and keeping one arm wrapped around her waist, securing her in the saddle. She held her body rigid, fighting the sudden fear that she was about to fall off the edge of a cliff.

"You can relax against me, Abby. I won't bite," Bo said. His voice held a husky tone that sent a shiver racing down her spine. She struggled to keep her back straight but there was no way and she realized this after just a few steps of the horse. When Bo moved Midnight into a trot she found herself snug against his chest automatically. His warm chuckle against the side of her neck sent skin-tingling sensations dancing through her.

"That's not so bad, is it?" he asked, his arm tightening, drawing her close against his chest. She felt his heart beating and it was as erratic as hers.

"I hope you didn't mind riding on one horse," Bo said against her exposed ear.

Shocked, she turned her head to look at him and found her lips very close to his. His eyes twinkled.

"Don't look so surprised You're safe. I'm just holding you. I'm not going to kiss you, though I'm very, very tempted right now."

Abby wanted to tell him to turn the horse around and take her back to the house. But she didn't. She couldn't explain it, but she felt lighthearted and free in this moment. For just a moment she could pretend that she was a normal woman flirting with a man. No sadness or guilt weighing her down. For just this moment she could pretend that she was free to enjoy the feel of Bo's arms around her, the press of his chest against her back, and the warmth of his breath trailing across her skin. It had been so long since she'd felt this. So long since she felt . . . anything. She was so weary from the numbness . . . the pain she'd been swallowed up in.

And just for the moment she let herself go, let herself enjoy the sensations. It had been too long since she'd felt anything like this. And she'd missed it desperately.

Without saying a word, she looked forward and gave into it. Closed her eyes, let Bo's strength surround her.

Let herself have that moment. Just for the time of the horse ride and then she'd let her good sense return. And the weight of guilt and grief would come flooding back with reality.

But for now, this was what she needed.

. . .

Bo wasn't sure what Abby was thinking, but to his surprise she leaned into him and seemed to enjoy the ride. Her heart was thundering and his was pounding triple time.

"I have to ride sometimes," he said, hoping to help the tension. "I'm cooped up in my workshop so much I lose this part of me if I don't get on a horse every once in a while." They had ridden away from the house and it felt good to be with Abby alone. Since meeting her they'd been with Pops or Levi almost all the time and he'd wanted to spend time with her that was separate from them. He was enjoying not having to worry that something was going to happen to either.

"You have a lot on your plate," Abby said, as if reading his mind.

He slowed Midnight to a walk and headed toward a shade tree on the hill. "Yeah, but I didn't really think so until Levi showed up. I'm so out of my element. I have all this new stuff flying around in my head. Heck, if you'd have showed up two weeks ago I would have been teasing you unmercifully. But since learning I'm a dad, I'm so tensed up I don't even feel like the same man anymore."

"I understand that feeling."

His hand tightened on her waist as he drew the gelding to a stop. He didn't waste any time sitting still with her in the circle of his arms like she was. He hopped to the ground then held his arms up to Abby and for a second he could tell she thought about refusing his offer and climbing down by herself.

Instead, she placed her hands on his shoulders and

let him lift her down. He backed away quickly, suddenly not trusting himself at all as he busied himself tying Midnight's reins to a Yaupon bush while Abby walked a few steps away watching the setting sun on the horizon.

"There is no difference in what you're feeling than when a doctor places a newborn into a daddy's arms right after birth. It's overwhelming. Remember that insurance commercial a few years ago? I can't remember which company it is anymore, but the young man takes his baby in his arms and suddenly he's transformed. It's universal. If you didn't feel a little overwhelmed then I'd think something was wrong with you."

He liked the way she thought. He liked everything about her. "Well, I have a feeling that you've had moments of putting me in that category."

She gave a sardonic look of agreement. "But I guess we all have our moments."

They were walking to the top of the hill and stopped when they crested the rise. Before them the pastures spread out in sections for a fairly far view. "It feels good to relax and know everything is under control back at the house though. At least for a few minutes."

"I'm sure it does."

"Not that I didn't feel that way when you were watching Levi. I meant it feels good to relax with *you* while all is in control back at the house."

She kept watching the horizon.

"You're nervous around me."

She offered a tiny hint of a smile. "There's no reason to deny it. We both know it's true."

He chose his next words carefully, seeing her shoulders tense. And a shadow cross her expression. "I can only imagine the pain you must have gone through when your husband died. What was his name?" He knew he was risking her walking away again. But he could not help wanting to understand her. Wanting to know more about her.

"Landon. Thanks for asking. I came here so I could gain some perspective on my past and move forward. That's what Maggie's advice spurred me to do—" She paused. "But it seems all I've done is think more about the wreck, about . . ." Her voice trailed off.

Bo stepped a little closer. "There's nothing wrong with moving forward, Abby. I'm sure Landon would have wanted you to."

She nodded, but her troubled expression didn't ease.

"Abby, what happened to Landon?"

She crossed her arms as if she was cold but it was a warm night.

"A wreck. We were hit by a drunk driver. I found out in the emergency room that I was pregnant. I lost the baby too."

Bo's stomach lurched. He hadn't known what he was expecting, but this wasn't it. No wonder she had moments when she looked so hollow he thought she would dissipate like vapor. No wonder the sorrow in her overrode everything at times. He knew about grief. He'd lost his dad and his mother in the plane crash. Their deaths had been overshadowed by learning what their dad had done and letting go of the anger had been his only way of coping with it. But nothing he'd been through could compare to having lost her husband and baby. "I'm so sorry, Abby. How far along were you?"

"Six weeks—I had no clue." She stared out over the pasture and he realized she was wiping tears from her eyes like that first night in his truck.

"Abby." His heart broke for her and he wanted to touch her, hold her, comfort her. But he felt uncomfortable now that he knew what she'd been through. "What can I do?"

She shook her head. "I don't know what I was thinking just now. I, Bo, I've never told anyone about the baby. The nurse, the doctor, only a very few people in the hospital trying to save me that night know."

"You didn't tell anyone?" Bo couldn't believe it. "Not your parents, your best friend?" How had she gone through this alone?

She shook her head. "I couldn't. It's complicated. I-I have so many regrets that I just can't breathe sometimes."

"Why would you have regrets?"

She gave a harsh laugh that didn't sound like the Abby he knew. "Oh believe me, the list is very long."

She looked so alone in that moment. And to realize she'd never told anyone the heartache that clung to her. That was what he'd seen in her eyes. He couldn't help himself, he crossed the space between them and drew her into his arms. Was he making a mistake? He wasn't letting himself think that far ahead. All he knew was she needed someone to hold her. She was stiff at first, rigid, as if she'd held this in for so long she couldn't release it and let him take some of the burden into himself. But she didn't back away, so he held on—tightened his hold and smoothed his hand slowly down her back, his fingers trailing through her hair. As if a dam released, her shoulders trembled and then she melted into him. Clinging to him while he held her and willed every ounce of strength he had to her.

When she looked up at him, teardrops glistening on her dark lashes, Bo's heart broke. He cupped her face with one hand and held her protectively with his other.

His gaze dropped to her lips and he suddenly found himself thinking about kissing her. What was he thinking? She needed him emotionally and he was thinking about kissing. He blinked and loosened their embrace a touch. "I have all night, Abby, if you want to talk. I don't know why you chose to share this with me. But it means a lot that you would do that. And it might help you if you let it out."

Abby stepped back looking as dazed as he felt. She walked to the edge of the water where a large flat rock jutted out. She looked so alone that Bo's arms tightened with the need to yank her into them and hold her again but that had just proven not to be the best move. He had his thoughts back in place now that there was some distance between them.

· · ·

Why hadn't she told anyone something so painful?

She took a deep breath. "I was very poor growing up. And I grew up determined to have more as an adult. I worked and scraped my way through college." Her shoulders sagged. "Right after graduation I married

Landon. He'd grown up in my neighborhood and wanted the same things I did. I was hired by a successful marketing firm right out of college and the work was challenging, and I loved it. I worked eighty-hour weeks, weekends, and evenings."

Bo was trying hard to fit her into the picture she was painting but he couldn't make it fit. She glanced at him and he gave her an encouraging smile because he feared she might stop talking. By the way the words were pouring out, this was something she needed. And he wanted to know. "I'm listening."

"I spent more time at work than I did at home. I have so many regrets and the main one is that Landon wanted to start a family. And I kept putting him off."

Bo's eyes narrowed. "But you love kids. It's apparent."

"Loving them and being ready aren't the same thing. I was building my name. My career was more than just filling in numbers—but that's beside the point now. I just wasn't ready. That didn't mean I didn't want children. I just wanted more investments in my portfolio before I committed to them. I'd put my work, my need to achieve success, money, recognition above everything. Even Landon." The last was barely a whisper.

"Abby, none of that sounds like the person I know."

She glared at him. "The person you know now . . . is me trying to find my way out of the hole I've been buried in for the last two years."

"You're being too hard on yourself."

"No. I'm not. I know what I know. I—"

"I don't believe that."

She glared at him. "It's true. There is no sugar-coating

it. I worked twelve-hour days at the office and then did more work at home. I kept thinking there was plenty of time."

She waved her hand in front of her face as if to fan away her sorrow. "I don't know why I started talking about this. Talking about it doesn't help. I'm trying to put distance between us. I'm trying to show you that I wasn't kidding yesterday when I told you I wasn't here for anything that had to do with a relationship. Bo, there's more . . ."

He crossed to her and pulled her into his arms again. "I don't care," he growled, and lowered his lips to hers. He wasn't thinking. He was tired of hearing her focus on only the things about herself that she regretted. He knew she was a good person.

He felt her arms go around him, clinging to him as he deepened the kiss, his mind reeling as every cell in his body reached out to her. When he finally pulled away, she looked stunned, but she wasn't talking. Wasn't saying negative trash about herself. He probably looked as dazed as she did when it was over. He leaned his forehead against hers as they both tried to catch their breath.

"I'm interested in you. I have been from the moment you nearly ran me over." He knew he could really be messing things up now. But he was winging it and too far in to stop now. "Look at me, Abby. Nothing you say is going to change that. But I'm listening and I can see too. I'm not going to push you."

"You're wasting your time to be interested in me. And with all you have going in your life you don't have any moments to waste."

He dropped his arms and lifted her chin to connect their gazes. "You're right that I don't have any time to waste. But wrong about the part that anything to do with you is a waste. Nothing could be farther from the truth."

The sun was almost gone. They'd be riding back in the low light of early darkness but Bo wasn't worried, he knew the ranch inside and out. He could ride it blindfolded.

"I better get you back to town."

He headed for the horse. His mind was racing with everything she'd told him. He started to climb into the saddle then turned to her instead. "Listen to me." He stepped closer. "I told you yesterday that I would be your friend." He trailed fingertips down the edge of her cheek, felt dampness that lingered there. "And that's what I'll be." He shrugged and gave as good a smile as he could muster up. "I've never been good at deep and meaningful relationships anyway. To be honest, where women are concerned, I've never been too good at friendship. I'm good for a little fun and that's about it. So this is probably the best course of action anyway. And now with Levi in my life, I have a whole set of new responsibilities on my shoulders that are all wound around growing him up and doing right by him. I could truly use a friend. And so could you. So like we talked about yesterday. What do you say?"

"Only friends. I mean it, Bo. No more kissing."

"Only friends. For now."

She considered him as if deciding if she could believe him. "Then okay, I'd like to help with Levi again if you don't mind. It's not an inconvenience. I want to."

Bo needed her and there was no denying it. But her being here every day, it was going to be torture. "Sure, can you start tomorrow?" he heard himself say and knew he had a tough road ahead of him because he'd never felt the feelings that Abby evoked in him. But there was more to her story and he knew it. He wasn't sure how he knew it, but he'd stopped her before she could say more. She needed him to be her friend first and it didn't matter how badly he wanted to see where they could go in a relationship . . . she needed him more without the complication of romance.

And that was exactly what she'd get—but it wasn't going to be easy.

CHAPTER 22

Trepidation filled Abby the next morning as she drove out to the ranch. She might have given Bo all that malarkey about being his friend but she knew she had a problem. She had loved Landon since childhood. Had been his best friend for all of their growing up years and had finally given into marrying him despite the drive to succeed that burned inside of her. He was her friend, he'd understood—at least in the beginning—her need to succeed and he'd felt the same need. Or at least she'd thought he had. And because of his understanding of that drive, she'd given in. He had admitted, when they'd started having fights about her unrelenting schedule, that he'd only been driven because he'd known he didn't stand a chance of winning her heart if he wasn't successful.

The sad thing was he'd been right.

She'd married him because she did love him—very much, but if he hadn't been driven and if he hadn't been okay with her making her goals of success a reality, she wouldn't have let herself marry him—no matter how much she'd loved him. Her desire to achieve financial freedom and be successful drove her too deeply— blinded her to what was important.

And thus their arguing had begun escalating. She'd had a vice president position in her sights within the next year and that would only happen if she'd increased her work time, not decreased it.

She closed her eyes and her heart felt as if it were chugging through sludge. Oh how she wished she could take it back. "Oh, Landon," she whispered. "What a mess I made of things."

But even so . . . her love for Landon had been based on many different things, but none of those things had been deep, undeniable need. If so, working all those hours might not have been so easy for her . . . She'd thought about this all night long and tried to deny it. But she feared denial was useless . . . if Landon's kiss had affected her like Bo's kiss, she would have had a harder time staying late at work every night.

A chill slid over her at the admission; guilt rolled in her stomach like molten lava.

What kind of person was she?

She pulled to a halt beside the garage and sat stiffly, trying to get her emotions in control before going inside.

With a sigh, she realized that the raw ache of guilt that clung to her was going nowhere. She headed across the yard and gave a quick knock on the door then walked into the kitchen and halted abruptly. The sight of five of the Monahan men in the kitchen, including the newest addition, greeted her. Pops stood beside Bo at the stove and appeared to be trying to help him flip pancakes. Tru and Jarrod sat at the table drinking coffee with Levi going back and forth in his swing in front of them. It was one of the most heartwarming sights she'd ever seen, yet also the polar opposite of the turmoil whipping up inside of her.

And of course her attention shot instantly straight back to Bo.

"Hey, Abby, watch this." He laughed and so did Pops who watched intently as Bo held the frying pan by the handle and shook it just right, causing the pancake to shoot into the air. It did a slow motion flip and landed back into the pan.

Pops threw his head back and laughed. "You got it, son. Still got it."

"Hey, I learned that from you. Okay, here we go, let's do it one more time, then this cake is all yours," he called. "Hey, hey, hey, Abby Knightley, one hot cake coming up for you after this one. Sound good?"

Her pulse shot to the moon despite every wish for him to have no effect on her. "That sounds like a deal," she managed. "What do you think, Pops?"

"It's a deal," he agreed, taking the plate Bo handed him.

"The syrup is over there at the table with Tru and Jarrod." Bo pointed toward the table, and Pops headed that way.

"Mornin', Abby," Tru said, and Jarrod tipped his hat at her and added his welcome.

She crossed the room, gave Levi a kiss on top of the head, then went to stand beside Bo at the stove. She tried to ignore the way every cell inside of her seemed to strain toward him. "You look like you know how to handle that pan like a pro."

"Aw, it's nothing. We can all do this. Pops is the master of hotcake flipping. Not so much anymore, but he sure does enjoy watching us do it."

"Yeah," Tru said. "We try to have a few mornings like this where we all come eat with him. I really enjoy it after I've been on the road. And my wife kind of kicked me out of the house so she could write this morning."

Jarrod stood. "I'm about to hit the road." He gave her a small smile.

Abby was always a little surprised when Jarrod smiled—given his generally pretty serious, even gruff, demeanor.

"So have a good day," Bo said to him. "See you tonight."

"No, I'm heading over to Corpus to the Sandbar Ranch. I'm going to pick that new cuttin' horse up from Brent. I won't be back till tomorrow afternoon."

"Goodness that's a trip," Abby said.

Jarrod shrugged. "Not so bad."

"Not by Texas standards anyway," Bo added, winking at her.

Tru stood. "Thanks for doing that for me," he said.

"I don't mind delivering the colt for you at all."

"I know, but thanks anyway. I'm heading out with you. Daylight's-a-burnin' and while you have a lot of driving ahead of you, I've got a lot of riding to do. Abby, nice to see you."

Abby watched the two brothers disappear out the door after telling Pops good-bye. Abby met Bo's gaze. "What all do you need me to do today?"

"Me and Tru can keep a watch on Pops. He'll be down at the shop with me and when Tru is here he'll walk over and watch him ride. That's his love. We have to watch *him*, though, or he'll start loading up the horses and try to head off to a competition somewhere."

Pops looked up at her from his hotcakes. He grinned. "Always a horse to show. And these boys are learning good, but I'm not done with their teaching yet."

A lump jumped into Abby's throat. "You're a great teacher, I understand."

He shrugged. "God." He studied his hands for a minute. "He put it here. Ability."

Abby looked back at Bo, amazed at Pops's clarity, and noted a sad light in his eyes, but then he blinked and it was gone and he grinned at her, causing the dimple to show playfully. "When a man's got it, he's got it. And Pops has always had it."

. . .

Abby went to church with Clara Lyn and Reba the next morning and mentioned that she was back working for Bo. Abby thought the two women were going to get up and dance a jig, they were so glad she was watching the baby again. They'd also volunteered to come over and help her get the last of her things organized on Monday. And Pebble planned to make cookies while she was there. Abby loved the idea of everyone in her home—as if it was the official stamp on her coming here and getting involved. If she thought about it, since she'd been here she'd been out and involved in some way almost every day—other than the few days she and Bo had been mad at each other.

She thought of Bo and their after-dinner ride on Friday night. The guilt she felt over her building attraction to Bo held on like a migraine, keeping her insides in turmoil.

And starting tomorrow she wasn't sure what would happen to the mix. Maggie was also coming to help today and bringing Levi. Bo had offered and insisted on a more than fair salary to her and they'd gotten a schedule figured out. Maggie would keep Levi on Monday and Wednesday when they were in town and leave the other days for Abby while Maggie worked on her column.

As a girl growing up in the low-rent areas of Houston, moving had consisted of loading the few rag-tag belongings that they owned in the back of the rusted out pickup truck that her dad drove and hauling it to the new place. A new place that was usually lower rent and only just saving them from being on the street. A moving company with men who actually came in and packed up everything and put it inside the huge moving truck with expert care was so unimaginable that Abby sometimes still felt like she was an actor playing a role. But in reality she was still that poor little girl. Yet while her parents had been poor, they had loved her more than life itself. Her dad, disabled from an accident at the packing company that he'd worked for, had struggled to keep a roof over his family's head and her mother had cleaned offices at night to help make up the difference. Because of their jobs, Abby was never a latchkey kid. Either her mom was home or her dad was.

Thinking about her roots, Abby had specifically

chosen this small place, because she'd wanted a comfortable home, but not extravagant. She was done with wanting those kinds of trappings. She had money in the bank, stocks in the market, and dead dreams.

She had lived modestly since the wreck. And she always would.

Today, she looked around the hustle of her little home and let herself enjoy the enthusiasm of her new friends.

"I think the couch should be catty-corner." Clara Lyn stood in the middle of the room with her hands on her hips and stared at the object being shoved around by Abby and Maggie at each suggestion. The moving men had set things inside and Abby liked the places they'd put them, but Clara Lyn and Reba Ann obviously had visions of starting up a home-staging business. And she was their guinea pig.

"Over just a hair," Reba Ann said, waving her hands like she was directing airport traffic to the front of the picture window. Throwing her arms wide she drew her hands slowly together and leaned to the side as if she was moving the couch herself. "Right there!"

"Yes," Clara Lyn yelped. "Perfect. Y'all did good, girls."

Maggie and Abby looked at each other and burst into laughter.

"Wait," Reba barked, reconsidering their handiwork. "It might work better if it was angled. What do you think, Clara?"

"Girls, would you mind scooting it the way Reba suggested? I think it's a fantastic plan."

Abby grabbed her end of the couch that weighed a

lot more than she'd realized when she bought it a year ago. Maggie grabbed her end and they got it shoved over. Then both collapsed on it with their legs sprawled out in front of them.

"Okay, okay, that's it for the moment," Abby gasped with exaggerated weariness.

Maggie flopped her head to the side and eyed her. "They're trying to do us in," she whispered loudly.

Pebble came in from the kitchen where she'd been getting things ready for cookie making. "You two leave those girls alone and stop making them shove that couch around and come help me. You have to see Levi bouncing in the contraption Maggie brought with him. The tot is a regular acrobat."

That was all it took for their taskmasters to abandon them.

"Well, that was easy," Maggie chuckled. "We should have slipped Pebble a hint to help us with diversion tactics an hour ago."

Abby laughed, and it hit her exactly how surreal the moment was that she was actually sitting on the couch in her new home beside Maggie Hope here in the middle of Wishing Springs.

"I like this," Maggie said. "With the chairs put in place and that beautiful rug rolled out, it's going to be very cozy. It's a good place for you to be."

Abby swallowed the lump in her throat, but couldn't speak. When she and Landon had first married, their apartment had been cozy. She'd scraped garage sale finds together and, thinking back now, it had been so lovely. Then she'd set her sights on bigger and better. There was so much to be said for cozy and simple.

"I think so too," she said, feeling good.

"Y'all hurry up, cookie time!" Clara Lyn yelled.

"She makes herself right at home, doesn't she?" Abby grinned at Maggie on the way into the kitchen.

Once there Maggie took Levi and cuddled him in her arms to feed him his bottle. He looked so adorable and peaceful in her arms. And Maggie looked peaceful too. It was clear to see that she would be a wonderful mother. Abby's hand went to her stomach. She'd been only six weeks or so pregnant and too busy to notice she'd missed her cycle that month.

Pebble pulled a batch of fragrant cookies from the oven and slipped another cookie sheet into the oven.

"Those smell amazing," Abby said.

From the kitchen breakfast nook they had a clear view of the house and the front yard. Not long after they began working Abby noticed Rand had come outside and begun working in his yard. It was the first time she'd seen him in his yard since she'd moved in. She was a little taken by surprise and then she realized that he'd probably seen Pebble's car sitting at the curb. Though she hadn't seen him in the yard, there was no denying that he had a gorgeous, well-manicured yard full of roses. The man did his own yard? He was just full of surprises.

She wondered if he'd been drinking. He hadn't said anything to her about the incident that first night, but that wasn't so surprising. They hadn't ever been alone . . .

Pebble saw him and Abby didn't miss the way her

gaze lingered on the view. Could Pebble really care for him?

"He's going to have a heat stroke if he's not careful," Pebble said, and then turned pink.

Abby was fairly certain she hadn't meant to speak out loud.

"You need to go over there and take him a tall glass of tea, Pebble." Clara Lyn paused placing the warm cookies on waxed paper. "That man has been working hard to make amends to you. He stopped drinking. At least that's what Doonie told me. And he's like a brother to those twins, so they should know."

Abby was shocked. Her temperature spiked. This would not do.

"He hasn't stopped drinking." She blurted the words out.

Everyone paused what they were doing to look at her.

"What makes you say that?" Pebble asked, her voice very tight.

"I haven't said anything." She hesitated, realizing she was new in town and she was about to say something derogatory about a very popular member of the community. But she had to, Pebble deserved to know the truth if the scoundrel was trying to pretend he'd stopped. As quick as she could, she told them what had happened and then waited for them to have the same reaction that Bo had had.

"Well, I'll be . . ." Reba's voice trailed off. "He lied."

Pebble's small pink mouth had snapped shut and formed a grim line—completely uncharacteristic for her. And Abby was sorry to realize that it showed the sweet lady did have feelings for that man.

Abby didn't even realize Clara Lyn hadn't spoken, as they stood there staring out the window, until the back door slammed shut and her sashaying backside was all that could be seen as she disappeared from view. They tracked her again through the breakfast nook window, marching across Abby's lawn toward Rand. The beauty operator was hot!

"Oh, this is not gonna be good." Reba spun and headed after Clara. In a display of bravado, Pebble marched out after them. Maggie and Abby hurried to follow, Maggie with Levi on her hip.

"What are you thinking, lying about your drinking, Rand Radcliff?" Clara Lyn looked about as mad as a mama badger after a snake.

"Rand, is this true?" Pebble asked. Her blue eyes flashed and she looked far less like the sweet knitter that Abby had seen so far.

The city councilman met Pebble's gaze and then he looked at Abby. To her surprise, she felt sorry for the man.

"It's true. But it was only—"

Without another word Pebble turned and headed toward her car. Reba followed her trying to calm her down.

Clara shook her head with pity in her eyes. "Rand, we thought you were okay."

With that statement Abby realized that none of them had ever had any dealings with an alcoholic. He wasn't just a binge drinker. Abby was pretty certain the man drank a little every day and hid it. That was the only way she could explain all the bottles in his trash. The town was enabling him and didn't even realize it.

What was worse, now that Pebble had found out what was going on, Rand was probably going to hit it hard tonight.

And that bothered Abby on several levels. She hated drinkers for many reasons. But the man needed help if he were going to overcome this. If he even had a chance of overcoming it.

"Rand, you have to get help," Clara urged. "I've been rooting for you to win Pebble over but now I'm thinking I haven't been thinking at all."

"Now, hold on, Clara," Maggie piped in. "Rand, what can we do for you? How can we help you? Tru would do whatever you need him to do—any of your friends would. Do you need him to take you to a rehab? Because he will. You can overcome this if you just set your mind to it."

Maggie—always the encourager. Abby rubbed the tension between her eyes and felt a headache coming on with a vengeance. It matched the heartache threatening to crack her chest wide open. Looking at the man whose eyes suddenly seemed conflicted, more guilt slammed into Abby.

Had she asked him if she could help him? No, she hadn't. She'd just tossed him on the bed that night and walked out and she'd barely talked to him since.

But Maggie was looking for answers for him. She was asking specific ways to be of service to him. And Abby knew helping him or any intoxicated person could very possibly save lives if it kept them off the road. And that was what concerned Abby.

Her heart ached with what she'd lost.

Rand stared at her. "You did this," he said, his shoulders slumping. "I was trying. I just had a little setback the other night."

Denial did not sit well with her. "I didn't do it. You did when you picked up that bottle. I'm concerned for you."

"I let you move into my rent house and this is how you repay me? Starting rumors—"

"Rumors—" Abby started then clamped her mouth shut, suddenly reminded that he was her landlord and while she did have a six-month lease, he could very well make her time here hard if he chose. "I stand by my comment. I'm concerned for you, Mr. Radcliff. You could hurt or kill yourself or someone else."

"I was at home."

"But how many times have you been behind the wheel in that condition? And just because you were home, doesn't it matter to you that you're harming yourself and Pebble?"

"You need to mind your own business."

"Rand, this is not like you," Clara Lyn gasped. "Not at all."

"Look," Abby said, a sense of urgency rushing over her. "You can beat this if you're really honest with yourself and want to be free of it . . . before it's too late. You can face it or blame me. It's *your* choice." She turned and walked away. She hoped he'd come to his senses, but at least she had said her piece. Her business or not, she couldn't live with herself if she swept it under the rug. And hopefully her new friends understood that.

"Hey." Maggie caught up with her. "That was pretty tough back there. On everyone."

"He needs to face reality."

"I agree. But I've also learned that until someone makes up their mind to change it won't happen. I guess what I'm saying is don't let Rand's problem eat you up."

As they got back into the house, Clara Lyn and Reba came back inside.

Reba looked a little flustered. "Pebble was so miffed she had to go. But she'll make it. That little gal is made of steel. No one would believe it looking at her, but she is. She knows what she'll put up with and what she won't and nothing will blow her off course. Rand has just slammed the door on any chance he had."

The room was silent for a moment. Abby felt a tug of sadness for the man and anger at him at the same time.

"Well, that's that." Clara Lyn sighed. She studied Abby. "Is there something else, honey?"

Anger fogged Abby's vision, and suddenly she knew she couldn't hide her past any longer. And in that moment she wasn't real certain why she'd tried in the first place. Not talking about it didn't make the pain go away. Hiding the truth deep in her heart didn't take away the heartache.

"A drunk driver killed my husband and . . . my baby."

CHAPTER 23

Bo pulled into Abby's drive, hopped out of his truck, and jogged to the front door. When Maggie had arrived back at the ranch from what should have been a fun time hanging out with the gals, she'd looked worried and told him that Abby had had a hard day.

He'd hadn't been able to stop thinking about her . . . and finally he'd asked Maggie if she and Tru would mind coming over to the house for a little while so he could come check on Abby. They hadn't minded a bit—they were enjoying being aunt and uncle. Tru, particularly, seemed so happy.

Though he and Maggie had gotten off to a rough start, he thought she was top notch now—kind and concerned and seemed to enjoy helping out. Tru had confessed to him that it came from a deep need to have a flock and family to love since she'd had it so rough as a kid.

One thing Bo never wanted to take for granted was his family. Sure, his dad had somehow gotten off track—much like Rand had, it seemed—but with gambling. Both had addictions that could be life-altering.

But he'd been a good dad, a loving dad, and that was

what made his behavior so bizarre. Addiction could take a good person and just botch them up bad. And in the process botch up the people they loved too.

As Bo walked to Abby's front porch the last faint ray of daylight disappeared. He knocked and his heart started doing odd little rat-a-tats inside his chest as he waited for her to answer.

When she opened the door Bo was struck by her beauty. Even in her bare feet, denim shorts, and an old Sam Houston State jersey she took his breath away. Her hair was pulled back in a ponytail and she had little if no makeup on and he could have looked at her all day. He smiled, liking everything about her.

"Hey," he said, his lips hitching into a grin. "Mind some company?"

She stepped back. "Sure."

He followed her into the house and stopped. He whistled. "Whoa, this is nice."

She wrapped her arms around herself and studied the room. "I like it. It's a haven."

Bo figured Abby needed a haven. He wanted to be that for her—a living, breathing, caring, and protective haven for her to run to when she needed someone to . . . to support her. Instinct told him Abby needed him—or maybe he was overthinking what was going on between them. The emotions that grabbed hold of him when she lifted those eyes to his told him he might be getting in over his head. And he had to remember that Abby only wanted and needed a friend right now . . . and he needed to proceed with caution on the feelings he had for her. What if he hurt her somehow? Abby couldn't handle any more hurt in her life and he didn't have the best record when it came to relationships with women. He forced himself not to think about that right then.

"Maggie told me you had a really tough day."

She cocked her head and her gaze cut to him. "Yup."

"She said she was worried about you. I decided I should come over and see if you are all right."

She rubbed her arms as if she were cold then turned and walked to the kitchen and out onto the porch. He followed. She sat down at the patio set there, but didn't actually scoot back in the seat. Instead she perched on the edge and her knee bounced in a nervous up and down.

"Abby?" Sinking into the seat next to her he leaned forward, elbows on his knees, and clasped his hands so as not to reach for hers. "Why was Maggie so worried about you?"

"I told them about Rand. I had to. Pebble was softening up to the man and I could tell it when she spotted him through the window. They started talking about how he'd stopped drinking. That was a lie and I thought Pebble had a right to know. Clara Lyn shot off like a rocket over there and I followed."

She stood up. She'd been talking low—seeing how Rand lived right next door, that was probably a good idea. Right after she stood up she plopped back down. "Clara Lyn gave him the what-for and then I joined in." She sighed and rubbed her forehead. "I have a right to be upset with people who drink and drive."

"Yes, you do. But from what I can tell Rand doesn't drink and drive. He lives two blocks from the town square and his office. And less than that to the grocery store. He loves to walk. I don't see any sign that he drives when he drinks."

"But he could."

"But he doesn't." He met her stare and wondered if she was going to ask him to leave.

"Maybe. It's just he lied to Pebble and was still trying to win her over. She deserved to know."

"Abby, I'm not going to disagree with you on that. She did deserve to know. If he really does have a drinking problem, then he's out of line trying to win her heart. Are you okay now? Is that why Maggie was so worried about you?"

"Maggie told you I had a bad day because when we got back in the kitchen I told them about Landon and my baby. It was time. I don't know why I thought I didn't want to tell anyone. I mean, it is what it is." She sounded so heartbroken, so lost.

"Abby, you need to let yourself grieve fully. Let it go. Get *mad*. Throw something. Heck, kick something, but stop trying to hold it in. And stop taking your anger out on Rand. The man needs help, maybe, if he wants it. But he's not your own personal crusade."

She glared at him. "I am not doing that."

"Looks like it to me." So, making her mad at him over Rand did not seem like a good thing to be doing. They'd just gotten over their last disagreement over the reporter.

"Well, you're wrong. If Pebble hadn't been here, I would not have even said anything and I wouldn't have gone over and confronted him if it hadn't been for Clara Lyn."

Bo wasn't sure why he was pushing her because it certainly wasn't in his best interest. He'd come here to see if she needed consoling or encouraging and here he was attacking her about Rand. "Look, I get that Pebble needed to know that you knew Rand was misleading her."

"He was lying."

"Okay, he was lying."

Abby got up and went inside the house, leaving the door open, so he followed. She headed to the sink, took a glass from the cabinet, filled it, and then drank . . . keeping her back to him.

He started to go to her, but stopped himself. There was so much about this woman that he didn't understand, yet he knew that losing her family because some drunk jerk got behind the wheel was driving everything she did.

What had she been like before this tragedy defined her? He bet she had life overflowing. He could only imagine that laugh that he'd heard just a few times would have bubbled out spontaneously. That her smile had come regularly—despite that she said she'd been driven and worked all the time. Or was he imagining everything he thought he knew about her?

Had he put traits in Abby that weren't really there?

These were things he wanted to know.

"Abby." He moved forward then and took her by the shoulders and turned her toward him. She came easily, her eyes wide, filled with anger and pain. He wanted to see laughter and joy there. He took the glass in her hand and set it on the counter. Then placed his hands on the counter, trapping her but feeling safer by not touching her. She didn't move, didn't look as if she were breathing.

"You're tied in knots. Something else is eating at you."

She stared at him. Tears filled her eyes.

"How do you know these things? How do you seem to look at me and know that there is more?"

The corner of his lip hitched to the side. "I see everything. I am all knowing."

She chuckled weakly despite the serious moment, probably releasing some tension.

"Truth is," he said, "I don't know for certain, I just feel it when I'm looking at you."

Her breath caught and drew his gaze to her lips. When he lifted his head, he met longing in her eyes that tore his heart out. He swallowed and told himself that if he kissed her he was going back on everything he'd promised her. But he could tell in the way her breathing hitched and her eyes mellowed that she felt exactly what he was feeling. He wanted to step in closer. Wanted to fold her in his arms. And he wanted to kiss her . . . but he didn't.

Instead he straightened and dragged air into his lungs, fighting to get much-needed oxygen to his brain.

"Bo, what I told you the other day was the truth. I worked too much and put achievement and money above my family. Dinner with clients, at the company president's beck and call, working late all the time and always expecting Landon to take care of things at home. What all of our friends don't know is that Landon and I had begun to fight all the time about it." She moved from the counter and walked to stare out the back window. He could see her reflection in the glass.

"He wasn't happy. He wanted me home. Wanted me

to be there more. Wanted to start a family. That was the reason we'd begun to argue so much." She turned to face him. "That night in the car. We were arguing. He told me he was thinking about leaving me. He told me the night of the wreck. Told me that I had to choose."

"What did you tell him?"

"I don't know. Everything after that is a blank. Wiped out. I don't remember anything until the next day about noon when I woke up in the hospital all banged and bruised." She stared at him, her eyes dead. "I keep getting flashes of Landon staring at me from the driver's seat. Staring at me as a light in my peripheral vision grows bright." She slammed her eyes shut. "I caused the wreck. He was angry at me and glaring at me instead of watching the oncoming traffic." Her voice broke. "I killed my family."

Bo's stomach knotted as the crush of her words pressed in around them. "Abby, no—"

"Yes. Bo, it's true," she snapped. "I have no memory of impact, but I keep seeing that one moment in time over and over and over again. Landon's eyes—so filled with hurt, digging into my soul as if he was so disappointed in the wrong choice I made. The drunk driver was a part of it . . . but it was me, my words that drew Landon's gaze away from the road. He would have seen that truck before it was too late if he hadn't been so upset with me."

Bo stared at Abby, praying for the right words. But there was some truth in her words. If she and Landon hadn't been fighting, then he would have been paying attention to the road. He wouldn't have been distracted.

What was he supposed to say to that?

- - -

Bo was staring at Abby as if she were someone he didn't know.

It was very close to the way Landon had looked at her. Abby knew she deserved the look of disappointment. Of shock.

She deserved it because she'd brought it on. No matter how she tried to rationalize why she kept having the dream—seeing Landon look at her in horror—she couldn't change it. There was no going back. He was gone . . . they were gone. And it was her fault.

Bo strode across the room and wrapped her in his arms. She pushed against him.

"Let me go," she cried as tears of regret and shame threatened to overflow.

"No," he growled. "No, Abby. Just stay."

The tears came, and she couldn't see past the salty rivers that poured from her eyes. She was a disgrace. How could she have thought she could change her past and move forward? "I don't deserve to move on with my life. Let me go."

Bo gripped her face fiercely between his large warm hands. "Stop, Abby. Just stop."

She shook her head, barely seeing him through the flood.

"Abby, Abby, Abby." His words sounded soft. Gentle. "So broken. And so wrong. Cry if you need to. Get this out. Release it." He leaned his forehead against hers. Holding her still.

His fingers were firm against her hair, yet gentle.

Her breath came in shuddering gasps as Abby sought to control them, but she couldn't stop. The dam had broken and the force was too strong.

"You are torturing yourself. You can beat yourself up. Torture yourself till the day you die and that does no one any good. Especially you."

Abby pulled out of Bo's embrace and wiped her tears. She'd vowed that she was over her tears, but obviously she wasn't. "Bo, I know what I did and there is nothing you can say that will change that. I just have to figure out how to live with it and go on."

"I agree that you must go on."

Abby pushed the tempting self-pity to the back of her mind and focused. "It would have been so much easier if I hadn't chosen this house to move into."

Bo's eyes narrowed. "You know, as crazy as this seems right now, given what you've been through, that does sound like the best thing. But what if there's a reason—"

"Yeah, me causing the whole town to get in an uproar. There is nothing about that that sounds right."

"Now you're exaggerating. Everyone isn't in an uproar or knows Rand's problem."

She shot him a glare. "Okay, Mr. Smart Stuff, you know what I'm talking about."

"I do. I'm just trying to lighten this up some."

Abby glared at him. "Why did I come here, Bo? Am I just running?"

"Maybe. But I choose to be an optimist. And I'm choosing to believe that you're here because you're supposed to be here."

She frowned. "Your optimism is a little irritating right now."

He grinned. "I'll do whatever it takes to get you off your pity party."

"My pity party?" She gasped. Was that what this was?

"Oops. Maybe I should have kept my mouth shut while I was ahead."

"No, I'm sure you're probably right about that—as much as I wish it weren't true." She glanced at the icebox. "Would you like some ice cream? No judging—ice cream makes me feel better."

"Load me up. What kind do you have?"

She pulled the door open and pulled out two half gallons of Blue Bell ice cream. "I have Brenham's best— Homemade Vanilla and Rocky Road."

He grinned. "You are a woman after my own heart. Pass that Rocky Road this way."

"How about I pass you a bowlful. I'm having it, too, and I've learned from the past that if I don't put it in a bowl, I'll go through a whole carton and then I'll not only feel bad but guilty . . ." She paused as she said the words. Everything always came back full circle. And feeling guilty was her beginning and her ending these days. That and undeserving.

"Hey, you in there." He gave an encouraging dimpled grin. "I'll take a bowl then."

She looked at him, knew he'd realized her mind had dived off the deep end again. "Coming up."

She filled two bowls then carried them over to the table where Bo had taken a seat. Setting his in front of him, she couldn't help thinking how nice it had been that he'd come to check on her. He hadn't changed her mind about how she felt, but . . . she did feel better.

"Thank you for coming," she said. "I was in a bad place and you've helped."

"Good." He dug his spoon into the rich ice cream then winked as he plopped the spoonful into his mouth.

She took a bite of hers, hoping it tasted half as good as he'd made his appear.

"What makes Abby Knightley tick?" he asked out of the blue. "I'd really like to know who you are when the heavy load you carry isn't weighing you down."

She'd just taken another bite of her chocolate and marshmallow mixture. She swallowed, her thoughts stilling as she tried to think of the person he was asking about. What did that girl, that woman, enjoy doing?

"Come on, spill. What makes you smile? Me, when I'm not working on my stirrups I like to ride horses, I like to do a little two-stepping on occasion. Do you like to dance?" He cocked his head and showed her a dimple when he smiled.

Abby set her spoon back in the bowl, suddenly imagining being in Bo's arms dancing the two-step . . . if she danced. "Well, I've never two-stepped . . . I've worked. I read." Until that moment she hadn't really thought about how few hobbies she had.

"You seriously don't like to dance?"

"I didn't say I don't like it, I said I never had. It all comes back to work. Everything I did was geared toward getting me ahead in the company."

"Then we are going to have to fix that. I'm taking you out dancing one night—" Bo's phone rang, the ringtone sounding like an alarm. He was standing instantly, pulling the phone from its harness, and he listened briefly.

"Hold that thought. I gotta run. There's a fire," he said as he punched the button and put the phone back to his ear.

Abby was standing too. "What can I do?" she asked, following him through the house as he hurried toward the front door.

"Nothing, just hang tight. I'll call you later."

Abby knew he was on the volunteer fire department. "But you could get hurt—"

"I'll be fine. We may be volunteers, but we have great training. Don't worry."

"But where is it?"

And he was gone. Abby couldn't help worrying as she watched him jog to his truck and drive away in the direction of downtown.

Suddenly, Rand entered her front yard. He didn't look good. He came straight toward her, weaved slightly as he came.

"I need you to drive me."

"What?"

He glared at her. "I need you to drive me or I'm getting in my car and driving myself—Pebble's motel is on fire."

"Pebble's? But how do you—"

"I have a scanner for the paper, so I hear everything. Now are you driving me or am I?"

CHAPTER 24

Abby raced inside her house and grabbed her purse, searching through it for the keys to her car as she ran back outside. Rand was already in the passenger seat.

"Come on, drive. Pebble needs me."

"I am," she said, cranking the car and backing out of the drive.

"Punch it. Go, go, go," Rand yelled as she rammed the shifter into drive.

"Hey, I'm just as worried as you are," she yelled back and stomped the gas. "So hold your horses, fella."

She was now not just worried about Bo, she was worried about Pebble.

"Oh, no," Rand said, gripping the dashboard as the motel came into view. It was dark, but even in the moonlight there was a white cloud rising above the main office. Pebble's apartment was in that building.

She slowed as the fire truck pulled ahead of them, sirens blaring. She followed it into the parking lot, pulling to the curb. Rand already had his door open, and though he stumbled, he managed to keep his balance and run toward the fire truck. Abby followed him, amazed at how agile and quick he was, even in what must be his early sixties . . . and drunk.

She'd had no questions about why he'd asked her to drive him. He'd gotten drunk after the upset in his yard today. She reached the fire truck, which blocked her view of the motel. As she reached it cars and people continued to gather nearby. It was hard to make everyone out in the darkness but she saw who she thought was Jarrod and Bo in the glow of the lights. It was hard to tell from behind with his gear, but then she caught Bo's profile. There was no mistaking him. He and the other man, who she was pretty certain was Jarrod, entered the building. Jarrod must have made it back from his trip. At least she knew the two brothers would have each other's back. Another man stepped in front of Rand, stopping him as he raced toward the building. It was obvious that he was telling him to back away. Rand was not happy. For a small man he bowed up pretty good. Abby's attention shifted back to the door that Bo had disappeared through. Flames could now be seen shooting from the roof—her heart pounded.

"Pebble!"

Abby whirled as Clara Lyn came barreling out of her car where she'd run it up on the curb and left her door open. Abby reacted to the woman racing past her by reaching for her. She did not need to go inside. Abby knew this, because she wanted to go inside with all her heart.

"Bo and Jarrod are in there, Clara. They'll bring her out." Abby knew this was true. Bo would bring Pebble out.

It seemed like hours were ticking by instead of minutes. Suddenly there was a huge crash and part of the roof fell in. Seconds later a fireman appeared through the flames and smoke with Pebble in his arms. It was Jarrod. The EMTs raced forward for Pebble. Abby's hand went to her throat—where was Bo?

Abby could barely hold herself up as thoughts of waking up with EMTs looking down at her after the wreck slammed into her—a kaleidoscope of lights merging as she faded in and out, her mind fuzzy as the question, "Where's Landon?" kept dying on her lips, darkness pulling her back.

Now, all she could think about was Bo.

Where was Bo?

The lone fireman picked his fire hose up and headed back inside the building dousing the flames as he did. Another fireman raced inside with his own hose, joining the fight. They were going back for Bo.

The fireman who had held Rand up was telling everyone to get back. And only then did Abby realize that Clara Lyn had joined Rand beside the gurney that they'd strapped Pebble to. They were administering oxygen to the sweet lady and that was at least a good sign that she was alive.

But what about Bo?

A moment later one of the firemen appeared from the flames—one was supporting Bo, who was moving on his own but barely. As soon as they were clear of the building, Bo collapsed . . .

. . .

The Kerrville hospital's emergency room was packed despite it being nearly midnight. Chaos reigned as word spread that Pebble and Bo were in the hospital.

"How are they?" Reba Ann yelled as she came rushing in through the doors. Her hair was in clips and there were hints of green facial mask still scattered over her face.

"They're okay," Clara Lyn assured her shrilly, still as hyper as she'd been when Abby had driven her to the hospital. Clara Lyn had been in no condition to drive, since she was so worried about her longtime friend. Abby had been upset, too, but both Clara Lyn and Rand had needed her to drive them.

"Bo got hit in the head by a beam, then pinned beneath it when he was getting Pebble out. Thankfully Jarrod got her out then went back for Bo. He's got a concussion and a dislocated shoulder."

"Oh, no," Reba gasped. "But he's okay, praise God. And Pebble. How's Pebble?" She looked from Clara Lyn to Abby.

"She's fine. She inhaled a lot of smoke and they are going to keep her overnight and hopefully she will get to go home tomorrow. But there is a chance they'll keep her for a couple of days. She was so lucky. God was watching out for her."

"How did it happen?"

"We don't know. But Jarrod thinks it was electrical. He's going back to figure it out after he checks on Bo."

"I can't believe it, just can't believe it." Reba shook her head.

Rand stood out near the hallway, looking worried but

sober. Abby had seen him talk with Jarrod before he'd gone back to check on Bo. Since Jarrod was the volunteer fire chief and Rand was the lone newspaper reporter for the town, they must have a lot of discussions after a fire in order for Rand to report in the paper. She assumed that no fire had ever been quite so personal to either of them.

Abby's nerves were keyed up even though they knew everyone was going to be okay.

Tru had come in not long after they'd made it to the hospital and he'd told her that Maggie had stayed home with Levi and Pops.

Doobie and Doonie had shown up, too, along with several other people that she hadn't met. The nurses finally came in and said that since both patients were in stable condition, everyone needed to go home and get some rest and come back during visiting hours.

• • •

Bo had had a very close call tonight. Even now, lying in bed staring up at the ceiling, it made her stomach sour just thinking about it. What if something had happened to him? Levi would have lost not only his mother but his father by the time he was little over a year old.

Abby closed her eyes at the thought. She knew if that had happened, Maggie and Tru would have instantly stepped in but . . . but what?

Bo was her friend. It was true, somewhere in the few weeks that she'd lived in Wishing Springs he had become her friend . . . and she was worried about him.

A chill came over Abby and she pulled her covers tighter about her . . . but it didn't help.

. . .

Pebble opened her eyes at the soft swoosh of her hospital door—it had been a revolving door since she'd arrived. Which was nice, her friends were just worried about her. But she felt adrift . . . and she wasn't sure why. She'd been feeling that way even before the fire. But the day after waking up in the hospital it had been worse. She'd glimpsed Rand in the crowd that had gathered around her at the fire, before she'd passed out and been transported to the hospital.

And the tortured worry in his eyes still haunted her.

"Pebble, are you awake?" a familiar voice asked gently. Rand.

Her heart thudded erratically. "I'm awake," she called, giving him a small smile. "You didn't have to come by. I know you've got a paper to get out."

He came closer and set a vase full of fall flowers on the table beside her. "I needed to deliver these to you and just make sure you were doing good."

"I am. Thanks to Bo and Jarrod I'm going to live at least another day." She coughed, something she'd be doing for a while, the doctor had explained.

Rand rushed to pour her a cup of water and handed it to her. Their fingers touched as she took it and she felt weaker suddenly than she had. "Thank you," she managed, keeping her eyes down. Pebble had been worried for a while now about the feelings she had for Rand.

It wasn't healthy and she knew it. He had a drinking problem. Yes, it seemed to be linked to times when she disappointed him. And that wasn't good in any way.

She and Cecil had had a wonderful, uncomplicated life. She'd loved him with all her heart—she'd chosen him. But she'd loved Rand too. A long time ago.

He'd been complicated back then too. When they were in high school, he'd taken too many risks, loved motorcycles, and drank some, not that she knew how much, just that he did. Pebble had been raised by Christian parents who hadn't allowed drinking and she had been fine with that, as she hung out with a like-minded crowd. Rand had found a rowdier one.

Falling for him had happened innocently enough, and had startled her, it was so unlikely. They'd been lab partners her junior year. He'd been so gentle and kind anytime he was around her, despite her not liking his lifestyle.

And then one day, she'd had a flat and he'd stopped and helped her. And they'd talked.

They'd met sometimes after that. Not making a big deal of it at school. It hadn't been meant to be secretive, but looking back on it, she knew she'd not wanted anyone to know.

Her parents wouldn't have been happy. And to be honest, if she'd let her heart lead her, she had no idea what kind of life they would have had.

She'd stopped the meetings before summer, realizing her feelings and knowing, fearing, he felt the same way. Rand had left after that and she'd heard he'd joined the navy.

She'd been brokenhearted over the whole thing.

And then, after a miserable summer a new boy had moved to town . . . and Cecil had been everything she'd ever dreamed of. He enjoyed living a simple, steady life like Pebble and she'd fallen for him completely . . . but she'd never forgotten Rand.

Pebble drew her mind back to Rand.

"Pebble, I've given drinking up. Completely."

"Rand—"

"I drink some, sometimes more than I should. But I'm changing. As of last night. I've been weak. I understand that now. But only when we've argued, or I'm worried about us."

Tears threatened to spill but she blinked them away. "Oh, Rand." She shook her head and looked down, hardening her resolve before lifting her gaze to meet his pleading eyes. "I can't . . ." she said, her heart as heavy as her breath. "You blame me for your drinking—" Coughing hit her and she couldn't speak. His words had hurt.

"Pebble . . ." Rand gently lifted her hand and wrapped her fingers around the glass he'd given her earlier. He helped her take a sip before she replaced the oxygen mask over her face.

"I'm so sorry," he said, then called the nurse.

And then he left.

Pebble watched him go and her heart broke all over again.

CHAPTER 25

B o hated hospitals. He hadn't slept well and had been sitting with his legs dangling off the edge of the bed wearing his hospital gown more than ready to put on his pants—if Jarrod would hurry up and get here with them.

The last person he expected to see walk in carrying his duffle bag was Abby but that was exactly who came in with it. "What are you doing here?"

"Um, well—" she started, then stuttered as her gaze fell on his bare legs. A smile tickled the edge of her lips. "Well, well, cowboy, looks like missing your trip to the beach this summer has made you grumpy."

He scowled and looked down at his white legs. Great. Just great. Abby seeing him dressed in a hospital gown, barefooted and—it wasn't exactly the picture of him he wanted in her mind. "Funny, real funny."

"I thought so, hero." She walked over and gently set the bag on the bed beside him. "Jarrod sent these to you and said everything you'd need was in there."

"Why are you picking me up?"

"It's my day to keep Levi, but Jarrod had a cow down or something like that. And Tru and Maggie are packing."

"Packing?"

"Yes, something has come up and they're having to leave a week early, so they asked me if I could pick you up while they got ready. I think they're leaving in the morning."

"But Jarrod's leaving in the morning." Bo reached for the zipper on his bag and winced as pain shot through him from the broken collarbone.

"Are you okay?" Abby asked, cringing.

"I'm fine. I just keep forgetting I have a broken collarbone."

"Here let me open that for you."

Bo watched her as she unzipped the bag. She smelled so good, he inhaled deeply and for the moment forgot his shoulder was killing him.

"Here you go." Her brow knitted as she looked at his sling. "Are you going to be able to get dressed with that arm in the sling? Do I need to call a nurse?"

"I can manage," he grunted.

"Then I'll step outside."

Once Abby closed the door, Bo pulled his pants from the bag with his left hand. Now how was he going to function with his right arm strapped to his body? And with strict directions not to lift anything at the risk of damaging the bone further and requiring surgery? If it was his left arm it wouldn't be so bad. But it wasn't.

The nurse stuck her head into the room when he had one leg in.

"Need help?"

"No," he yelled, feeling about as nice as a grizzly bear.

He was going to have a talk with his brothers when he got home. He managed to get the other leg into the pants while he was sitting in a chair, but the hard part was standing up and getting the jeans up around his hips without tripping over the blamed things and breaking his neck. If that part was hard, he hadn't even tried getting his pullover on.

He was breathing hard by the time a knock sounded on the door and his doctor walked in.

"Ah, you're dressed. Good for you."

"If you can call it that," Bo growled. He had one arm through the sleeve and then he'd managed to get the shirt pulled down over his incapacitated right shoulder and left it there. He'd walk out of the hospital looking like he had one arm. There was no way of getting this pullover over a fractured collar bone. "How long do I have to wear this?"

The doctor closed his chart. "It's just minimally displaced, but you'll need to keep it stable for ten to fourteen days. And no lifting for three weeks. Then, you should be able to resume activities as long as you don't overdo it. We'll let you go home today. Call my office to set up an appointment in a week."

Bo watched the doctor leave . . . he had a problem. A big problem. How was he going to take care of Levi while his brothers ran off and abandoned him?

. . .

While Abby waited on Bo to get dressed and speak with his doctor, she walked down the hall to Pebble's room. Abby knew they'd come close to losing her the night before.

"Knock, knock," Abby said, rapping gently on the open door and leaning into the room.

"Abby!" Pebble said, happiness in her voice—well, it was nice someone was glad to see her. She thought Bo was going to snap her head off.

Pebble's skin was sallow but her blue eyes were bright above the oxygen tube, IV, and monitors. "What are you doing here? It's awful early," she said, and then coughed. When Abby hurried over and reached to hand her a glass of water she took it.

"Don't look so worried, Abby, I'm fine. This will pass. The doctor says I'll live. Now, sit down here." She patted the bed and Abby eased down beside her.

"You scared us terribly."

"Well, the Lord kept me safe and sent your handsome hero to rescue me."

"Oh, he's not my—"

Pebble winked. "I'm just going to call him that then. I like the thought of it."

"I hope all that smoke didn't suddenly make you a matchmaker."

"Maybe."

Abby decided not pressing the issue was the best plan of action. "Speaking of heroes, I should mention that I drove a very worried newspaper reporter to the motel last night. If one of the firemen hadn't blocked his way, I'm pretty sure he would have plunged into that building to get to you."

Pebble looked troubled as she let her gaze shift to the

window. Abby wondered again how deep her feelings really went for Rand.

"I just thought I should tell you that," she said. "I mean, I told you the other so I should tell this, too, right?"

Pebble patted her hand. "Thank you for being honest with me. Rand is a good man. He's not perfect. But he's a good man. Our friendship goes back a long way, and it's complicated."

Abby squeezed Pebble's hand, feeling close to the innkeeper. "I hope I haven't complicated it more. I never meant anything bad. I was just worried about you."

"I understand. I needed to know. My Cecil was a good man. He was very uncomplicated." She took a sip of her water and laid her head back on her pillow. "It was the kind of life I wanted—easy, risk free."

Abby remembered someone saying that Rand had loved Pebble when they were young. She suddenly wondered if Pebble had loved him. Had she chosen between complicated and uncomplicated?

It was none of her business. She'd already done enough. "I better go check on Bo. He's being released today and I'm driving him home. If you need anything, please let me know. I'm sure you're going to have a lot of offers of that though."

"Yes, they've already started."

Abby gave her a quick hug and headed toward the door.

"Abby—"

She paused at the door and turned back. "Yes."

"Why did you drive Rand to the fire?"

Abby cocked her head to the side. "Because it was so

important to him . . . and he asked me instead of getting behind the wheel and driving himself despite how desperate he was to get to you."

. . .

Bo sank into Abby's car trying not to jar his shoulder too much. He figured that if he did things exactly as the doc had said, then he would have no complications and he'd be back to his normal routine quicker than if he pushed it. With the way his luck was going, if he pushed it, he'd end up having surgery like the doc had warned him before he left. He didn't want that. He had a baby counting on him and a business to run and Pops to look out for and no time to be gambling with this injury. And right now he had to figure out how he was going to deal with this while his brothers were off doing their jobs.

Once again it came down to him imposing on Abby.

And he wasn't happy about it. But on short notice what else did he have? If she said no, then he'd just have to deal with it and figure something else out. Still, he didn't mention it. He stared out the window and watched the town of Kerrville fade away and the familiar landscape of rolling hills and scrub dot the landscape. And his thoughts kept going to Abby.

When he'd been trapped under that beam, and Jarrod had to leave him there in order to get Pebble out, he had thought of nothing but Levi and Abby as the fire closed in around him.

"You sure are quiet," Abby said finally.

She was probably wondering if he was mad at her. If she knew what he was thinking, she'd be the one mad at him. Bo looked over at her and wondered if she had worried about him.

She'd said twice that she only wanted to be friends. And up until now he'd backed off, but now, he knew what he wanted.

He just had to figure out how to get it. And maybe his brothers suddenly running off like this was just what he needed to get it.

. . .

It felt awkward being the one to pick Bo up at the hospital and once they were in the car driving it was even more awkward. But what was she supposed to do when Maggie asked her to do it? It seemed odd to Abby and she wondered if Bo thought so too.

Then again, the situation at the Four of Hearts Ranch wasn't a truly normal situation. There were so many variables that made it complicated. His broken collar bone only being part of the equation. The other was the still unwanted complete awareness of the man beside her. It radiated throughout her like a jackhammer on steroids. And it only grew worse when he turned those devastating blue eyes on her. Those eyes instantly had her thinking about a walk on the beach, holding hands and kissing in the moonlight *all* at the same time. *And* . . . she pushed the "and" away. She'd stopped thinking about *that* after Landon died.

But those eyes, drat them, they were like a lighthouse

beacon and this ship was caught in the powerful beam. "So, I was thinking you're going to be in trouble when Maggie leaves. I mean, we talked about her leaving and me watching Levi full time when that happened. But now, with your shoulder, what are you going to do?"

He looked troubled. "I've been sitting here thinking about the very same thing. I can manage with Pops, but Levi could pose a problem with me only having the use of one arm. I think maybe I'll need to go ahead and find some nighttime help too. Just in case something were to happen while I'm the only one with both Pops and Levi. I mean, I'm capable but for the baby's safety I wouldn't want to take chances."

Abby understood his concern and admired him for realizing that there could be a safety issue. "I agree." She bit her lip, her mind whirling. "Lifting Levi is going to be a problem for you." She started thinking about everything that could happen changing a diaper with one hand, and as if he were reading her mind, he frowned.

"If he gets to squirming while I'm trying to change his diaper, it might not be pretty—it might be doggone awful now that I think about it."

If he wasn't so obviously stressed about it, Abby would have laughed, but she didn't.

"I gotta find help. I'm not willing to take that chance, for his sake. It's not fair to him. Maybe one of Sergio's sisters could help. Or a niece. "

He was rambling and Abby found his nerves reassuring. He was as much out of his element here as she was out of hers. And the truth was, what else did he have? Demand that his brothers stay? From what she had gleaned from their conversations about his dad's gambling, they still had some debt hanging over their heads and it took all of them to make the payments. And Maggie had confided that part of this trip was for a column promotion.

Abby knew that they couldn't afford to have any individual piece drop out of that structure.

And Bo had had a lot dumped in his lap suddenly and he was trying so hard to do the right thing. "I can do it," she blurted. Instantly, she tensed and wanted to take the words back. But she'd said them now. The thought of Levi being around people he wasn't used to drove her crazy. The baby had been moved and shifted who knew how much in the last few weeks, months. Everything they could find out about his life seemed rooted in his mother being ill and him being shuffled around while she tried to survive.

"No, I couldn't ask you to do that."

"You're not asking. I volunteered," she said with more conviction than she felt. He had no idea what this was going to do to her emotionally but she had to do it.

"Look, you have an extra bedroom. I can come stay for a few days. No big deal. I'd take him home at night with me, but the poor kid has been moved around so much I think keeping him in his own room and getting him a routine is the best thing. I'll come stay, and when you're better, I'll head back to my place." She wanted to slap her forehead in dismay, hearing what she was saying—disbelief stung as if she'd done just that.

She knew saying nothing would have been the best

policy. Especially where Bo was concerned. But Levi deserved better than the cards he'd been dealt. And there was just nothing she could do but offer to help.

Levi needed her.

"I don't mind, really." The words came out sounding as strained as she felt. And looking at Bo, she figured that was only going to grow worse with every passing moment she was in his presence.

"Seriously? No, I can't ask you to do that."

"No, Bo, listen to me. That baby has been through a lot. Right now he needs people around him he's comfortable with and he needs the security of his own bed. His own room. I'd cart him to my house every night but that would be selfish on my part. This will be best."

He studied her for the longest moment and she thought he might turn her down. Finally, he slowly nodded. "You're right. This is what's best for Levi."

Butterflies and bees tangled together inside her chest. "Everything's going to be okay."

She just wished she felt as confident as she sounded.

CHAPTER 26

They didn't waste any more time rethinking the situation. Bo had help from the ranch hands with the cattle, and truthfully he could find someone to step in to help him with Levi. But the baby was comfortable with Abby and she had grown so attached to him she hated the thought of not being the one caring for him. And though she was terrified in many ways, she couldn't help but wonder if God had placed this challenge in her path. This was one more step forward and she was doing it. Still, Abby got the feeling that Bo was as uncomfortable with the situation as she was but he was considering Levi too. It could potentially be unsafe for Levi if Bo had any trouble during the night. Not to mention that he also had to take care of Pops. She wouldn't sleep well knowing she'd refused to help. Especially just because she was afraid that being around him twenty-four hours a day might make her start feeling emotions that she didn't want to feel.

Selfish.

So she found herself in her room packing an overnight bag with enough clothing for several nights. By her calculation she would be there for at least a week.

Maybe two since Bo explained that Jarrod was on his way to the Houston Livestock show with a load of their best show cattle. She'd thought for a moment that she'd been set up when they'd all suddenly had to leave after Bo got hurt. But she knew the brothers and they'd hardly act that way, she chided her overactive imagination.

She chose a few makeup items and her shampoo and hairspray from the counter in the bathroom and then her toothbrush and caught the worried expression on her face in the mirror.

"Why are you so nervous?" she whispered, shooting herself a glare. "You'll be taking care of Levi. And you'll enjoy that. You know you will." Automatically her hand went to her lower belly where her baby had once lived so briefly. She'd believed that being around Levi would make the pain of losing her baby worse. And she'd been right initially. But now, the very thought of Levi brought a smile to her lips. She could do this. She would do it. And she'd deal with the awakening that seemed to be going on inside of her with every glance Bo sent her way.

But on this she was clear. She would never change her mind about risking her heart again. Pebble talked about her relationship with Rand being complicated. Well, Abby knew all about complicated.

Grabbing her bag from the bed, she walked into the living room where Bo stood among her things. He seemed to dwarf the room with the sheer magnitude of his presence. And Abby was hit all anew that she'd be saying both good-night and good morning to him. Complicated—her rioting insides would agree wholeheartedly that she knew more than she wanted to know about complicated.

Because there was that part of her that no amount of talking could coax from the ledge and the overwhelming temptation of taking a dive straight into trouble.

. . .

Bo's entire shoulder was radiating with pain by the time he led the way into the house. The small break did hurt but the stress of realizing he was going to be sleeping down the hallway from Abby for probably two weeks had him tensed up like a barbed wire fence.

It did help realizing that he wasn't the only one feeling the pressure. Abby was about as keyed up as he'd ever seen her. Every time their eyes met her cheeks flushed the becoming pink blush of a fresh field of Texas buttercups. And that only made his situation much more tense.

"This is your room," he said, standing in the doorway. "It was my grandmother's sewing room. A lot of pretty things were created here, like that quilt on the bed." His grandmother was a safe subject.

Abby had paused just outside the doorway in the hall and he could see the vein at the base of her jaw ramp up. At the mention of his grandmother, she smiled, relieved, he figured, to have something to focus on other than that pounding that was apparently going on inside her.

He had his own drumbeat going and nothing was easing up about it.

Abby swept past him in a flurry of sweet spring flower mix.

"This is gorgeous, Bo," she said, bending forward to run her hand over the intricate pattern of colorful patches of material.

He set Abby's bag just inside the door, but didn't go in. "Yeah, Gram loved to sit for hours and create quilts. She finished them in here, but while she was on the road with Pops at shows is where she did a lot of cutting and piecing. I don't recall a lot of memories of my Gram where she didn't have a pretty square or triangle of material in her hand."

"I bet she was a lovely, contented woman."

He smiled, and he felt the dimple that he'd inherited from his Gram crease his cheek. "I was a kid, pretty young when she died. But from everything I remember and from everything I've heard, I'd say so. She loved her family. That chest there—the one at the foot of that bed, it used to be over there under the window. It was used as a window seat back then when there was no bed in here. But it was also where she stored her treasure."

Abby tilted her head and she beamed an intrigued tell-me-more expression his way. She was about the most beautiful woman he'd ever seen and it had more to do with the spirit that illuminated those amazing eyes of hers. He wondered what it would take to make her a contented woman. Because he knew she wasn't and he understood why, knowing she'd lost her husband and her child. How could he begin to think that he could ever take that pain and bring her heart, her soul, contentment? Especially him, the cowboy who had always had a problem with commitment.

Abby didn't need to be hurt again, a man like him was not what she needed—did he even trust himself and the strength of his feelings when he was around her?

He pushed the sudden thoughts away and focused on his Gram's treasure. "She'd sewn each of us a quilt and a wedding present. Even though she didn't live to see any of us graduate from junior high school she'd created each of us a special quilt."

"And she called them her treasure?"

"Yeah, when I'd come in here as a boy and climb up there to sit and watch her work she'd tell me I was sitting on treasure."

"I'd love to see your quilt someday. You've got my curiosity up."

"I'll show you. I keep it at my place, but maybe while you're here we'll go see it."

"You don't live here full time?"

"Nope, I do own a home. It's not snugged up right here in the middle of the mix, but over on the ranch's south side. It was just too far away for when Pops needed me and so I closed it up and moved over here. My shop's here, too, so it made sense."

She considered that statement for a long moment and he wondered what she was thinking.

She walked over and looked up at him, her eyes as serious, as intense as he'd ever seen them.

"You're a good man, Bo Monahan."

He wasn't so sure of that—not with how he'd hurt Darla. Before he could react or say anything, she'd walked past him and headed down the hall toward the living room.

And despite the swift kick of doubt, he couldn't help the silly grin that plastered itself on his face at her compliment. Abby thought he was a good man.

And that gave him hope.

$\cdot \quad \cdot \quad \cdot$

"You're a lifesaver. I feel so much better knowing you'll be here."

Abby hugged Maggie and took Levi from her arms as Maggie gave the little tyke one last kiss.

She juggled Levi in her arms, loving the feel of him against her and the weight of his little body. "We're going to have a great time. You go and do what you have to do. This media tour your paper has set up for you sounds wonderful. Maybe more of the people you've touched will follow you home and settle in town," she teased.

"I'm sure Bo would love that." Maggie chuckled.

Abby caught Bo rolling his eyes. "Yup, just what I'd like to see."

"You better watch what you say, brother-in-law. Abby there decides to walk, you'll be stranded up a creek without a paddle as Doobie and Doonie say."

"Okay, looks like everything's loaded and we're ready to hit the road. You ready?" Tru asked, striding up from the back of the trailer where he'd been doing some last-minute loading.

"I am." Maggie kissed him then turned back to Abby.

"Call if you need anything. You, too, Bo. We really are sorry about this."

"It's okay, we'll be fine," Abby assured her, shooing her toward the truck. "Really."

Abby had to chuckle as Tru opened the passenger door and had to practically pick Maggie up and stuff her into the cab. Maggie immediately rolled the window down as the screen door slammed and they all turned to see Pops striding from the house carrying a duffle bag of his own. And a saddle.

He'd been outside with them a few minutes ago and then he'd turned and headed inside, not an uncommon thing for him to do, but now, it was clear that he'd gone inside for a reason. He now wore a crisply starched shirt that had been buttoned crooked and he had on a pair of gleaming boots and a buckle practically the size of a hubcap taken off his trophy shelf. The saddle was also one of the championship saddles that sat in a corner on a saddle rack.

"Hey, Pops," Bo said, meeting him as he reached the truck. "What ya doin'?"

"It's a good day to win." He grinned, and Abby's heart did a complete double rotation as a boulder-sized lump lodged in her throat. Solomon came barreling through the screen door toward them, howling all the way.

"Pops, why don't you stay here with us today? Solomon is having trouble thinking about you leaving him behind." Abby saw the pain in both Tru and Bo's eyes.

"But I have a horse to ride."

"Your ride is tomorrow, Pops," Bo said, as she watched Pops grow distressed.

"I thought it was today. With Tru."

"No, tomorrow, Pops," Bo repeated and confusion came into Pops's eyes. "Tomorrow will be a better day to win."

Pops looked at Bo and after a minute he nodded. "I'm gonna win."

And then, as quickly as he'd grown confused he was fine. And he waved to Tru and Maggie, watching them as they drove away.

Jarrod had left before dawn that morning with one of the ranch hands and a large trailer full of black cattle. Beautiful black cattle. Abby hadn't seen the actual cattle operation—that part was on another area of the large ranch. The part around the house was more for the horse operation. It made her all the more aware of how large a place the brothers were managing.

All the more aware of the hard work that Pops had put into building the place and what his son had almost lost had it not been for the hard work of Bo, Tru, and Jarrod.

Looking at Pops standing there beside Bo Abby felt a sense of urgency.

Life was so precious. Time was so precious . . .

She hugged Levi and he giggled his contagious cackle that always sent joy coursing through her.

"Moo," he said, bouncing and straining toward the cows that were grazing along the fence near the side of the house.

"Moo." She laughed back as he continued talking to the cattle that were totally ignoring him. He didn't even say daddy or anything yet, but he was suddenly saying moo.

Pops turned and grinned then came over.

Bo did too. "Wow, his first word."

Abby laughed at their expressions of awe. "Well, I guess that makes it official. He is a cowboy."

Smiling, Abby turned and led the way inside, feeling completely, inexplicably happy that she was here.

CHAPTER 27

"Pebble, are you sure you are okay?"

"Clara Lyn, I've told you I'm fine. And no, I don't need to stay with you or Reba. I'll be fine here. Besides, it'll be easier for me to stay in one of my motel rooms while the office is being renovated. I'll still be able to run the motel and watch the work as it's being done."

They were sitting in some of the colorful chairs outside the room where Pebble was going to be living. Clara wasn't happy about it, not one little bit, but Pebble was being more stubborn than usual. And for a tiny woman she could be as firm as a rock when she wanted to be.

"But your lungs are still not completely healed," Reba said. "What if you start coughing and . . . and you need someone to bring you a drink or something?"

Pebble closed her eyes and tilted her head slightly as if she were praying for patience. She probably was. They'd been after her since yesterday at the hospital when she'd told them her plan. "Girls, I'll be fine. I'm not an infant. I'll put a glass of water beside my bed and there will be nothing to worry about."

Clara Lyn knew when she'd lost. "Fine. But you have my number and you can call any time."

"Of course I will."

"So, what about Rand?" Clara asked. Now that she'd given up getting Pebble to go along with her plan she wanted to get to other things. "Did he come to see you yesterday?"

Pebble toyed with her skirt. "No. I told you he came that first day and not since."

"Well, what did he say? You have been extremely close-mouthed about the entire issue." Clara had been persistent and had gotten nowhere with Pebble and it was driving her crazy.

"That man was one worried puppy about you that night. He looked about as sick as a dog when they wouldn't let him in there to try and get to you."

Pebble sat up straight. "Clara Lyn, if you must know, he'd been drinking that night. Did you ever wonder why he asked Abby to drive him? He probably was sicker than a dog."

Reba's mouth fell open. "I tell you, I feel like going over there and . . . and locking him in his room until he gives this bad behavior up. Doesn't he know what he's doing?"

Clara sighed and plopped her elbows on her knees and looked at the ground. "I never took myself to be gullible or naïve, but I feel downright foolish right now."

"The truth is," Pebble said, "I do too. But I spent the last few days going over this in my mind. And I wonder if I've been looking at this all wrong."

Clara looked up. "What do you mean?"

"I have been so mad at him I haven't once asked myself how I could help him."

"How could you help him?" Reba said, with a sigh. "If you try to help him, he'll probably think you're interested in a future and then if you're not, that'll just drive him to drink again. It's just a vicious, vicious circle. Besides, how would you ever be able to believe him again?" Reba tucked her hair behind her ears and frowned as she slumped in her chair.

Clara knew exactly how her friend felt. "Look, Pebble, I've been a bit of a ninny over this romance blooming in my mind between you and Rand. Why, crazy me actually thought back last year when he got drunk and sang "I Will Always Love You" like a hound dog howling at the moon, well, I actually thought it was kinda cute and romantic . . ." Clara scowled in distaste. "When in fact I should have immediately encouraged you to hold to your guns and keep your distance. And then when he got drunk again and you had to hit him over the head because he wouldn't go home and leave you alone and Jake came and hauled him off to the clink . . . what was I thinking? There's nothing funny or the least bit romantic about any of that. You've been using your common sense and I've been acting like a silly fool. You needed to hit me over the head and have Jake haul me off to jail."

And here she thought she gave good advice. Always prided herself on giving advice in the salon.

"Now, Clara and Reba, both of you need to calm down. For starters again, may I remind you that I am no china doll. I don't know if either of you noticed, but I have always had a mind of my own. So, what I do or do not do is not your fault or your responsibility.

And that's the same way I feel about Rand. He's made choices that I as a longtime friend have never agreed with. And if you really want to know, once I came very near to agreeing to marry him—"

"I knew it!" Clara gasped. "You never admitted it but we knew that you and he had a thing going on back in school."

Pebble gave a halfhearted chuckle.

"So, what stopped you?" Reba asked.

"I thought about any future life with Rand—there were so many variables of the way life with him could have gone. He was exciting. I never knew exactly what he was thinking. He drank some then, of course. He wanted to see places and do things that just seemed would be hard with a wife. And as a girl I was still very practical, and I wasn't sure how he would pay for all these dreams. I just didn't see myself as a motorcycle chick."

Clara Lyn laughed and so did Reba. "Just you saying 'motorcycle chick' is hilarious."

"Well, I didn't think it was that funny," Pebble said indignantly.

Clara tried to stop the chuckles. "Believe me, it is. When I picture you on a motorcycle it's like trying to picture the Queen of England on the back of a motor-cycle. It just doesn't compute."

"Fine. I didn't care for the picture I had of myself either. I just didn't laugh at it." Pebble huffed the last part and tugged at the collar of her prim shirt. "Anyway, I told him I couldn't marry him. And he left and joined the navy. And as you know he has seen the world."

"And he came back here wearing loafers, khakis, and

starched dress shirts and opened the newspaper and joined the city council." Clara arched a brow.

"Gave up that career in advertising out in California to come back here trying to be the man you would marry," Reba said, her eyes wide.

"But he still drinks." Pebble looked out across her yard at the burned shell of her motel.

Clara wasn't often at a loss for words. She was at the moment. Reba, too, given the silence coming from her corner.

"I've never asked him what I could do to help him. And I think it's about time I did."

"But—"

"I said that a lot over the last few days as I thought about this and you know what? I'm all butted out. There are no more buts about it."

.   .   .

Bo walked into the kitchen clobbered by the knowledge that he had two weeks to start winning Abby's heart. To hope that he could get her to think that there was more love out there for her. Specifically, right here. If anyone had asked him a month ago if he was ready for love, marriage, and a baby he'd have laughed. But that was then and this was now, and he wanted Abby. He had a baby and he was looking for marriage and more babies with the woman he loved.

"So," he said, as he followed Abby through the kitchen. "What are you thinking?"

Abby led the way into the living room where the

playpen was set up and she sank down on the floor to play with Levi. He immediately got on his knees and crawled across the floor to Bo. Pops trailed off into the den and Solomon followed him.

"Will he be okay in there?" Abby asked.

Bo heard the TV click on. "He'll settle into his recliner for a little while and watch *Walker, Texas Ranger* or some other rerun that he loves. He's fine."

He bent to grin at Levi who immediately crawled back to Abby cackling joyfully as he went. He grabbed Abby's fingers and pulled up, then grinned like he was king of the world.

"I think that Levi is just starting to get busy."

"Really?"

She looked up at him and his heart skidded to a halt.

"He's really starting to move around. Babies usually start walking anywhere between ten and fourteen months, so he's right there."

Bo sank down on the floor and held out his good arm. Levi instantly grabbed his hand and held on. When he started to teeter Abby gently placed her hands on the baby's torso and supported him. Her long and slender fingers wore no rings. Bo could see one there in his imagination and found himself wondering what kind she'd like.

"He adores you, you know."

Bo jerked his thoughts back to his son. "I feel the same way about him. It doesn't seem possible that I didn't know he even existed a month ago. And now I can't imagine him not being in my life." He felt the same way about Abby. He looked from his cherub-faced baby to Abby, her eyes sparkling, happy.

"Love, it's amazing."

"Yeah, it is." He only had one good arm and Levi had ahold of it. And that was a good thing because otherwise Bo would have touched Abby then. Trailed a finger along her jaw or touched her silky hair. He cleared his throat and pulled his finger from Levi's, not worried about if he would fall since Abby was holding him up. Bo got to his feet. "I better go check on the work at the shop and see if I can do anything with one hand."

She smiled. "I'd tell you to take a painkiller for that collarbone, but I have a feeling it would just be a waste of breath. So, have fun and we'll be here."

"I like the sound of that. See you in a little while."

He stopped by the den and asked Pops if he wanted to go to work and that's all it took to find a shadow.

It was going to be a good, good day.

.   .   .

"He's sleeping like a baby," Abby said that evening as she walked outside where Bo was sitting on the porch step staring up at the sky. His hat was off and his dark hair curled slightly at the nape of his neck. She'd found herself repeatedly studying that little bit of curl and wanting to touch it.

He'd decided to go work just in the nick of time. For a woman who wasn't interested in opening the door to her feelings, she had been feeling pretty good as she'd looked into his eyes and listened to him talk about loving his son. That husky emotion that had come into his voice had sent a shiver through her, a longing that had had her barely able to act normal. Normal as in not having just wished he had been speaking about her.

Of course that had been that morning. She'd had all day to talk sense into herself and to distance herself from any kind of irrational behavior.

She'd reminded herself that she didn't deserve to feel happiness in this situation. That she'd been blessed to have any time at all with Levi, but that this was not permanent. One day, when Bo found a full-time nanny or a wife, she wouldn't be around. She reminded herself of all of that, and the harsh reminder of what it cost to love and lose had sent her guard up when she walked outside.

And now, here she stood looking at the curling hair at the nape of his neck and thinking foolish thoughts about running her fingers through the rest of his seemingly straight hair and seeing if it would curl at her touch. Foolish didn't begin to describe what she was being.

"Thanks for putting Levi to bed. There would have been no way I could have managed without you. I mean, his bath alone would have been impossible. Can you picture me trying to hold that slippery little body with one hand? Nope, even the thought has disaster written all over it."

Abby laughed hard at the picture in her mind. Everything he said was the truth.

He patted the step beside him. "Sit, take a load off. You certainly deserve it."

"Sure." She moved to sit beside him, instantly regretting it when he leaned in and bumped their shoulders together.

"So, how did you hold up?" he asked, cocking his head forward and looking across his shoulder at her.

Abby almost groaned as his voice, a gentle rumble in the silky darkness, melted through her like warmed chocolate. *How was she holding up? Not so good at the moment. He was obviously into asking trick questions tonight.*

She inhaled to clear her head and instantly regretted that when his woodsy scent enveloped her. "Good. I'm doing good," she lied.

He smiled that dangerous smile that spread slow, and then *bam*, the dimple popped and his entire face came alive. Combined with the moonlight and the blanket of night and the day they'd shared . . . Abby was feeling out of sync with her reality. Was he feeling it too?

"Good. I'm glad. Levi likes you being here. He didn't wake up at all last night. At least I never heard him and the three times I checked on him he was sleeping soundly."

"You checked on him three times?"

"Yeah, I do every night. It scares me when I wake up and realize I haven't heard him on the monitor in a few hours, so I get up and check on him and on Pops too."

"Then I can safely say that they were both well watched over last night because I checked on them three times, too, for the exact same reason. And both of them were out. We were obviously on different schedules. You didn't check on me, did you?"

He laughed hard at that. "Yeah, I forgot to tell you I opened your door and heard you snoring like a racehorse in there. I had to close the door fast before it woke Pops and Levi."

She grinned. "You are so full of it."

"Yeah, I am. I did not open your door."

"Good."

"Didn't say I didn't hear you snoring though."

"Hey, buster, careful. You have a hurt shoulder that could get poked if I wanted to."

His eyes twinkled, catching the light. "You wouldn't, Abby Knightley. You wouldn't hurt a flea."

His words splashed over her like a bucket of ice-cold water. "I better go in now, I'm feeling a little tired."

"Okay, sure." He stood the same time she did and when she wobbled, he grabbed her arm with his good one and steadied her. "Are you okay?"

"Just feeling tired. I-I'll see you in the morning."

"If not before," he said, but she was already across the porch and entering the house by then.

Abby went into Levi's room and stood beside his bed to watch him. She touched his soft cheek and tenderly smoothed his tiny tuft of hair. He was so precious.

"I love to watch him sleeping," Bo said, startling her by coming up behind her. She felt his warmth radiating through her back. Abby stood very still, her fingertips lingering on Levi's sweet cheek before pulling away. Bo moved to stand beside her, angled so he was facing her and looking down at his son.

Abby tore her eyes off of Bo and returned them to Levi. "I'm so thankful that that friend of his mother's dropped him off on your front porch," she said softly.

"Yeah, me too." Bo's voice cracked.

Abby's throat ached. "What would have happened to him if we, if *you*, had never known about him?" She looked up at him, wishing he had stayed safely on the front porch.

Bo pulled his gaze from his son, the tenderness for Levi still lingering in his eyes. He lifted a strand of her hair from her shoulder and gently rubbed it between his fingertips. Abby couldn't breathe. "I've thought about that every night since he arrived. And I thank God that He brought my son to me. I . . ." He paused. "That's the only way I can think about it."

Abby nodded. "Good-night," she said, and this time she went to her room and didn't look back, closing the door firmly behind her.

CHAPTER 28

"Y ou will keep your distance," Abby told herself the next morning. "You are here to do a job, snd you will do it." She glared at herself in the mirror. "And no funny business."

She heard Levi's morning cry and rushed from her room and into his. She'd checked on him before getting dressed herself but she'd spent a little too long giving herself a pep talk in front of the mirror. "Good morning, sunshine," she said, picking him up out of his crib and snuggling him. "Oh my, you are not smelling like sunshine this morning."

"Levi—" Bo came hurrying into the room and stopped when he saw her. "Mornin'." He smiled, ramming a hand through his already rumpled hair.

Abby knew he was normally an early riser but this morning he looked like he'd hardly slept. "Mornin' to you." Her stomach tumbled around and she felt breathless at the lack of oxygen in the room.

He looked so good, rumpled and all—especially rumpled.

"If you've got him, me and Pops will get breakfast."

"Can you manage it with one arm?"

"I can. No pancake flipping this morning, but nothing else should pose a problem."

She smiled. Despite all the turmoil he created inside of her, he could make her smile with ease. Abby turned back to Levi, grabbed a diaper, and took care of baby business. "You can make me smile, too, little one."

She took a clean shirt from the basket and looked around the room that was simply a spare bedroom Bo had moved the baby bed into that she'd helped him pick out at the store that first day.

She pulled Levi's shirt over his head and then tugged on a pair of jeans. She had come to Wishing Springs to find her way back into life. And looking at Levi grinning at her, she knew that she had accomplished that and more. She could smile, though she still had to keep her guard up. The guilt still lurked. And when it hit her, the sadness came with it. But if she was careful, she was okay.

And she was happy.

She just had to keep on the path she was on and not cross the line like she had been tempted to do last night.

That kind of happiness she didn't deserve or want. That kind of happiness required more than she could give. More than she could risk.

"I can do this . . ." She hoisted the baby she adored to her hip, swung around in a circle, and watched his expression go from happy to gleeful in a quick instant.

Walking into the kitchen, she forced herself to ignore the way her heart leapt in her chest at the sight of Bo whistling as he stirred eggs in the skillet. Pops smiled as she entered.

"Mornin', Abby girl. It's a great day in the neighborhood."

Abby laughed. "Oh, Pops. Yes, it is. Bo, are the guys making it okay down at the shop?"

He glanced over his shoulder. "Actually, they are. I had to delegate the branding of each stirrup to Sergio and we hired one of his cousins. They're getting the work done. I'll have to alter my Monahan promise, but I believe if we maintain quality, it'll be okay."

"You're making a choice for the better good of your child." Abby's heart clutched in her chest. "You're a good man, Bo. A good daddy."

He looked a little embarrassed by her words then gave her a gentle smile that set the butterflies free inside of her.

"I've been doing a lot of thinking—I'm determined to be the best daddy I can be. God gave me this blessing and I'm not going to take it lightly."

Abby wished she'd not taken Landon's desire to be a father so lightly. She wished . . . that she'd said yes to having a family. That she'd agreed and that they'd never argued in that car.

"You'll do a wonderful job with that attitude." She admired Bo. He'd taken a hard situation and he'd handled it with flying colors.

What a truly wonderful man he was.

. . .

Before breakfast was over, Pops got up and headed off in the direction of his room. Bo watched Abby feed Levi, teasing him and playing with his son as the baby ate like a horse.

"He's going to hurt himself if he keeps eating like this," he said.

"He's a growing boy, but you're right. I think he'd eat as long as I put a spoon or a bottle in front of him." She wiped his little mouth and chuckled when Levi giggled at her. Her eyes sparkled. Bo could have looked at her for the rest of his life like this. It made him happy. And knowing she loved his kid made him even happier.

He wondered if she knew she loved Levi. He wondered if loving Levi was helping her move forward past the sadness of losing her own baby. He found himself praying that it was so.

He wondered if . . . if . . .

He pushed that half thought away, deciding now wasn't the time to wonder about anything past today.

"Bo," Pops said, coming into the room carrying an armload of stuff. He had an old stuffed horse that had been Bo's and he carried a baby blanket that Bo remembered had been on Tru's bed when they were little. And a child's felt cowboy hat dangled from his fingertips by the chin string. "Toys for Levi." Coming over to them, he grinned at Levi.

Levi reached for the stuffed horse and Pops let him have it.

"Where did he get those?" Abby asked, taking the hat and the blanket from him. "Oh, Pops, this is so cute."

"My grandmother made that," Bo said. "Pops, where was all of this?"

"My room." Pops crooked his finger at them to follow him and headed down the hallway. Solomon padded along beside him.

"Let's go see," Abby said, already lifting Levi out and placing him on her hip.

"After you," Bo said, curious about what Pops had found.

He'd opened the door to a hall closet that Bo knew his grandmother had used for storage. They found him and Solomon standing among several large plastic containers from which he'd removed the lids. Inside were stuffed toys and things from Bo's childhood that he'd long ago forgotten about.

"The boys' toys," Pops said. "He needs them."

Abby was smiling like she'd just been awarded grand prize at the county fair.

"Bo, is this stuff from your and your brothers' childhoods?"

Bo reached for a familiar John Deere tractor that had been his. "Yeah, I played many times in the dirt with this hoss."

Pops chuckled and pulled a yellow tractor from among the various stuffed animals. "Boys." He seemed to fumble for his next word. "Dirt. Work."

"That's right, Pops. These will get it done."

"Let's decorate Levi's room with some of the things," Abby said, delight in her words.

"Sure, use whatever you want. And if we need to get anything else just let me know."

Abby studied the boxes. "I bet I can manage with what I find in here."

"Then go for it. I'm here to help."

Bo hadn't seen this much excitement in Abby's eyes before. There was something about the look in them that seemed more alive. And he was grateful to see it.

"Pops, this is great." In more ways than he'd ever understand, Bo thought.

. . .

"This is going to be the best little boy room ever," Abby commented the next day when Bo came in for lunch.

She'd gone through the boxes and pulled out a lot of things. She'd enjoyed seeing the cute blankets and pillows that Bo's grandmother had sewn for Bo and his brothers. They were brightly colored and some had western themes with lots of reds and tans. The stuffed animals that she'd saved were in great shape also, along with tractors and trailers and plastic horses and farm animals. Bo had also told her, if she saw anything in any of the bedrooms that she could use, to let him know and he'd move them for her. She helped him move a cute chest and a small bookshelf into Levi's room. She'd had to help since he could only use one arm, but they got them moved. Then she'd gone to work.

He looked into the room and his mouth dropped open.

"You're not kidding. You've done all of this with what you found in the closet?"

Abby used everything she'd found that was horse-themed. And then decorated with toys in various areas that Levi could grow into later.

"Pops loves the horses and cowboy theme—this is awesome," Bo continued.

"Pops has left y'all a wonderful legacy. It's only right

to carry it on. He is, after all, the best champion quarter horse trainer ever in my book," she said, and meant it.

"He is in my book too."

"And his great-grandson will agree," she said quietly, and found herself looking up at Bo with a tenderness filling her. She hadn't felt so alive and happy in a long time as she had the last twenty-four hours working on Levi's room. Pops had hovered about grinning and talking. Sometimes making sense and sometimes not.

Levi had played and cooed and pulled up on everything imaginable.

And Abby had loved every moment.

CHAPTER 29

A bby spent a restless night thinking about Bo. And that became a relentless process over the next couple of weeks. They'd start their days over breakfast, then he would come and go all through the day checking on them, or sometimes loading them up and taking them to town for lunch. That was always fun, because everyone was interested in talking to the adorable baby.

But for the most part Abby spent her time at the house contentedly watching Levi. They took walks down the lane to visit the horses and stopped by the stirrup barn to see Bo. Sometimes Pops walked with them or sometimes he busied himself in the shop with Bo. October had arrived with cooler weather and rain and rainy days were spent mostly inside. And almost overnight Levi began toddling precariously, reminding Abby that the baby was plenty old enough to start walking.

Abby had been at the ranch for almost two weeks and she knew that by Friday she'd go home to her place and start working the regular schedule of every other day or so while Maggie and Tru were back in town. But it wouldn't be exactly the same. She wouldn't be sleeping in the room beside Levi's and she wouldn't be able to get up and rock him back to sleep when he'd had a bad dream. And she wouldn't be sleeping down the hall from Bo, running into him sometimes at night when they would end up checking on Levi at the same time . . . this didn't happen often and she wondered if it was because Bo tried as hard as she did to avoid those times. There were sweet moments watching the baby sleep or Bo getting a bottle while she rocked Levi back to sleep. Teamwork and also sleepless nights.

Still, Abby loved every moment that she was there and hated the idea of leaving and returning to her own place. She had these few days, though, and she was going to make the best of them. She had fallen in love with . . . Levi.

There were a few things she could control and one was loving Levi and making him laugh when she was around. And that was what she gave her energy to. She held nothing back if it would make him laugh.

Holding him now, she looked down at him on her hip giggling with delight as she danced with him around the kitchen. The sound of his giggle sparkled though her like gold dust. In the blink of an eye everything could be gone. How she wished she could stand time still and know that working, that money and stature, were not what she wanted. Not what she needed.

Not ever again.

Longing so deep cut through her—she'd needed and longed to hear her child's laughter . . . but that had been stolen from her. Levi would never know his mother's laughter. The thought struck her hard looking down at him. But he would know his father's. And his father would hear his son's. And that gave Abby joy.

And he would know her laughter—laughter that he was very much responsible for.

She hugged him close as they moved around the kitchen. Pops had gone down to the shop with Bo and she had felt the need to dance with Levi to set them both laughing. The need to give this child what he didn't have took hold of her more strongly by the second.

She'd told herself she couldn't get too attached. Too late—she'd already crossed that line. Her time here in the house had put complications in her way that she'd begun to think about continually.

There had been that one brief kiss that had happened nearly two weeks ago, yet Bo had kept his promise and there had been no more. Not even on those nights they tended to Levi together.

However she'd been waking up at night thinking about that kiss. She'd tried not to . . . tried hard to put it from her mind. Where once she'd been burdened down with guilt over the way she felt around him, now she couldn't stop thinking about it. Talk about not being in control. It was impossible to stop thinking about how his lips felt on hers, about the way he made her feel.

That he made her feel at all.

But she knew it was useless. Her heart of hearts just couldn't go there. She'd failed.

She knew she'd contributed to her loved ones' deaths, in part. She knew that if she gave into the needs and wants that had begun to slip into her heart that she was potentially setting herself up for heartache.

She couldn't.

She forced the thoughts from her mind and kissed

the top of Levi's head, concentrating on him as she two-stepped around the room in a crazy sashaying version that got him smiling. And when she dipped him, Levi cackled gleefully and her heart swelled, filling with the joy of his laughter. It was as good for her as it was for him.

"Now that's what I call some good dancing."

Abby whirled around and found Bo grinning wide, leaning against the door frame watching them.

"How long have you been standing there?"

He laughed. "Long enough to know you have some moves, woman."

Her cheeks shot hot and she knew they were glowing red. "I thought—you were supposed to be working." He'd started helping more this week since his collar bone wasn't as painful and a little motion of the lower arm and elbow was a good thing.

"Oh, I am. I just forgot my gloves." He strode to the table, watching her all the way. "And I have to say that I might just start forgetting these every day. Levi is sure enjoying the dancing."

Her heart pounded watching him walk over. He stopped beside her and Levi smiled at him, his eyes bright. Abby realized she probably looked just like Levi in that minute.

Bo kissed the top of Levi's head but his gaze clung to hers as he did so.

Abby's pulse raced. "Want to hold him?" Before she realized what he was doing Bo wrapped his good arm around her, holding her and Levi as he swept them in a slow circle, his gaze never leaving hers, Levi's laughter ringing between them like the sweetest song on earth. "I need to get back, but carry on." He chuckled and headed toward the door.

Dazed, she watched him go, feeling breathless.

Bo Monahan was a heart stopper and one day some lucky woman was going to fall head over heels in love with him . . . *Like you?*

Abby froze, watching as Bo reached the door. She loved him. He turned back and winked at her. "Go ahead, dance. I'm gone now."

I'm gone now.

Abby closed her eyes. Somehow, despite everything she'd done she'd still fallen in love with Bo.

I'm gone now . . . She'd fallen in love with Bo and just like Landon and her baby, he could be gone in an instant.

. . .

Bo made it outside and grinned all the way back to the shop. Abby was something. Pops nodded at him as he approached the bench where Pops sat outside enjoying the afternoon.

"Hey, Pops. You ready to help me with the stirrups?"

Pops frowned. "I been waitin'."

Bo laughed. "Yes, sir. And I've been dragging my feet. Sorry about that."

Pops shook his head and went inside with Bo. Bo was madly, deeply in love with Abby and he didn't know how he was going to get that across to her without running her off.

She was fragile.

And in order to have a chance with her he knew he had to get through the heartbreak of her past. But could he do that?

CHAPTER 30

Abby took Levi to town the day after Bo had briefly danced with them. She'd been thinking about that moment, that beautiful moment in the kitchen with the three of them together and she didn't know where to go from here.

Running errands got her out of the house and gave her time to think. They went to the discount store and picked up diapers. The time at Bo's had flown. Her mom called while she was in the store and they talked about the move into her new place, but despite the progress they'd made in regaining their relationship, Abby found herself holding back telling her about Bo or Levi . . . but before they parted, her mother told her she sounded happier than she'd sounded in a very long time.

She didn't dig or push or ask why, but continued to give Abby her space. Abby found herself smiling when she said good-bye.

Almost instantly she was swamped by guilt. Feeling off-balance at the emotional rollercoaster she seemed tied to, she stopped by the real estate office to drop off her rent check since they managed the property for Rand. It made it a lot easier on her not to face her neighbor, and she wasn't expecting to run into Rand the moment she walked into the office.

She hadn't seen him since she'd carried him to the fire. And she'd managed to keep her mouth shut that night even though he'd admitted that he'd been drinking.

He was sitting in the waiting area of the office having coffee with Doobie and Doonie and Doc Hallaway, the local vet. She'd met Doc, as everyone called him, on her first trip to The Bull Barn.

"Hey, there, Abby," one of the twins greeted her. "It's good to see you. And you brought the little fella with you."

She kept Levi on her hip knowing they weren't staying.

"How's it going out there at the ranch?" Doc grunted. "Solomon hasn't bitten you yet, has he?"

"Everything's fine. And Solomon's a good dog. He loves the baby, but we don't let him get too close. Bo said he only bit Maggie that time because he was stuck under the bed." Bo had told her about Maggie's first meeting with the dog.

"That's right. But you can never be too careful around a little one."

"Yes, sir. We are." She told herself to relax, to calm down. Be civil. But she didn't want to be around Rand. Despite the fact that he'd been so concerned for Pebble the night of the fire.

"Here's the check for my rent. I can't stay. Y'all enjoy your coffee."

She turned and left the building. Her hands shook as she buckled Levi into the car and they were still shaking when she climbed behind the wheel.

"Abby."

No. She didn't want to talk to him. He hadn't killed Landon and her baby. But he represented everything she despised. She'd helped him the night of the fire and she still wasn't sure why—yes, she'd told Pebble it was because he asked instead of getting behind the wheel and that was true. But she'd been holding out that maybe his eyes would be opened. That he would change, but she feared he hadn't. She'd lost patience with that.

Anger surged like a wildfire inside of her now, and she barely looked at him as she tried to get control. "What?"

"I wanted to come and tell you that I'm sorry about your loss. I never told you and, well, I'm sorry."

She glared at him. His words only added fuel to the anger roaring inside of her. "*Sorry?* Those are empty words, sir. What if you're behind that wheel some night and it's *your* vehicle that comes across the line and wipes out a family like mine? Sorry doesn't exactly hit the mark coming from you."

Their gazes locked, then Abby slammed the door and drove away, leaving him standing in her rearview.

Hands and insides shaking, she drove very carefully all the way to Bo's.

. . .

Pebble drove to Rand's home and calmed the quaking in her heart as she walked to his front door. She said a prayer for guidance, then knocked. She'd been praying all through the day knowing that she was going to make this visit after Rand came home from the office.

When the door opened, she smiled with trepidation.

"Pebble," he said, his expression and tone telling her just how startled he was to find her standing on his front steps.

"Hello, Rand. May I come in?"

"Yes, sure," he said, stepping back so she could enter.

She fought to ignore the way her heart thundered as she stepped across his threshold. "I came to talk. Can we do that?"

"Yes, of course." He led the way down the hall into a nice room with a caramel-toned sofa set and wide bookshelves lined with books.

It was a lovely room, and Pebble couldn't help but walk over and look at the book bindings. There were books from all genres. Hardbacks and paperbacks—he wasn't particular. There were travel books and cookbooks from all over the world.

"You love to read."

He came to stand beside her, his arms folded across his chest. "I do."

Pebble moved away from him, putting space between them as she took a seat on one of the cushioned chairs. He took his cue and sat down in the chair beside hers. "How are you feeling?"

"Much better. I'm coughing less every day. How are you doing?" she asked.

"I'm making it. I've hired a reporter, an old friend who is going to come in and take over the paper for a few months for me."

"Take over?"

He nodded. "I check into a rehab tomorrow. It took me a few days to pull something together that wouldn't leave the town stranded without a paper."

Pebble was confused now. "You're going to rehab?"

He smiled and she felt it all the way through her. "I knew you were right the other morning at the hospital. I've been very unfair to you, Pebble. I've been essentially placing my problem in your lap by allowing our relationship to be responsible for my moments of weakness. That is not your fault. And you were right to point it out to me. I'm going to fix that. And when I'm out of my program—ninety days or longer if they decide I need longer—then maybe for once in my life I may have a chance with you."

"Oh, Rand, I can't guarantee that."

"I know, and that's a risk I'm willing to take. One I have to take."

Pebble held her hand out across the small space between the chairs. Rand looked at her hand and then gently took it into his. Pebble's pulse stuttered, then kicked into gear. It had always been that way when they held hands. Even from that first moment when he held her hand after fixing her tire. "I came by because I need to apologize to you and ask you to forgive me."

He recoiled. "You don't have anything to apologize for and you've certainly done nothing that needs forgiveness."

"Yes, I do. You see, I've known you had a problem. And it made me mad, and sad, that you would do such a thing and then that you would expect me to be okay with it. That you would expect me to sign on for a life with you that would most likely just bring me a front-row seat to you self-destructing. That's selfish on your part. And for a man who has claimed to love me all of your life, it shows me only that you are thinking of yourself. And that's angered me as much as the drinking. I'm sorry I haven't explained myself better. Yet if you understand why I'm withdrawn, then maybe it will help you to overcome."

His eyes filled with sorrow. He hung his head. "You're right. How could I have ever expected you to love a man like me?"

Pebble wanted to stomp her foot and yell. How could she get through to this man? She had to be strong. "And that right there is part of the problem. Look at me, Rand. That isn't the man I knew once, the young, strong man, the kind man that I fell in love with that year in high school. That's the alcohol speaking. The manipulator who has lied to me, to everyone, to himself, who's hiding behind a façade. I can't and I won't enable you, Rand. Letting you get away with those kinds of words isn't okay. It would be the worst thing I could do. After you came to see me at the hospital, I realized that I was a liar too. I care about you, but I've been so busy pushing you away that I forgot to offer you my support. And that's why I've come. I came to tell you that if you would commit to getting help and enter a rehab that I would be there for you—as a friend. Only a friend. No promises."

Rand's Adam's apple bobbed and his shoulders squared as he straightened, still holding her hand, his fingers gripping hers as if she were the lifeline to heaven. "I want you to place your faith in God, Rand. Not in man. Not in me. I want you to go into this rehab for you. And I want you to succeed for you. And when it gets hard, and it will, I want you to be strong and to hold onto God's hand like you're holding onto mine. Do you promise me that?"

A hint of a smile stole across his dear face. Pebble thanked God for giving her strength in that moment. "Do you need me to take you to the rehab?"

"No, Doonie and Doobie are driving me down there. And they're going to come cheer me on in their own special way as soon as I can have visitors."

Pebble chuckled. "I can't decide if that's a good thing or a bad thing."

Rand's thumb made small, gentle circles on the back of her hand. Pebble let the feeling seep through her knowing this could very well be the last time she allowed herself to let her guard down with him. "Rand, I'm not promising you anything but my friendship and support. You understand this . . . right?"

"I do," he said.

She laid her free hand against his cheek. "You can do this. And it may take longer than three months and one visit."

He stood and pulled her to stand also. "I know. But I'm going to do this, Pebble. I promise."

Pebble started walking back toward the front door and paused. "Promise yourself."

He nodded. "I promise I will do this. I'm stronger than I've been acting. And, seeing the pain in Abby

Knightley's eyes slammed that into me as if that truck had hit me instead of her family's car. Pebble, I've only been lucky so far that I haven't killed anyone. I don't drink responsibly. I know that. I'm not kidding myself anymore. It very well could have been me who ran my car across the road on that night two years ago. And when Abby looks at me, that's what she sees."

Pebble nodded. She squeezed his hands and pulled hers away and walked out into the evening. "I'll be praying for you."

She walked away then, with hope in her heart.

•   •   •

Bo was signing off on a delivery when Abby drove into the yard. Even with the distance between his shop and the main house, he could tell she was upset. "Thanks," he told the delivery man, handing him his pad. Then he strode toward the house.

He found Abby in the baby's room putting a sleeping Levi under the covers. "Hey, you okay?"

"No. I'm not, Bo. I'm not at all," she said, anguish in her voice, her expression crushed.

Bo automatically opened his arms when she came his way, and to his surprise, she walked into them, wrapped her arms around him, and held on tight.

"I feel so lost." She trembled and her shoulders shook. She was crying.

Bo tightened his arm around her and held on, wishing he had both arms to hold her with. She smelled of flowers and sunlight. "How can I help you, Abby? How?"

She shook her head, lifted her face from his chest, and sniffed. "I'm just so angry inside. I've tried and I think I've made progress and then I see Rand and he represents everything that I'm furious about. He actually told me he was sorry about my family."

"That's a good thing. Right?"

"I guess, but I can't get past it."

"Come here." He led the way to the couch in the living room. Pops came into the room and seeing the tears on Abby's face, immediately came over to her.

He patted her knee. "You'll do better tomorrow," he said, smiled, then walked out of the room looking for Solomon.

Abby sighed. "Wouldn't it be nice if it were that simple?"

"It can be. You're going to have to forgive him, Abby."

"Who?"

"The driver of the truck. I know he died, too, but you're still going to have to forgive him. And you're going to have to let this go. It's eating you up."

Her face was puffy from tears and she swiped at them. Her eyes flashed. "I won't do that."

"That's not healthy for you. You'll just get angrier and angrier and that's not going to do anyone any good. You'll never let yourself love again."

"I don't want to love again. Bo—"

"Abby, you do and you know it."

"I don't."

"I don't believe you. You've fallen in love with Levi."

She crossed her arms and looked away. "So, yes I have and it terrifies me."

Bo felt warmth seeping back in around him. For a minute there he'd worried that he'd been wrong. "I was going to say you'd turned into the ice queen if you hadn't fallen in love with that little cowboy. And I know you aren't the ice queen."

"How do you know that?"

He shook his head. "Because," he growled. Then throwing caution to the wind he bent his head and kissed her. It was a soft gentle brush of his lips across hers first and he felt her freeze, as if afraid if she moved something would break. If Bo had his way something would, it being the chains locking her emotions away. Not satisfied with her reaction, he brushed his lips across hers a second time, as every cell in his being joined into this kiss. Clarity came as her warmth began to enfold him and he decided that this might be the last kiss he ever had the chance to share with Abby. With that in mind he tightened his arm around her and tried to kiss her all the way to her stubborn, guarded heart.

.   .   .

Abby reacted to the touch of Bo's kiss like she'd been lost in the desert for years. Her arms went around his neck as he deepened the kiss, and every emotion she'd been fighting, denying, came to life with scorching cheers. And the kiss went on.

It was as if Bo set out to make her fully and undeniably aware that she was a woman. A warm-blooded woman with God-given longings and desires. And that no amount of denying was going to change that fact.

When he finally pulled back, he looked like he'd given everything he had to the cause. Abby felt dazed, amazed. And angry.

"What do you think you're doing?"

Bo wasn't looking at her like he regretted the kiss one bit. He grinned, that slow grin that spread across that handsome face of his then lifted into a full-blown smile that had the wattage to blow the lights out of every house all the way to Houston. And then his eyes twinkled like Christmas. "Well, Abby Knightley, I'm giving you fair warning that I love you. And I don't care how long it takes to wake you up, I'm not giving up. Because you know, and I know, that Levi isn't the only one you love."

Abby's heart ached and longing so sharp and sweet throbbed through her. "That's unfair."

"Abby Knightley, when it comes to you I'll do whatever it takes to bring you to life."

"Bo, I-I'll admit that I've come to care for you despite not wanting to. Living here, being around you and Pops and Levi, how could I not? But I don't love you that way. I won't—"

"You're a liar."

"How dare you." She was actually glad to be mad again. She shot to her feet. "You stay away from me. You hear? Keep your distance." She didn't waste any time standing there arguing. She was too scared to. Instead she hightailed it to her room and shut the door behind her.

CHAPTER 31

Abby was so mad she would have slammed the door to her bedroom, but that would have wakened the baby in the room next door and she couldn't do that.

Still she wanted to slam it.

And later, lying in her bed, arms crossed as she stared up at the ceiling, steam shot from her ears every time she recalled Bo's arrogant attitude. How dare the man think that he could just pull her into his arms, kiss the daylights out of her, and she would automatically fall madly, deeply in love with him.

Of course the problem was that she'd already admitted to herself that she did love him, but he wasn't going to know it. Especially now.

She flopped over and buried her face in her pillow. No luck, so she raised up and punched it hard a few times to fluff it up, then flopped to her back, trying to get in a comfortable position that would allow her to fall asleep and not think about this for a few blissful hours.

Not happening.

In the end she lay there, continuing to stare up at the ceiling, counting the moments till morning . . .

somewhere during that time she fell into a restless sleep and instead of thoughts of Bo . . . she dreamed of Landon.

He stood on the edge of the horizon looking so handsome, so dear to her heart that tears welled inside of her. She wanted to touch him and she reached for him, but he was just out of her reach.

He smiled. "Not me, Abbs. It's time for you to be happy again."

Abby cried and tried to say no but the words wouldn't come.

Landon's beautiful, kind brown eyes softened and his lips lifted into the sweetest smile . . . it dug into her heart until it ached. "I'll love you forever and always . . . but let me go. Let it go."

Let it go . . . let me go . . .

"No," Abby cried, yanking herself awake. Disoriented for a moment she sat up, her heart thundering. *Landon.*

She blinked the blurry dredges of her restless sleep away and tried to still her clamoring heart. It was a dream. Just a dream. And yet . . . she could almost feel Landon in the room.

She dropped her forehead into her palm and sat there as the soft fingers of moonlight filtering in through the curtains washed over her. It was just a dream. But it wasn't a nightmare.

Abby looked up. It wasn't a nightmare.

Let it go. Let me go.

She scrambled out of bed, thrusting the thoughts away. *Levi!*

She needed to see Levi. Pulling her housecoat on

over her pajama bottoms and T-shirt she padded quietly into Levi's room. In the shadows of the night she gathered the sleeping baby into her arms and carried him over to the rocking chair. Sinking into it Abby cuddled the precious baby close, buried her nose in his tousled hair, and just rocked gently.

The turmoil inside her calmed . . . but the question echoed in stillness, *"How can I walk away from this child?"*

Because one thing she knew was the emotions passing between her and Bo were no longer containable. If she wasn't going to let their relationship progress then she couldn't keep this job. She had to let them go.

She just couldn't do it anymore.

· · ·

Abby wasn't acting like herself. Bo was working in the shop doing what he could with one arm, straightening and organizing. He'd gotten out of the house as soon as breakfast was done and she'd taken Levi into the living room to play.

He had messed up. He'd been awake most of the night and gone to check on Levi only to find Abby cuddled with him asleep in the rocking chair. Her beautiful face rested peacefully on Levi's little head. Dear Lord, how he loved them.

He'd been rooted to the spot unable to look away.

After a moment, he backed away and went out to sit on the porch where he'd waited on the sunrise. And prayed.

Now he was keeping busy, giving Abby room. He could only hope he hadn't run her off.

A scream broke the morning, shrill and startling. He dropped his branding iron and ran.

As he rounded the corner of the barn he could see Abby running toward him, carrying Levi. Pops was trailing behind her, but what Bo focused on was the blood that seemed to be pouring from Levi's forehead.

"He, he was trying to climb the bar stool and hit—" Abby screamed almost incoherently. She was pale as watered-down milk. Blood was all over her.

And she was still standing.

Just as Bo reached them, her knees seemed to give way and she sank to the dirt clutching a wailing baby to her as the gash on his forehead pumped blood out like a high-powered sprinkler system.

"Help him," Abby gasped, looking up at Bo.

Bo grabbed the hem of his shirt and ripped the tail off. Wadded it up and pressed it to the bleeder. "Come on, Abby, we need to get this stopped and get him to the clinic."

She nodded, and let him take Levi into his arms. Pops was frantic, but all Bo could think about was his boy. "Y'all come on, climb into the truck." He hurried to the truck and Abby, who still had managed not to pass out over all the blood, helped Pops get to the truck. Tru was gone today of all days.

Abby got Pops in the backseat then jumped into the passenger's seat and Bo handed over Levi, realizing they had a problem with maneuvering the car seat and keeping pressure on the wound. "Hold that tight," he said, studying her white face and knowing he had to get Levi and Abby both to the clinic. Her eyes were hollow and he could only imagine what was going on inside her head.

She nodded, took Levi back into her arms, and held the now soaked rag tight.

Bo drove. Laid the gas pedal to the floor and headed for town.

Levi was screaming. Pops was yelling. And Abby was having trouble breathing. Bo shot her a glance. "Breathe, Abby, don't hyperventilate. Levi needs you."

She nodded and he could tell she fought to get control.

"He, he hit his head on the . . . corner of the cabinet . . ." she managed, barely audible over Levi and Pops.

"It'll be okay, Abby."

Town came into view and he was thankful there were no stop signs between him and the nurse's office. And today was a day the nurse was in town. Wishing Springs shared their nurse with another small town clinic about eighteen miles down the road.

If Bertha hadn't been in, he'd have headed to the vet. But one way or the other, someone would have seen Levi.

Bo was out of the truck and opening Abby's door the minute he got the truck stopped. He led the way up the steps carrying Levi and Abby hurried to get the door open.

"My baby cut his forehead open," she cried as she threw the door open and led the way in. Instantly the receptionist jumped up from the desk. "Bertha!" she yelled and came to help.

The large nurse came barreling out of the back, assessed the situation in a glance, and motioned for Bo to follow her.

Stumbling behind them, Abby entered the room and sank into the chair by the door. Pops paced in the hall.

"What happened?" Bertha asked, her tone brisk but professional as she lifted the dripping rag to see the gash. Instantly more blood spurted straight into the air. She didn't even have to ask for the thick gauze pad that the receptionist/assistant grabbed from a cabinet and handed her.

Abby watched them, the horror of the blood from her past haunting her as she sat there. She dropped her forehead to her hands and bit back tears and fought off the spinning of the room.

It had happened so fast. She'd been cleaning up after breakfast, washing dishes, and letting Levi crawl on the floor. She'd had her back to him when he must have decided the bar stool looked inviting. All she could figure out was that while holding on to the bar stool to stand, he fell and hit his forehead just right on the bottom corner of the cabinet . . .

Abby began to shake. She couldn't lose her baby—he had lost so much blood though.

Her baby . . . Abby's heart thundered and she cried silently sitting there wishing she could do something. Wishing she'd been paying more attention . . . wishing she hadn't turned her back to wash the dishes.

"Are you bleeding anywhere?" the receptionist asked gently.

Abby looked up, dazed. She wiped her eyes then shook her head and looked down at herself. She was covered in Levi's blood . . . Her stomach lurched and the room spun for a moment but she willed herself not to faint. Instead she stood. "I'm fine. It's Levi's."

She crossed the room and placed her hand on Levi as the nurse worked while Bo continued to hold the terrified baby.

"Foreheads bleed like nobody's business," Bertha explained, glancing at her. "It'll scare the life out of you, that's for sure. Your baby's going to be fine. You can stop worrying."

And all Abby could do was nod.

. . . .

Bo was worried about Levi and Abby but so proud that Abby was fighting the turmoil he saw in her eyes.

Bertha looked down at the wide eyes of Levi. "Now see there, your mama is here. You can calm down. Mama, take his little hand and hold on while I do this."

Levi instantly looked at Abby as if he understood the words and she took his hand and kissed the top of it. Bo had to belt back the emotion that swamped him.

"It's okay, darlin', I'm here," Abby told his son. "It's going to be all right."

Bo swallowed the lump that lodged in his throat seeing Abby comfort Levi, knowing there was blood everywhere and she was still standing. He loved her. Loved her more than she could even imagine. But was that going to be enough to get through the walls surrounding her?

. . . . .

By the time they got back home, he'd called Jarrod who, thankfully, had arrived home the day before. His big brother was waiting on them when they drove into the driveway.

Pops, still shaken, went immediately to the fence to look at the cows. Bo figured it would calm him down just watching the placid animals graze.

Bertha had put five stitches in Levi's head, and the poor baby was so worn out from crying he had fallen asleep in Abby's arms before they'd gotten out of the nurse's office.

Jane, the receptionist, had given Abby a clean nurse's scrub top to replace her bloody shirt and now she wasn't looking quite as pale as she had.

But she wasn't saying much and he wasn't pressing. He'd told her she'd done good hanging on and not passing out but he wasn't sure where her head was right now.

And he was worried that they'd put Levi in his crib and then she'd pack up her things and go home. And the door would be closed.

"Y'all don't look so good," Jarrod said, taking them in with concerned eyes. "Is she okay?" he asked Bo softly when Abby just nodded and walked into the house carrying Levi.

"I don't know. This has all been hard on her with the wreck and the blood. She stayed strong from sheer will, I think. Didn't even pass out. But Levi is fine. He hit the bottom corner of the cabinet at a perfect angle when he fell and foreheads bleed a lot . . . But I'm worried, Jarrod."

His brother paused in the kitchen. Abby had already

disappeared heading toward Levi's room. "Bo, let me watch him. Why don't you take Abby to your place? Let her relax. Maybe talk to her."

Bo nodded. "Thanks. You sure you got it?"

Jarrod grinned. "Uncle Jarrod's got this. You two take your time off."

CHAPTER 32

Bo had insisted Abby leave Levi's side and come with him. He'd told her to grab some clean clothes so she could shower at his house while he fixed them something to eat. She had agreed only after Jarrod assured her that he'd call if they were needed

Abby wrapped her arms around herself, chilled and numb. The effort to walk to the truck took concentration. She had to bite her lip to hold back the quiver and hold her emotions at bay. She sat silently looking out the window as Bo drove to his home—a well-kept older home that had probably been on the ranch for a very long time and remodeled. He'd told her it had been on the place when they'd bought a neighbor's ranch and combined it with the Monahan ranch. She liked it, though she was a little too numb at the moment to really appreciate it.

Once inside Bo led her to a bedroom and showed her where the shower was. "Take your time. I'll grab one in my room and get a late lunch going for us. You relax, okay?"

She stared into his eyes, so concerned, and her heart ached more.

After he left, she got into the hot shower and stayed there—closed her eyes and let the dried blood wash away. The words that had been clinging to her for hours echoed through the steaming hot spray. *Let me go.*

Tears. Deep, drenching tears mixed with the hot spray washing over her, and Abby let her sobs come . . .

. . .

Bo took a shower fast, washing the dried blood off of himself, then dressed and headed to the kitchen. His mind was on Abby and where her mind was right now. He loved her and knew that he would spend the rest of his days trying to win her heart, trying to help her realize that her heart was big enough to love again. He didn't want to take Landon's place. He knew she'd loved him and was happy that she'd known his love. But he knew in his heart of hearts that she loved him and she loved Levi. She just had to admit it. Take a risk on happiness.

He could hear the water still running in the other room as he pulled two steaks from the freezer and put them into the microwave to defrost. Then headed outside to get the grill going. He was glad it was a beautiful afternoon. A cool breeze was blowing, but nothing that would keep them from eating on the porch if she wanted to.

By the time she came walking into the kitchen forty-five minutes later he had steaks on the grill and some vegetables simmering on the stove.

She was a little pale and her hair was damp and pulled

back in a ponytail. Just looking at her caused his heart to ache.

"You look better." He filled a glass with ice. "Tea?"

She nodded, glancing around his kitchen. "I like your home."

He grinned at her as he poured her drink. "I like it. It's kind of empty right now with me never here, but I still enjoy stealing a few hours here every once in a while."

He handed her the glass and their fingers touched. She thanked him and moved to stare out the window to the pasture and the woods out back. He went to stand beside her.

"Steaks are almost done. Midafternoon that's a heavy lunch, but there weren't a lot of choices in my freezer."

"I'm not very hungry, I have to admit. But I'll eat a little."

"Whatever you can do. I just knew you needed to eat something." He opened the door. "Want to sit outside while I flip them?"

She smiled and went out onto the porch and sat on the deck chair. "Bo, I need to talk."

He flipped the steaks, closed the lid, and went to sit in the chair beside her. "I'm here."

"I was so scared when Levi was bleeding." She closed her eyes for a moment.

"That had to be hard on you. I'm so sorry. But you did great—you didn't even pass out."

The hint of a smile crooked her lips. "I couldn't, Levi needed me. I had a dream last night. I dreamed that Landon forgave me, told me to let it go. To let him go."

Bo leaned forward and placed his hand on her knee. "Are you okay?"

"I am. I-I can't guarantee you that a few rough days won't be ahead. But I realized today that I can deny that I love you and Levi all I want, but that won't stop it from being true."

He couldn't move. She'd just admitted that she loved them.

She smiled sweetly, tenderly. "When I thought"—she blinked back tears—"when I thought Levi was dying—because there seemed to be so much blood—all I could think about was that I had denied my love for him. That I'd lost one child before I'd even had the chance to know he existed. And that I was losing another child I'd denied myself the opportunity to love. And that I was pushing you away when all I really wanted to do was grab hold of you for the rest of my life."

Bo moved from the chair to his knees in front of Abby and cupped her face with his hands. "I love you, Abby. And I'm here ready to hold on to you for the rest of my life too. I'm here for you. But I won't push."

"Could you maybe start some of that holding right now? I could really use it."

Bo didn't waste any time. He gently pulled her into his arms, pulled her close, and let her head rest on his shoulder as their hearts beat together just like they were meant to.

And when she lifted her face to his, he kissed her. "You know," he said after a minute, "you're going to have a hard time getting out of my arms this time."

She breathed deeply, contentedly. "I'm counting on it."

Bo grinned. "Well, darling, one thing you'll always be able to do is to count on this cowboy to hold on tight and love you forever."

She smiled and pulled his lips back to hers.

. . .

Later, after the steaks had almost burned and the beans had burned, Bo took Abby back to the house to check on Levi. Her heart was so very full of love for both of them.

Levi was sitting in his high chair and pinned big brown eyes on her and smiled his wide smile. "Moo-ma!"

Moo-ma! She stopped in her tracks. Levi had just called her mama . . . it was only appropriate that he'd combine "moo" with the words he'd heard Bertha calling her.

Abby sucked in air and met Bo's electric gaze. He gave her that smile. The one that turned on the heat then whacked her with the dimple. Her heart thundered like a raging flood was coming, and it was if she didn't keep the waterworks intact. She sank to her knees beside Levi. "Oh, precious, precious baby."

"Moo-ma. Moo-ma!" Levi chanted, grabbing a handful of her hair and tugging her forward. She got his little grip to release its hold and Bo's hand wrapped around both hers and Levi's.

Abby blinked, Moo-ma ringing in her ears and the feel of Levi's small innocent fist and Bo's protective, strong hand securing them all. Tears filled her eyes once more. And before she could speak or move, Pops laid his weathered, aged hand over Bo's.

"It's gonna be a good day to win," he said, and Abby's gaze went to Bo.

Her heart, so fearful yet so full, swelled and she heaved in air trying to steady her emotions. "I love you, Bo. And Levi. And Pops."

"Hey, what about me?" Jarrod called from where he was standing at the stove.

Abby glanced at him over her shoulder. "I love you, too, Uncle Jarrod."

He grinned. "It's good to know someone does." Walking over he pulled Levi out of the high chair. "Pops, why don't you and me and this butterball go play in the other room and give these two some time alone."

Abby didn't bother to point out to him that she and Bo had just come from having time alone.

"Thanks, Jarrod," Bo said and pulled her into his arms.

Pops winked and followed the others out of the room.

"I'm willing to wait forever if that's what it takes for your heart to heal. I love you. Will you marry me?"

"I will. But only if you kiss me like you mean it."

He smiled. "Always and forever." And then he lowered his lips to hers and kissed Abby like there was no tomorrow. And in her heart of hearts she heard those same words echo through her and she knew that she was blessed beyond measure to know that kind of love not once but twice . . .

"Always and forever," she said with a sigh and held on to Bo with all of her might.

DISCUSSION QUESTIONS

1. Abby has been through tragedy. She's lost her husband and her child. Why has she come to Wishing Springs? Does she get more than she bargained for? How?

2. Bo has sworn off dating when the book opens. Why?

3. We learn early in the book that Abby feels unworthy of a new start. Have you ever felt you didn't deserve a fresh start?

4. Bo regrets his relationship with Levi's mother. Why?

5. Bo is really shaken up when he finds Levi on the front porch. But he accepts responsibility that Levi could be his and he falls in love with his little boy. He is worried that Maggie and Tru will have a hard time learning that he has a son. Why?

6. This book deals with some hard issues: the loss of a spouse and a child and drunk driving and the horrible consequences of making the choice to drink and drive. Do you know someone struggling with grief from having lost a loved one due to alcohol? Pebble and Abby both have strong reactions to excessive drinking and the dangers. Do you think they were justified?

7. Abby felt guilty for what? She had a lot on her

shoulders that happened before the wreck. Do you or anyone you know carry burdens like hers? Do you need to let it go? Do you need to talk to the Lord about the problem?

8. Abby realizes she can love again. Her love for Bo happens despite her not wanting it to happen. Her love for Levi happens this way too. It just takes time to let a wounded heart heal. She could have made the choice to walk away from her new love though. Why do you think she would have done this—because of fear? There are so many reasons to walk away . . . but there were so many reasons to grab hold and envision a different future than she'd planned. Discuss with the group.

9. One of the reasons Abby had sought to step out in faith and move to Wishing Springs, in an effort to help herself move forward, was because of words she'd read in Maggie's column. Maggie had said, "Sometimes it takes courage to make a change and take steps to become joyful and seek fulfillment again after tragedy." Abby believed this to be true and decided to push herself to make the change. What do you think?

10. Are you or someone you know going through a storm in your life that is causing you great sorrow? I lost my first husband and walked this path that Abby has walked and so many others. And I know that I found peace in knowing that God was with me through it all. The Bible says in Philippians 4:13, "I can do all things though Christ who strengthens me". I know He gave me

courage and strength and I just had to let myself lean on Him. When you are going through a storm in your life do you lean on the Lord? Discuss this with the group.

ACKNOWLEDGMENTS

I want to thank my editor, the talented Becky Monds, for her wonderful influence and input into the development of this story, and also, my line editor, Krista Stroever, for her insightful contribution in helping me bring it all together.

I want to thank the entire Thomas Nelson team who worked to make this book a reality. You are all amazing and your dedication is so appreciated!

And my agent, Natasha Kern, thank you for all you do!

ENJOY DEBRA CLOPTON'S FOUR OF HEARTS RANCH ROMANCE SERIES

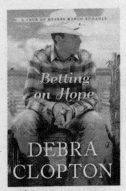

Available in print and e-book.

Available in print and e-book.

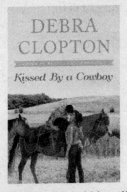

Available in print and e-book February 2016.

It all started with an ad in a mail-order bride catalogue . . .

This charming bouquet of novellas introduces you to four Hitching Post Mail-Order Bride Catalogue prospects in the year 1870, all eager for second chances . . . and hungry for happiness. Year in, year out, they'll learn that love often comes in unexpected packages.

AVAILABLE IN PRINT, E-BOOK, AND E-SINGLES

In 1885 five western preachers sit around a campfire talking about unlikely couples they've seen God bring together.

AVAILABLE IN PRINT AND E-BOOK

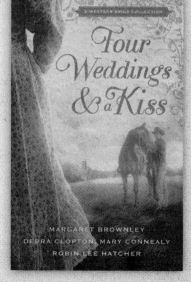

ABOUT THE AUTHOR

Debra Clopton is a multi-award winning novelist first published in 2005 and has written more than 22 novels. Along with writing, Debra helps her husband teach the youth at their local Cowboy Church. Debra is the author of the acclaimed Mule Hollow Matchmaker Series, and her goal is to shine a light toward God while she entertains readers with her words.

* * *

Visit her website at www.debraclopton.com
Twitter: @debraclopton
Facebook: debra.clopton.5

ENJOY AN EXCERPT FROM THE
FINAL BOOK IN THE FOUR OF
HEARTS RANCH ROMANCE SERIES,

KISSED BY A COWBOY

CHAPTER 1

Strawberry Hill. Cassidy Starr's headlights shined on the faded words of the wooden sign, which looked nearly ready to collapse. She knew exactly how it felt.

Taking a deep breath, she pushed her kinky mass of red hair behind her ears, then took hold of the steering wheel of her truck and drove up the dark, tree-lined lane. Up the hill, the two-story, yellow Victorian appeared in her headlight beams, and a wave of nostalgia and relief washed over Cassidy. She was home.

Humiliated, but home.

Tears dampened her eyelashes and she blinked them away. "I will not get emotional. I will not get emotional," she chanted to the silence around her.

She was done with tears.

Seriously done.

So over them.

These days the only thing tears did was make her mad when they dared to threaten.

Coming back here must have been pulling these feelings from her, because it had been months since the divorce, since she'd walked away. Coming back to Aunt Roxie's was just . . . well, it was emotional.

She hadn't planned on getting here this late, but on the way her truck's battery died in some tiny town in the middle of nowhere. She'd been lucky when an older man had finally come along and given her battery a jump-start.

Pulling to the rear of the house, she parked, then nearly rocketed out of her skin when the truck backfired. The engine sputtered and died.

"Terrific. Par for the course."

She was suddenly shrouded in darkness as her truck lights died. She groaned—it was blacker than Texas oil out here. Other than the ones coming from the ranch house half a mile away, there wasn't a light or even a moonbeam anywhere to be seen.

Cassidy swallowed hard and tried to crank her engine. It made a sad attempt, but then the battery completely flew the coop as just a clicking noise sounded when she turned the key.

"Well, how do ya like them beans?" she muttered while fumbling around for her cell phone. When she finally found it and turned it on, she groaned again— the battery life meter registered in the red. Two percent life was all she had—this wasn't looking good.

Clicking on the phone's flashlight app, she reached for the truck door. She had to act fast before the little light she had ran out. The heated air of the early June night hit her as she climbed out of the truck, then slammed the door extra hard, trying to make noise, just in case any unwanted visitors were roaming around. Hopefully the noise would scare them off. She remembered that once when she'd been here as a girl, she'd met a skunk face-to-face. Not a good situation at all.

"Yah! Get on outta here!" she yelled loudly into the night. She remembered Pops saying that when he wanted to move cattle along. Pops owned the ranch next door, and she'd been able to tag along with him and his grandsons a few times on roundups. She didn't want to round up anything now, but yelling should run off things too.

At this moment, all she wanted was to get inside Aunt Roxie's house—her house now. It had been six years since her aunt passed away and left the house to her, as if she'd known Cassidy would need it someday. And she'd been right. The thought settled depressingly on her shoulders and she shoved it away.

A bed and sleep were all Cassidy needed for now. It had been an exhausting day of travel from Plano, which had started with catching all the morning commuters in Dallas and then gone downhill from there. If it could go wrong, it had, and all this was more of the same.

Heart thundering, Cassidy moved toward the back porch. Memories greeted her as she approached the house, but now was not the time to be waylaid by them. So she shoved them away too and trudged forward.

She stomped up the steps and stooped down to

feel beneath the flowerpot that had sat next to that back door since she was a kid. No key.

She should have made certain the Burke brothers, who kept watch on the place, still kept it in the same spot. She just hadn't thought to ask about that when she'd made arrangements to have the electricity turned on.

The eerie sound of a Hoot Owl sounded from the direction of the barn's hayloft, and Cassidy shivered despite the warmth of the summer night. She shined the phone's light that direction just in time to see the bird fly off into the darkness.

She swallowed hard, then turned back to the door and gave the handle a twist, hoping that maybe . . . Nope, nothing. She eyed the doggie door with skeptical eyes. No, no way. Striding over to a window on the porch, she tried opening it. No budge.

She was worried about her phone battery too.

"Why couldn't there have been a full moon tonight?" she grumbled, then promptly tripped over the step as she hurried off the porch. Managing not to fall, she found the rock that sat in the flower bed beside the porch and lifted it, hoping maybe . . . A couple of bugs scurried away, but there was still no key.

Clomping around the house, she tried each window and the front door.

"Come on!" Weariness was starting to get to her.

She should have felt some excitement at being here, but instead she felt weighed down by the trepidation swirling in the pit of her stomach. She was here, but it was not looking good.

Stop that. She might not be inside her new home yet, but she would find a way. She would—"

Umph," she grunted as she fell facedown on the ground, her phone flying out of her hand. She knew instantly that she'd hit the water spigot that had always protruded from the earth in the middle of the yard. She'd forgotten it was there despite having tripped over it several times growing up. Either it had rained at some point or the water hose had been leaking, because dampness instantly began seeping through her clothes. Then her phone light died, the battery evidently giving out.

"Great. Just great."

She jerked up to her hands and knees and felt around on the ground. Finally she gave up, knowing she'd find it in the morning. Her knees were soaked now, and her determination was wavering.

Sleeping in the hot truck might be her only option. Her head was starting to thump, a lingering ailment from the accident that had pushed her to move to Strawberry Hill. Being hit by a car and spending two days in a coma made a person take a serious look at her life. Rubbing her temple, Cassidy scrambled up and eased around to the back of the house, still wary of what critters she might run into.

She seriously needed to be in the house and get some light. Her stomach was churning, her head was thumping harder, and now her knee throbbed where she'd hit that metal water spigot. She grimaced with each uncertain step.

Aunt Roxie would have plowed through this inky black and dared something to jump out at her. Her aunt had lived her entire adult life single, independent, and self-sufficient. She'd been able to do anything. Cassidy remembered the roof once sprang a leak during a rainstorm and there went Roxie, stomping out to the barn, grabbing her ladder. The next thing Cassidy knew, the woman was up on that roof with a blue tarp and tacks, covering it up until the rain stopped.

"It's just going from point A to point B," she'd tell Cassidy. "You can do anything you want in life if you think about it like that—and read lots of books." To prove that belief she had shelves and shelves of books on every subject imaginable.

The bottom line was her aunt Roxie wasn't afraid of anything. She'd lived fully and on her terms until she'd dropped dead in her garden. She was probably up there in heaven right now with her big, floppy, brimmed red gardening hat and her oversized chambray shirt and her gardening gloves, telling the Lord where she wanted the strawberries, tomatoes, and marigolds to go.

And he was probably saying, "Have at it, Roxie. Things have never looked so good before."

Cassidy smiled in the darkness, consoling herself with the knowledge that her aunt had died doing what she loved. Working in her garden, living her simple, uncomplicated, single life.

And that was exactly what Cassidy had come home to do.

She made it to the back porch by feel and memory, then knelt down and felt for the doggie door. When she'd been younger she'd fit through this opening. Loopy, Aunt Roxie's cocker spaniel, hadn't been big, but she hadn't been tiny either. If Loopy could fit, maybe Cassidy could. She pushed on the heavy flap and felt it give. She weighed the idea of sleeping in her truck, no light, and no shower against sleeping in a bed, light, hot water, and all the comforts of Aunt Roxie's things around her.

It was a no-brainer. She needed sleep tonight. She had a lot to do. Starting tomorrow she was making plans for her organic strawberry farm and beginning the process of making her new home into a bed-and-breakfast.

You won't make it on your own. You need me.

Jack the Jerk's chiding words echoed through her mind, words he'd smugly tossed at her the day they'd signed the papers that had cut their legal ties.

But like Roxie, she could make it on her own.

She *would* make it on her own.

Because from here on out that was the way it would be.

A fist of fear knotted in her chest, but she ignored it as best she could and stuck her head through the doggie door. She was going in.

The story continues in Debra Clopton's,
Kissed by a Cowboy . . .